"You have one too." She nudged her chin in his direction.

"Do I?" He looked down at his vest.

"Here." Maddie reached out to retrieve the leaf from his shoulder, but he was somehow taller than she realized and farther away than she calculated. She tipped too far forward, lost her balance, and rested her palm on his chest to catch herself. He pressed a hand to her waist to help steady her, but an instant later they both let go.

It had been one brief touch, so quick she might have imagined it if not for the tingling heat where his hand had rested.

Now that they were close, nothing seemed to escape his notice. She sensed him appraising the faded scar at the edge of her jaw, the beauty mark near her upper lip, and the wisps of hair that had slipped their pins.

This near, she noticed things too. Aspects she hadn't detected when she'd been struck by his chiseled beauty from across the hall. His eyes weren't truly black. They were the darkest of browns. And while there were deep grooves between his brows, laugh lines hugged his mouth.

Perhaps he wasn't as grim as he seemed, or at least he hadn't been once upon a time.

"I . . ." She didn't know for sure what she'd meant to say. She needed to go. That was all she knew for sure.

He was far too handsome, and her heart was doing odd things in her chest. And none of it mattered.

By Christy Carlyle

The Love on Holiday Series
DUKE GONE ROGUE

The Duke's Den Series
A DUKE CHANGES EVERYTHING
ANYTHING BUT A DUKE
NOTHING COMPARES TO THE DUKE

The Romancing the Rules Series
RULES FOR A ROGUE
A STUDY IN SCOUNDRELS
HOW TO WOO A WALLFLOWER

The Accidental Heirs Series
ONE SCANDALOUS KISS
ONE TEMPTING PROPOSAL
ONE DANGEROUS DESIRE

ATTENTION: ORGANIZATIONS AND CORPORATIONS
HarperCollins books may be purchased for educational, business, or sales promotional use. For information, please e-mail the Special Markets Department at SPsales@harpercollins.com.

DUKE GONE ROGUE

A Love on Holiday Novel

CHRISTY CARLYLE

AVONBOOKS

An Imprint of HarperCollinsPublishers

This is a work of fiction. Names, characters, places, and incidents are products of the author's imagination or are used fictitiously and are not to be construed as real. Any resemblance to actual events, locales, organizations, or persons, living or dead, is entirely coincidental.

DUKE GONE ROGUE. Copyright © 2021 by Christy Carlyle. All rights reserved. Printed in the United States of America. No part of this book may be used or reproduced in any manner whatsoever without written permission except in the case of brief quotations embodied in critical articles and reviews. For information, address HarperCollins Publishers, 195 Broadway, New York, NY 10007.

First Avon Books mass market printing: December 2021

Print Edition ISBN: 978-0-06-305449-3
Digital Edition ISBN: 978-0-06-305438-7

Cover design by Amy Halperin
Cover illustration by Judy York
Cover images © iStock/Getty Images
Rose chapter opener art © mikwa59/Shutterstock, Inc.

Avon, Avon & logo, and Avon Books & logo are registered trademarks of HarperCollins Publishers in the United States of America and other countries.

HarperCollins is a registered trademark of HarperCollins Publishers in the United States of America and other countries.

FIRST EDITION

Printed in Lithuania

21 22 23 24 25 SB 10 9 8 7 6 5 4 3 2 1

If you purchased this book without a cover, you should be aware that this book is stolen property. It was reported as "unsold and destroyed" to the publisher, and neither the author nor the publisher has received any payment for this "stripped book."

To J.M. Your friendship, encouragement, and belief in me through the past year helped make a hard year bearable and this book possible. Thank you, always, for everything.

Acknowledgments

*E*ndless thanks to my brilliant editor, Elle; my great agent, Jill; and my funny, creative, and endlessly supportive Avon sister, Charis. Without your ideas, feedback, and support as I developed this series, this book would never have happened.

Heartfelt gratitude to everyone at Avon who touched or will be a part of getting this book into the hands of readers. Thank you.

And my deepest thanks go to readers who give this new book in a brand-new series a chance.

DUKE GONE ROGUE

Chapter One

February 1894
St. James's Square, London

William Hart, Duke of Ashmore, was a practical man. He had no time for fancies and didn't believe in impossibilities. Give him facts and figures. Give him what he could see and touch and measure.

Over the previous two years, the duties of a dukedom and the death of his mother had entirely worn away the impulsive young man he'd once been.

Or so he'd believed. Tonight, rogue impulses rang in his mind.

Walk away. Choose better.

He looked out into the London night and then at his companion across the expanse of his carriage, musing over two options. Practical Will urged him to have the coachman turn around and return the lady to her residence and face the consequences of that choice. But some flickering remnant of Reckless Will made him want to fling open the carriage door, jump from the moving vehicle, and escape into the night.

He let the idea play out in his mind and imagined the mention in scandal rags.

In the long Ashmore tradition of doing asinine things . . .

No one would be surprised to see the Ashmore name on those pages again. His father had given them plenty to print, and London society had expected Will to take on the old roué's debauchery the moment he'd inherited the title.

Gossipmongers still watched him at social events, waiting for him to spark a scandal.

Will was determined to defy them all.

His father had been a man of destruction, breaking vows and betraying trust every day of his life. *Indulgence, excess, impulse*—those had been his bywords.

So Will devoted himself to putting things right. It had become his constant endeavor—uncovering his father's dishonesty, making amends, offering recompense to those the old devil had duped and swindled.

All he wanted from London society was for the Ashmore name to stay off their tongues. Which meant jumping out of the carriage was out of the question.

But that still left him on the eve of a battle he neither desired nor knew how to win. His jaw ached from how tightly every muscle in his body had coiled during the quarter-hour crawl through London's thick fog.

The skirmish was coming. He just didn't know when.

He drew in a breath to break the silence that had dragged on too long.

Lady Davina Desmond finally came alive, bristling before he could speak. "We shall put in an appearance and be on our way," she said in an arctic tone.

"As you wish."

An odd sound came then, a huff of utter disdain. Then she finally turned to him, shoulders ramrod straight, her face an emotionless mask. She was the consummate well-bred noblewoman.

It was, after all, why he'd agreed to their engagement.

"This invitation was accepted weeks ago," she said while staring his way but not truly meeting his gaze. For all he knew, she was staring at the blue velvet upholstery behind his head. "It wouldn't do to decline the Countess of Trenmere." This pronouncement came with a vicious tug at the elbow of each of her gloves.

In every word and movement, the lady telegraphed fury.

"We should do our duty, of course." It was the goal he set himself each day.

"Duty?" she scoffed.

He frowned.

Duty was what had led them both to an engagement brokered by her father, a meeting in which they both agreed that their marriage would be sensible. Nothing as fanciful as infatuation. That nonsense never lasted. Their bargain was better. An arrangement that benefited both parties in the most practical of ways.

The equation was simple. He had a title; her father offered an enviable dowry. And at the time, his dukedom had needed funds. Desperately. Now the Ashmore coffers were healthier. His sisters could finally feel a bit more secure, socially and financially. He'd been able to recoup much of what their father had squandered via investments.

His engagement was not as necessary as it had once seemed, which allowed him to notice one very relevant fact. His fiancée loathed him. Perhaps it was that he was too joyless, as she'd once accused, or didn't enjoy parties as she did. Or maybe his own need had blinded him to her reticence about the match from the start, despite her family's glee over matching their daughter with a duke.

He didn't miss the irony of Lady Davina hating him now for the very propriety that had persuaded him to marry her in the first place.

"There are matters more important than duty, Ashmore."

"Such as?" He was baiting her but couldn't help himself. He preferred plain speaking, and she'd been prevaricating for days.

"Family," she said emphatically, then notched up her chin.

"Family *is* a duty, Davina. Perhaps the most important of all."

"You can't believe that. Not after what you've done to mine."

Will let out a sigh and pinched the bridge of his nose. "Your uncle bears that responsibility." The man had swindled a circle of friends, bilking each nobleman out of sums approaching a thousand pounds. Enough to leave at least two of them paupers. Will had uncovered the man's malfeasance while investigating his own father's crimes. He'd never told a soul, but he had confronted Davina's uncle—both as a warning and to discover the extent of his father's involvement. For whatever reason, the man had confessed the whole sordid business to the entire Desmond clan.

"*Your* father started the scheme," she hissed at him.

"With your uncle. They were equal partners."

"And would you have ruined your own father too?"

"Gladly." He sometimes dreamed of turning back time and uncovering his father's misdeeds before his death. How he would have relished seeing the man face some kind of justice for the damage he'd done to their family and the dukedom.

"My goodness, you are cruel."

Perhaps he was. He'd been told as much before. He found it hard to forgive those who hurt others for sport, and impossible to overlook harm done to his family. "My only wish is to do what's right."

She let out a bitter chuckle. "Ah, yes, the oh so very proper son of the devil duke."

Will clenched his teeth and tasted blood. Any mention of his father dredged up an endless well of anger inside of him.

"He's not the duke anymore. And it falls to me to restore my family's reputation."

Davina remained freakishly still, as if she held her breath.

He was prepared for tears, shouting, or even the possibility she might leap across the carriage and bash him as her glare told him she wished to. Words seemed to catch in her throat. She swallowed, opened her mouth, yet said nothing. Only her hands moved, gloved fingers tightening around the tufted edge of her bench.

"Say what you must. Do your worst, and let's get this over with," he finally said.

Her blue eyes narrowed. "Have you ever failed, Ashmore? Made a mistake? Brought scandal to yourself and your family?" Her low, whispering tone sent a shiver down his spine.

"Never." He rasped out the word.

She spoke his greatest fear.

"One day you will." She raked her gaze over him from head to toe. "It's in your blood. Your birthright, some might say. When that day comes, you'll understand how a man can make a mistake and not deserve to have his life ruined."

"I merely sought the truth from your uncle, Davina."

"What if his name finds its way into the papers? He'd be shunned by society and lose every friend he's ever had."

"I've spoken to no one, though he may confess to whoever he chooses. But for the sake of the dukedom, I must put things right," Will repeated. More than an explanation, it was a plea for her to understand his motives.

But she didn't.

Leaning over, Davina pointed a finger toward his chest. At the same moment, the carriage rolled to a stop and she settled against the squabs. With a deep breath, she seemed to transform into the poised noblewoman he'd first met months before. She even managed the semblance of a smile.

A footman opened the carriage door and offered his hand to assist her. But she waited, staring at Will a moment longer.

"You're not as perfect as you pretend. You'll topple from your pedestal one day, Ashmore, and I only hope I'm there to see it."

MADELINE RAVENWOOD HAD come to London to do what she loved most.

"Let me bring you up to London to paint Trenmere House with greenery and blooms," the Countess of Trenmere had offered. Her London town house's garden required a redesign, and the party this evening was to be festooned with hundreds of blooms.

Maddie couldn't resist any opportunity that called on her love of flowers and garden design. She tried to put aside her worries about the business she'd left behind in Cornwall for the duration of her short visit to the city, but it was always on her mind. A weight on her heart. She'd taken on the running of Ravenwood Nursery to honor all of her parents' hard work after their passing, but it left little time for anything else.

Her first trip to the city had been a true treat.

In two days, she'd met half a dozen of Lady Trenmere's friends, some of whom had spoken of calling on her to design their own garden spaces. And yesterday she'd slipped away to visit the British Museum and attend a lecture by a famous botanist. This would be her last night in the city, and her sense of wistfulness about departing shocked her.

"You can take one if you'd like," Maddie called to a maid who'd stopped to smell a vase of freesias as she walked by with a tray of refreshments.

"Oh, miss, I couldn't."

"I bought those myself in Covent Garden this morning and added them to the bouquets for a touch of scent." Maddie approached, took a fragrant bloom from the vase, and presented it to the girl. "So, you see, they're mine to give."

The girl beamed as she walked away. Maddie smiled too.

If only the joy-inducing power of flowers could solve every problem.

As she worked to arrange floral centerpieces in the dining room, resonant vibrations from the hired musicians echoed in the hallway. Maddie tapped her toes compulsively to the rhythmic sound mixed with the titter of conversation filtering out from the overcrowded drawing room.

Maddie's curiosity gnawed at her like a caterpillar worked at a leaf.

As soon as the maid departed and the dining room was finished, she made her way to a spot across from the drawing room's open pocket doors. Two mature, lush Kentia palms stood opposite the doors, and Maddie stepped behind them, parting two large fronds to gaze into the lively room.

The mix of colors rivaled a garden in late-autumn bloom. Gentlemen dressed in black and formal white tie contrasted with ladies wrapped in silk and velvet in rich, dark colors: plum, sapphire, crimson. They filled the space in clusters, some reclining on settees while others mingled in corners.

A small soiree, the countess had said, but Maddie counted no less than twenty-five guests.

"The flowers look perfect. Thank you, Madeline."

Maddie jumped at the sound of the countess's voice and turned to face the woman she'd come to know well. Lady Trenmere was a young widow, and with an age difference of only seven years between them, they'd become less formal than patroness and botanical adviser.

"You're very welcome. I thought you'd already be in the drawing room."

"Oh no, my dear. Never enter a room first." Susan smiled, and her bellflower blue eyes twinkled. "Always wait to make *an entrance*."

Maddie grinned, as much at the advice as at the notion that she might ever put it to use. Her life would never include making a grand entrance or catching everyone's notice. Unless it was when she accepted first prize for her roses at the upcoming flower show in Haven Cove. That was one bit of acclaim she did want. If she could stir some interest in her flowers and garner attention for Ravenwood Nursery, maybe she could save what her parents had spent so many years creating.

But Lady Trenmere persisted in believing another future lay ahead for Maddie. *You're the grand-daughter of a viscount*, she reminded her often. She and Maddie's mother had been friends. Perhaps Lady Trenmere knew that Mama had been disowned for marrying Maddie's father, the family's groundskeeper, but she was too polite to mention that history.

"Are you certain you don't wish to join us?" Susan offered her arm as if inviting Maddie for a stroll in Hyde Park.

"No." Maddie returned her warm smile. "My train leaves early tomorrow."

"Very well." Susan let out a dramatic sigh. "It's not fair for me to admire your diligence and keep you from your responsibilities, I suppose."

"Next time you throw a party at Allswell, I promise to attend if you wish."

Allswell was Susan's retreat for much of the year, a Cornish manor gifted by her late husband shortly after their wedding. Maddie had been maintaining its gardens and helping Susan cultivate prizewinning camellias there for years.

"Rest well, travel safely, and remember me to Haven Cove." She started across the foyer and then turned back. "A carriage will be ready to take you to the station as early as you wish to depart."

"Thank you, my lady."

Maddie watched her glide across the hall and fought the impulse to follow. It was the music that drew her. Her mother had taught her how to dance and to play the violin, but she rarely found reason to practice either.

There'd be no dancing for her tonight either. What could she have to say to ladies who spent their days planning their next social engagement? She was a businesswoman with a heap of work waiting for her in Cornwall. In the morning, she'd head home and stop imagining what it might be like to attend elegant dinner parties.

Still, the colors, the music, the laughter in the drawing room drew her like a hungry bee to nectar. She stepped toward the enormous palms again, hoping to see but go unseen. Voices had lifted in excitement when Lady Trenmere swept into the room. Before leaving, Maddie wanted to get one last glimpse of her, happy and drawing all the attention she desired.

Guests swarmed around the countess, and Maddie rose onto her toes to get a better view. One man stood out from the rest. Tall and broad-shouldered, he blocked her view of everything else. She maneuvered a little to the left to spot Susan, but the blasted man stepped left too. Then a young lady approached him, and the pair blocked Maddie's view entirely.

Oh well.

Lowering onto her feet, she moved to squeeze out from the nook where the potted palms stood and tripped on a brass leg of the planter. Reaching out, she grasped the trunk of one palm to steady herself. The leaves shook, and she let out a little squeak of alarm and then prayed that no one in the drawing room had heard. Once she got her footing, one glance assured her that no one had noticed her clumsiness.

Then *he* turned. The tall dark-haired behemoth with view-blocking shoulders. She was in a corner. In the shadows. Wearing a dark dress. He couldn't possibly see her. And yet his gaze held on her, steady and intense and as velvety dark as the inner petal of a poppy.

One brow, as black as his gaze, arched up as he gave her a disdainful perusal from the palm frond near her head to the spot where the hem of her gown hung over the leg of the planter.

Breath tangled in her throat, and she froze. The man possessed a hard face, all sharp angles and elegant edges, as if he'd been carved or hewn. Only his mouth held the potential of softness. Perhaps if he smiled. And yet the narrow set of his eyes and unrelenting squareness of his jaw promised nothing like mirth.

Maddie held still. Didn't move. Didn't breathe.

She yearned to flee and yet feared moving and drawing the notice of more than one man.

If only he'd forget her and her foolish stumble.

Turn away. Good grief, why did he glower at her when he had a pretty young woman at his elbow? With those broad shoulders and chiseled jaw, it was a wonder there was only one lady seeking his attention.

Finally, he pivoted to face the lady beside him, but his frown remained. He seemed an entirely glum man, even if he was distractingly well-made.

Maddie took advantage of his moment of inattention to slip out of the hallway and into the countess's conservatory. The warm, high-ceilinged space was the one place she never lost her footing. The scent of damp earth and the green of new growth soothed her nerves.

Thank heavens she hadn't given in to Lady Trenmere's invitation to attend the party. She would have hated the necessity of attempting conversation with anyone as grumpy and arrogant as that horribly observant man.

Chapter Two

Will glanced toward the hallway again. The young woman was gone.

What a strange, awkward creature. With that auburn hair of hers, lurking was ineffectual, no matter how large the plant she chose to hide behind.

He hoped she wasn't one of those surreptitious wallflower types who watched quietly from the edge of a social event and then went home to a typewriter and fashioned wild tales to print in gossip rags.

Truth be told, the minute he'd spotted her, he'd envied the red-haired observer. Now that she was gone, even more so. If he could escape this ridiculously cramped drawing room and the razor-sharp glares Davina kept throwing his way, he'd count himself a lucky man.

His impulse in the carriage had been correct. Attending the party with Davina had been a mistake. As she stood beside him, she was all but vibrating with frustration, and even her usual practiced facade wasn't enough to conceal her misery. The conversation he needed to have with her was long overdue.

The sigh of relief he let out involuntarily when a lady friend called her away from across the room was probably audible to everyone around him.

He glanced toward the hallway. Still no lady in the palms.

"You're in for an unpleasant evening, Ashmore. Your bride-to-be seems displeased." Lord Esquith didn't sound at all sympathetic as he spoke the words in a confidential tone and took a spot next to Will near the threshold.

The man had once shown an interest in Davina, despite being thirty years her senior and very recently widowed.

"Perhaps it's not the best night for a party." Will had confronted Davina's uncle months ago, but it seemed she'd only learned of it recently. Maintaining the pretense of their practical engagement was becoming impossible for both of them.

"Do you ever enjoy a party?" Lord Esquith couldn't seem to speak without smirking. He'd been a crony of Will's father, though Will had uncovered no crimes on the middle-aged lord's part, aside from a penchant for attending the late duke's wild house parties without the accompaniment of his wife.

"Very rarely."

"So unlike your father."

Will walked a few steps away to keep himself from saying something reckless and took a dainty aperitif from a passing servant. He wanted a whiskey, but needs must.

The urge to find a balcony and escape for a breath

of fresh air had him darting his gaze around the room.

Lord Esquith failed to notice that Will did not care to continue the conversation. Instead, he'd followed Will.

"At least your father could enliven a party."

"Yes, while he was swindling you behind your back." Will did his best not to crush the little crystal glass in his hand.

"He was a generous host and a jolly man. People liked him." Esquith sniffed haughtily. Loudly. For some reason, the fool wanted to cause a scene.

Will turned and took a step closer. "If you wish to provoke me to violence in the Countess of Trenmere's drawing room, please continue."

The nobleman had the good sense to take a step back in retreat, but he didn't depart and hovered on the verge of saying more.

"How dare you threaten me? You're nothing but a boor who will never possess an ounce of the charm your father did."

"I don't need his charm." Will somehow managed to unclench his hand long enough to hand his empty glass to a footman. "I have his title, his dukedom, and a record of all his crimes."

The aristocrat turned as white as his tie. Perhaps he *had* been party to some nefarious undertaking of Will's father. Whatever the cause, Lord Esquith's lower lip trembled as he offered Will one final sneer before turning on his heel and walking away.

Will didn't want a scandal. It would destroy all the respectability he'd been trying to achieve for years. Worse, any impulsive mistake of his wouldn't simply further tarnish the dukedom, it would harm his sisters.

Their future was his to protect.

Scanning the room, he caught Davina's gaze, but only long enough for her to glare and turn her back on him.

"Excuse me." Will barked the words again at a nobleman blocking his way.

Will recognized him as a viscount who'd joined an investment scheme with his father. Was there a single nobleman in England who hadn't been in thrall to the man?

Will sidestepped him and passed through a gaggle of couples to cross the threshold and emerge into the hallway. He stared at the glossy palms where the girl had stood.

Where had she escaped to?

He strode down the hallway in search of either a balcony or a drinks cart. After several minutes he'd found neither, but light filtered out from a whitewashed, earthy-scented conservatory, and it seemed an acceptable haven.

TEN MINUTES IN the conservatory, and Maddie's thoughts were fully occupied with plants and ideas about the countess's garden design. Only a faint reverberation of music now and then reminded her that a party was going on, and she tried especially hard to forget the odious man with a marble jaw who'd scowled at her across the hall.

She took one last wander through the collection of palms, geraniums, and flowering vines the countess favored. As she started toward the far door that let out near the house's staircase, she heard footsteps on the conservatory tiles. Heavy steps.

She swung around to see who'd intruded on her peaceful moment.

It was him. The grim statue of a man.

Her heart slammed against her ribs at the notion that he might have sought her out.

But, as she watched him, it was clear that he wasn't seeking anyone or anything but solitude. He glanced behind him as if concerned he might have been followed. Then he stalked to the edge of the conservatory, planted one hand on the cool glass wall, and ran the other through the black waves of his hair.

Fingers balled into a fist, he pounded once against the window and then turned away.

She had a wild urge to step into view and demand to know why he had stared at her in the hallway. But what she truly wanted to know was why he looked so miserable.

She dragged in a deep breath and took a step forward. And stopped in her tracks.

"How dare you?" A woman's voice echoed off the glass walls. As she came into view, Maddie recognized her as the young woman who'd stood near him in the drawing room. "I was just coming to speak to you, and you simply walked away."

The man whirled to face her but didn't approach.

"I left the drawing room for your sake," he said with a tone of calm. "You're unsettled, and neither of us wishes to spark gossip. I'll depart if you prefer. I can call on you tomorrow, or you can come to me."

The lady shook her head vehemently. "No. We'll do this now. I desire no further visits from you, nor do I wish to call on you."

"Very well." He nodded once, seemingly unaffected. But his carved jaw firmed, and the lines between his brows deepened. "I hold you to nothing and will say whatever you wish."

She tugged furiously at one of her long white gloves, fumbling over the pearl buttons. "Whatever I wish?"

"Of course. I bear you no ill will."

She tugged at her last button and stripped off her left glove. Her cheeks flamed as she pulled at a ring on her finger and then threw the glittering band. It bounced off the broad expanse of the man's snug waistcoat and pinged as it hit the tile floor.

"I wish you to say that *I* broke our engagement. Some will think me mad to jilt a man of your rank, but then they'll remember your cruelty and joylessness. In the end, I think I shall come out all the better for it."

He drew in a long breath, and the tight set of his shoulders eased as he exhaled. "Then, it's settled.

I'll say you broke the engagement. I'll even admit to my joylessness." Oddly, he smiled then. Dimples flashed at the edges of his mouth. But it was a sad expression, heavy with the words she'd just thrown at him.

"You're a heartless man. He's my family. You might simply have never spoken to him of what you learned."

Sighing deeply, he raked a hand through his hair once more. "He possessed information I required about my father's dealings."

"Your father is dead and can't pay a price for his wrongs. My uncle is alive, and what you've uncovered will forever hang over him."

"I'm sorry."

"You're not. Not truly. People warned me of your rigidity, but I never dreamed I could loathe you this much." The lady spun on her heel and rushed from the room in a whirl of taffeta and silk.

Maddie moved backward, trying not to make a sound. If she could cross to the edge of the conservatory, she could exit through the far door. But her boots weren't silent no matter how gently she stepped.

The gentleman's head snapped up, and he turned in her direction. "Whoever you are, show yourself."

Maddie gnawed at her lip and decided sneaking about and getting caught would be far more mortifying than facing the man and pointing out that *he* had intruded on her solitude. She stepped out of a cluster of vines and faced him.

"Of course it's you." He tugged at his tie until it hung loosely at this throat. "The lady hiding in the palm."

"The gentleman blocking my view of the drawing room."

A black brow shot skyward. He almost seemed offended by the accusation. Then his eyes swept over her as if he was looking for something. "Do you work for Special Branch or a newspaper, or is eavesdropping just a hobby?"

"I wasn't eavesdropping. I was just—"

"You could have entered the drawing room instead of lurking in a plant. Are you not a guest of Lady Trenmere's?"

"I am." She didn't wish to explain the rest. He wasn't the sort of man she wanted to converse with any longer than necessary.

He stared at her expectantly, his gaze flicking down to her mouth. "Perhaps you're wise. I should have avoided that drawing room myself."

Maddie glanced in the direction the lady had gone. "Should you go after her?"

He let out a huff, but Maddie couldn't tell if he thought her question absurd or amusing.

"Go after a lady who loathes me? Doesn't seem like the best idea. Besides, I'm heartless, remember?" He shrugged those brawny shoulders, stretching the fabric of his suit jacket so tight she could see the threads in the seam. "The lady was well within her rights."

He sounded cold, just as the woman had said.

But there was something in his expression. Maddie didn't even know the man's name, but she recognized regret.

"Is it true?"

"That I'm heartless? Completely." He set his shoulders back, lifted his chin, and crossed his arms across his chest. His evening-suit fabric stretched taut again, and he almost seemed to be holding his breath. He'd become a statue of stone, impervious to anything as soft as a lady's denunciation.

Except for his eyes.

Maddie got caught up in staring at his inscrutable gaze. Then, pointlessly, she noticed that his hair only seemed black, and a few strands of umber caught in the gas lamps.

The nobleman seemed as good at watchfulness as she was. Better, perhaps. It was almost too much to be examined by him. Surely he noticed how out of place she was here at Trenmere House. He swept his gaze over her clothing, even sparing a glance for her unfashionable boots. She suspected he'd notice the cut-flower stains on her fingers soon.

Maddie turned her glance to a trellis nearby, just to be free of his assessing perusal. Sleep was what she needed most. This silent standoff was ridiculous, and if anyone found them, the questions would be equally so.

"If you'll excuse me." She nodded and hoped that was sufficient leave-taking for an encounter with a heartless stranger in a conservatory.

"Wait." He spoke the word as a command, and Maddie had the distinct impression he was quite used to ordering others about.

Then he took a step that brought him much closer and planted himself in her path.

"You have a . . ." He raised his hand and gestured toward her head. "Just there." He pointed at a spot above her temple.

Maddie lifted a hand to pat at her disheveled hair. She'd been working for hours, and her red curls never remained neatly tamed for long.

He stepped closer. Maddie took a step back.

That little flicker of a grin curved his mouth. "You needn't fear me."

"She did say you're cruel." Maddie held his gaze as he extended his hand toward her and tugged at something in her hair.

"This was clinging to you." He presented her with a little desiccated leaf in the center of his palm.

"It must have fallen," she explained in case he thought she adorned herself on purpose. She glanced up at the decorative tree that stood near the center of the room.

He still held his palm out, waiting for her to retrieve the leaf. She did and drew in a sharp breath at the warmth of his bare skin.

"A ficus leaf." Suddenly her voice had gone breathy, and her heart was tapping such a fearsome tattoo she wondered if he could hear it.

How long had it been since she'd stood this close

to a gentleman? Been alone with a gentleman? A long time. And even then, the young man in question hadn't been anything like this stranger.

Then she noticed that a leaf had caught him too. As tall as he was, it was a wonder there was only one. It was impossible not to pass the shedding ficus on the way into the conservatory.

"You have one too." She nudged her chin in his direction.

"Do I?" He looked down at his vest.

"Here." Maddie reached out to retrieve the leaf from his shoulder, but he was somehow taller than she realized and farther away than she calculated. She tipped too far forward, lost her balance, and rested her palm on his chest to catch herself. He pressed a hand to her waist to help steady her, but an instant later they both let go.

It had been one brief touch, so quick she might have imagined it if not for the tingling heat where his hand had rested.

Now that they were close, nothing seemed to escape his notice. She sensed him appraising the faded scar at the edge of her jaw, the beauty mark near her upper lip, and the wisps of hair that had slipped their pins.

This near, she noticed things too. Aspects she hadn't noticed when she'd been struck by his chiseled beauty from across the hall. His eyes weren't truly black. They were the darkest of browns. And while there were deep grooves between his brows, laugh lines hugged his mouth.

Perhaps he wasn't as grim as he seemed, or at least he hadn't been once upon a time.

"I . . ." She didn't know for sure what she'd meant to say. She needed to go. That was all she knew for sure.

He was far too handsome, and her heart was doing odd things in her chest. And none of it mattered. She was returning to Cornwall, and he would be wanted in the drawing room.

"You're a peculiar young woman."

Not exactly the assessment she'd anticipated, but she couldn't deny it.

"Yes, well, if you'll excuse me." Walking away was what she should have done five minutes ago. But this time when she attempted to skirt her way around his sizable bulk, he skimmed a hand along her arm to keep her from going.

"I must ask something of you."

Maddie considered bolting from the room.

Speaking to the man was folly. Remaining in his company, more so. Letting him touch her wasn't even debatably proper. It was, as Lady Trenmere might say, beyond the pale. She owed the imperious aristocrat nothing except to leave him alone.

Yet she found herself locked in place and the desire to escape waning.

"What is it?" The words came out with more of an irritated bite than she'd intended.

They were standing far too close now. They'd already touched each other, and she didn't even know his name.

"I plan to escape through those doors at the back of the conservatory and spare my former fiancée any further distress."

It seemed a reasonable strategy. Maddie couldn't imagine what her part might be.

"What is it you want of me?"

"Your discretion."

"Of course." What she'd witnessed would be mortifying to most people, let alone to nobles who held themselves to standards set by dusty etiquette books. He and the lady would both make up polite stories of how they'd parted ways, and only the two of them would know the truth.

The two of them and Maddie.

"You needn't worry, sir. I'll say nothing. I'm leaving London tomorrow and likely won't return."

"Ever?" He frowned, and there was something like disappointment in his tone.

But Maddie decided that was her own fanciful nature making silly assumptions. Shouldn't her departure please him beyond measure?

"Possibly." Her life, her business, and the community she was a part of were all in Cornwall. Regardless of the wistful sadness she'd been battling at the thought of leaving London.

Of all she'd seen and experienced, this odd encounter would be the strangest of her memories.

"Farewell, heartless gentleman."

The glower on his face held, and then he shocked her. His lips twitched up in a smile that transformed him. Amusement made him come alive. His eyes brightened, his jaw softened, and he was suddenly more than handsome. He was tantalizing.

"Goodbye, lady of the greenery." His voice wasn't the harsh bark of before. It was warmer, intimate, just for her ears.

None of it mattered. Not his velvet voice or his bone-melting smile.

She would never see the man again. She was leaving. And, finally, that's what she did.

After one last look at him, she walked away.

Chapter Three

Three months later
Grosvenor Square, London

A lady screeched, and the sound lanced through Will's sleep-dulled brain like a hot blade.

Stop. Did he speak the word, or was it just rattling around in his throat yearning to get out? Speech wouldn't come. His mind was fuzzy and clouded. Beyond the echo of the lady's wail, he heard only one word. His father's title, which was now his. Then the honorific he'd always loathed because he'd grown up hearing it when others addressed his father.

Your Grace. The two words came again and again, relentlessly and with increasing volume.

"Your Grace." A man's voice. Familiar too.

Will opened his eyes, and his body jolted as if he'd been given a dose of Mr. Edison's voltage. Everything hurt—the painful twist in his neck, the ache in his back, and the headache dancing a ring around his head.

Squinting, he surveyed his dimly lit study and made out the owner of the voice that had awoken him.

"Whittier." The butler he'd hired because he could no longer trust the one who'd served his father for decades. "Good god, man, did you truly let me fall asleep during a meeting?"

"You merely closed your eyes for a moment, sir." Whittier lifted his very thin, very pale brows. "You seemed to require it. Besides"—he held up a glinting crystal glass containing a scant finger of amber liquid—"it gave me a chance to nip at my whiskey."

"It's the afternoon."

"It is evening." The middle-aged man's eyes flashed with concern. "You offered me a drink when I arrived in your study, Your Grace. We were discussing preparations for tonight's dinner party."

"Were we?" Will couldn't remember. Restful sleep hadn't come for weeks. Months. Fatigue was beginning to make him forgetful, and he hated it. He loathed admitting to any failing.

"Indeed, sir."

His own unconsumed drink, a generous pour compared to Whittier's mere finger, sat on the blotter in front of him. He gripped the glass, and the cool cut crystal felt soothing under his palm.

"Are you unwell, Your Grace?" The butler's gaze was assessing, worried.

"I'm well. Only a bit tired. I shall get through dinner and then retreat early." Whether he would manage any sleep was another question. "How many are we expecting tonight?" Will swigged down the whiskey. Might as well stop wasting the man's time and go and do his duty as host.

"The usual number, Your Grace."

"What was that god-awful noise?" He could no longer hear the voice of the lady who had awoken him, but her singing wasn't what anyone could call harmonious.

"It's the soprano Lady Daisy is considering for her upcoming engagement party. I believe she's been invited this evening as a sort of trial performance."

"Wonderful." Will bit back a groan.

"If that's all, sir, I shall go and see that all is in place as guests begin to arrive."

"Very good." Will watched as the butler drained his glass and placed it along with an abandoned coffee cup on his tray before heading for the door.

Once Whittier had gone, Will allowed himself the groan he'd been holding back. He dreaded this evening's dinner, even though it would be small and intimate compared to the bash his sisters were planning to host in a few days.

And it wasn't just the dinner or this party. After weeks of fitful sleep, doing the usual sorts of social rounds filled with pretense and inane small talk had begun to chip away at his patience.

"For Daisy," he mumbled to himself. Anything was bearable for his sister's sake. Whatever financial straits or social scandals their father had left them to untangle, Daisy would never suffer the consequences. Not if Will could help it. The dukedom's finances were healthy enough to give her the kind of day she deserved.

Her wedding would be lavish. So grand that none

in London society would guess at the way their father had depleted the Ashmore coffers.

Will closed his eyes and pressed the heel of his palm between his brows where pain hammered at his skull.

He let out a sigh and tried not to move or breathe or do anything that might unsettle the moment of calm. He'd never liked social events, never developed the skill of conversing easily and choosing the right thing to say at the right moment. The truth was that he didn't have time for soirees and frivolity, even if his sisters seemed to think it was their family's duty to entertain half of London as aggressively as their father had. Indeed, his sister Cora insisted that engaging in *good* society was part of the work of redeeming the Ashmore name.

Will stood and headed for the drawing room.

"Pardon me, Your Grace."

A few feet from his study, a footman called out, and Will stepped nearer the wall so that a parade of maids and footmen carrying silver bowls teeming with foliage and blooms could pass. One maid struggled with her towering floral arrangement and thwacked him with an enormous pink flower on the way by. The footman behind her gasped, stopped in his tracks, and stared at Will wide-eyed as if expecting the lot of them to be fired.

"Carry on," Will told the young man through clenched teeth.

A moment later, he stepped into Ashmore House's large front drawing room.

Heads turned. Voices stilled. A cluster of ladies pivoted toward him as one, whipping their fans as if they were brandishing weapons.

He recognized two of them as close friends of Davina. Months later, he was still considered an ogre among her circle, and even gentlemen he'd once considered friendly acquaintances couldn't seem to meet his gaze.

When the room grew uncomfortably quiet, Daisy stepped into the center of the carpet. She was feigning joviality, but Will noted the pinched pleat of her brow even as she smiled broadly.

"Let's have more music before we dine." She cast a look toward the piano where one of her friends had taken up the bench.

On cue, the young lady's fingers danced across the keys as she played a lively concerto.

Eventually, guests lost interest in Will's presence, except for a few ladies who studied him as if he was a puzzle to be solved.

Clearly he was a distraction, and not a welcome one. His presence was putting a pall over the whole gathering, and his sisters wished for each of their dinner parties to be a success.

Cora might harangue him later, but he took it as an excuse to slip away.

He made it all the way to his study, poured a glass, and slumped into the wingback in front of the fire before someone rapped on the door.

"Not now."

He just needed half an hour of relative silence, and with any luck, the whiskey would take him.

Another knock. A little louder. More insistent. He knew exactly who it was.

"Go away," he said lightly.

"We should go in together." Daisy's voice carried through the closed door. She couldn't conceal her overflowing vivacity with a whisper.

"I'll speak to him first. Soften the way." Cora, the middle sibling and more practical than all of them, spoke in a tone that Will knew meant she would brook no refusal.

Leaning back in his chair, he stared at the wood panel of the door, willing one of them to decide and come speak to him so that he could either drink or sleep. Just on the point of standing to usher them both in, Cora knocked twice before stepping inside the room alone.

"You heard us," she said matter-of-factly.

"Mostly Daisy. But yes." Will noticed the way his sister clasped and unclasped her hands. She was nervous but looked frighteningly determined. A chill skittered down his back. "What are you two scheming?"

Individually, his sisters were formidable. Combined in their efforts, he imagined they could hold back the Thames by sheer will if they put their minds to it.

Cora smiled, and Will's belly dropped to his boots. She was a lady who did not give her smiles freely, and this one was a bit too wide to be the least bit believable.

"You left the drawing room rather abruptly."

"I thought it best once I saw Davina's friends."

"They're nieces of Lady Tidwell. It would have been a snub to not invite them."

"Of course, and I'm content in my study."

"What do you think of the soprano Daisy chose?" She spoke in a tone that told him music was the last thing she truly wished to discuss.

"Don't make me equivocate, Cora. She's dreadful."

"I prefer to think of her as memorable."

"You haven't come to discuss music."

"I did." Cora was a whip-smart young woman, keen about opera, fond of walks in Hyde Park, better at organizing and planning than anyone he'd ever known, and the worst liar in London. "Or at least it was one of the things I intended to mention."

She stepped forward, her inquisitive gaze taking in the pile of notes and correspondence he'd used to assemble the details of their father's scheme. Will flipped the letter he'd been reading so that she couldn't see its contents.

"What is it you've been working on? A lecture for the Architectural Society?"

He'd only ever given a single lecture. Though he'd studied architecture at university and found it fascinating, being the center of attention and trying to hold the interest of an audience filled with judgmental scholars didn't interest him at all.

"Or are you sketching again?" she asked with a hopeful lilt in her voice. "It feels as if you've done nothing you truly enjoy since we lost Mama."

The assessment felt harsh, mostly because it was completely accurate. An irritable impulse made Will want to reply with some biting commentary about the burdens of overseeing a dukedom. But she knew.

"No. This is a matter related to Father."

"You've found something else he did. Something terrible."

The worry in her tone was what he wanted to avoid. He'd kept much of what he'd learned about their father's infamy to himself, just as his mother had shielded all of them while she'd lived. But he couldn't stop working to discover the extent of the man's misdeeds. Making amends was the only way he knew to undo what their father had done.

"You needn't worry. I shall deal with all of it."

The grim set of her mouth tightened.

"Don't fret. We'll see this through. Daisy's wedding. Yours, eventually."

She grimaced at that.

"And yours?" She pinned him with an expectant stare.

"Eventually." Marriage, he knew, was high on the list of requirements he'd taken on when he became duke. He'd thought to fulfill that duty with Davina, but he'd misjudged. Badly.

Now all of his energy was devoted to righting the

damage done by their father, recompensing those he could, accepting responsibility in ways the late duke never had.

"You've done a great deal to redeem the Ashmore title." Her words were stated plainly and didn't feel like praise. "I know it's a burden, and you look exhausted."

The comment took him aback. Ladies didn't comment on his looks except in exuberant tones, especially now that he'd inherited a dukedom. And, of course, he was exhausted. He'd found that trying to be a duke the right way was a hell of a lot more difficult than simply sinking into debauchery as his father had been content to do.

"Have you considered a holiday?"

"A holiday?" Will would have been less surprised if she'd asked him if he'd considered stealing the crown jewels or plundering a ship on the high seas.

"Yes. You know, a trip one makes for the purpose of recuperation and relaxation." Her mouth twitched as soon as she got the sentence out. Then one dark brow inched up her forehead.

"Have you ever said the word *relaxation* before in your life?"

"I'm certain I have." She was peeved now. Her voice climbed an octave.

"And have you ever taken a holiday to achieve it?"

"None of us have. We both know Father hoarded all the recreation for himself."

"I know." Will gestured at a pile on his desk. In two organized stacks were documents relating to the debts his father had accrued over years of frivolous holidays and house parties. One heap contained those that had been paid, the other consisted of the few that remained.

"Well, now we have the opportunity to take some recreation ourselves. As other people do quite regularly. To the seaside. To the continent. To the Highlands." She smiled. Cora had always longed to visit the Highlands. "Some take them every year and—"

"Yes, yes." Will raised a hand to forestall a longer explanation. "I do comprehend the concept. I merely don't understand how you can think one is in order. For me. Now." He pointed toward the door where he suspected his baby sister's ear was pressed against the polished wood. "Daisy's engagement party is less than a week away."

"Precisely."

"I am serving as host, am I not? I hope to bloody hell it's still being hosted here at Ashmore House. Otherwise, my nerves have suffered weeks of noise and chaos for nothing."

Cora glanced at the carpet, took a deep bolstering breath, and squared her shoulders. "Our family is hosting the party here at Ashmore House."

"And I am the head of our family." Will spoke slowly, drawing out each word, recognizing the absurdity of speaking the obvious to one of the most intelligent women he knew.

"You are."

"Thank you." He shot her a smirk, but her expression remained immovable.

"I still think a holiday would do you good."

"Cora, it's not the right time. The party—"

"Lady Davina Desmond will be in attendance."

"I see."

"How could we avoid inviting her?"

Will thought one less invitation would have made his sisters' lives easier, but of course, this one was more delicate than the others.

"Her cousins are close friends of Daisy. And apparently her family is connected to Andrew."

Andrew was Daisy's fiancé, and though Will hadn't known of the connection to Davina, it didn't surprise him. The ties between noble families were many and tangled.

"I'm sorry if it pains you."

"It doesn't. My engagement never felt right, just practical. I wish her well, but I take it she doesn't feel the same."

Cora shot him a look that was something between shock and disappointment. "That's more than apparent. Whatever happened between you two, she seems to loathe you. More than most."

Will took a swig of his drink, but the familiar burn didn't bring him any comfort. Then his sister's words registered through the fuzziness of fatigue.

"What do you mean, *more than most*?"

She let out a sigh. Will had the sense that now, finally, she would arrive at the point of why she'd come to his study.

"I know you're very committed to discovering all of Father's sins. I even understand why. But it seems to have made you rather . . . unlikable among our acquaintances."

Dare he tell her that some of those acquaintances disliked him because by investigating their father's misdeeds he might uncover their own?

"You mean those who were fond of Father while he was merrily destroying our family's reputation?"

"It's hardly destroyed," she insisted. "A bit tarnished."

"Broken, Cora. Still limping. Trust me, the damage runs deep, and I suspect I haven't discovered all of it. Every day I find something he'd covered up."

"He is gone." His sister's voice rarely rose in anger. Other than Daisy, they weren't a family of shouted words and rows. Their father took that chaos with him when he passed on.

Will set his glass on the desk and approached his sister and waited.

"We mustn't focus so much on the past. The best way to change how others perceive our family is to live our lives well now. Shouldn't we move toward the future?" Without letting him answer, she added, "That's what Daisy is doing, and nothing can be allowed to mar her happiness."

"And my presence at her engagement party will."

The study door burst open, and Daisy stepped into the room. Her expressive green eyes welled with tears. "I don't wish to banish you, truly. But—"

"You want your party to be perfect." Will wanted nothing less for her.

"It's just, people think of you as—" She gulped

and stared at Cora, unwilling to finish her declaration.

"I understand." Will approached and chucked her trembling chin. "Cora is right, as she usually is." He cast their sister a mock serious look. "I am long overdue for a holiday."

"Thank you." Daisy launched herself into his arms.

As he hugged his little sister, Will's gaze met Cora's. They might not always agree on how to go about redeeming their family name, but they would never quarrel about making sure Daisy was happy.

"I must return to the party," she told him excitedly. "Cora?"

"I'll be along soon, dear."

Will waited until the door closed behind Daisy. "What *do* people think of me?"

Cora was terrible at demurring, but she attempted it. She reached down for one of the decorative pillows on the settee and plumped it.

"Just tell me." Will crossed his arms. "Heartless?" How could he forget Davina's condemnation?

"Perhaps a little. But also a bit of a . . . curmudgeon."

"That's a word for old men who refuse to be charitable and shout at birds in Green Park."

She stared at the thin line of sky visible through the drapes. "You don't seem like a young man. Since inheriting the dukedom, you've become old beyond your years. And you seem to have forgotten how to enjoy yourself."

"Well then." Her words left him feeling hollow.

He had worked so hard to cultivate a spotless reputation, striving to be the opposite of what their father had been. "Perhaps some time away is just the thing." Why stay in a city where everyone apparently thought of him as a man who'd ruin a party?

"Now it's just a matter of deciding where to go." Will emptied his glass and tried not to focus on how he hated the idea of leaving just when he was making progress reorganizing the workings of the dukedom.

"I have a suggestion."

Will smiled. "I suspected you would."

She lifted a folded piece of newsprint from inside the belt of her evening gown. The clipped piece was an article from a magazine called *The Merry Wanderer*.

Will read the first line aloud. "If a traveler relishes wild and unrivaled scenery, there is no place in all of England like the farthest southwest coast."

She came closer, practically bouncing with excitement. "From handling the family correspondence, I know Father purchased a property in Cornwall."

"Do you know anything about Carnwyth?"

The question seemed to surprise her. "I know where it is and that we own it. And that you've never visited." She pointed to the clipping. "Most importantly, I know that Cornwall is reputedly lovely, especially at this time of year."

It was true that he'd never given the property much attention. Indeed, there was a short list of properties their father had purchased—a Scottish hunting box, a house for a mistress in Hampstead, a town house for wild soirees in Cavendish Square, and this Cornish manor where, if rumors were true, their father had hosted bacchanalian house parties that lasted for weeks.

Because of its infamy, he'd been avoiding Carnwyth and the question of how to dispose of it. Perhaps this *holiday* would be an opportunity to do so.

Cora watched him, waiting, all but holding her breath.

"Fine. I'll go to Cornwall."

She grinned triumphantly. "It's a much-needed holiday, and I suspect you will find it enjoyable."

Will doubted that entirely, but staying and putting a damper on Daisy's party wasn't an appealing prospect either.

"I'll wrap up a few matters and make arrangements to depart in a couple of days."

"Arrangements have been made." She rushed to the door, stepped into the hall, and then quickly returned with a little pile of documents. "I've purchased a train ticket. I also wrote ahead to the staff, and Mr. Bly, the butler, returned this list of those currently employed at the manor. Oh, I also clipped a few other relevant pages from *The Merry Wanderer.*"

Cora's preparations didn't surprise him. She always thought several steps ahead.

But Will didn't feel ready for any of it. He took the documents from her and tried to offer a reassuring smile. Then he saw the date and time circled on the printed train timetable and looked up at her in shock.

"I know it's soon," she said with a touch of sympathy in her tone, but then she smiled. "Prepare yourself for relaxation. You start your holiday tomorrow."

Chapter Four

May 1894
Haven Cove, Cornwall

*M*addie held on to her straw hat as a cool breeze rushed across the flower fields. The wind carried the scent of the sea, and it was dense with rain that would soon follow. An hour earlier, she'd reveled in the warmth of the early-morning sun. Now storm clouds darkened the horizon, and the dip in temperature made her shiver.

A gust spun a little pile of fallen rhododendron petals, and a few brushed her skin as she reached for her tools. Standing, she felt one clinging to her hair and reached up to pull it out.

Sweet and sharp, a memory came of a tall, darkly handsome man tugging a ficus leaf from her hair.

Silly musings. There was no point in thinking of him. She was certain he'd never given her a second thought.

"Where is Eames?" she called to James, one of the garden workers she employed to help maintain Ravenwood Nursery.

"Back edge of the nursery, miss, in the hardwood fields. Preparing the order for the new hotel."

Maddie couldn't see as far as the back side of the nursery from where she stood. She eyed the bicycle she kept outside her office for quick travel around the fields, but rather than use the cycle to find Mr. Cedric Eames, her head gardener, she decided she could secure the greenhouses on her own.

Eames was where he needed to be. The order he was preparing was perhaps the most important in Ravenwood Nursery's history.

In a fortnight, Princess Beatrice would descend on their small coastal town, lodge in the new Haven Cove Hotel, dine in the hotel restaurant run by a famous chef the proprietor had enticed over from France, and oversee their town's annual flower festival. Each vendor that she visited and each item she purchased would take on a kind of minor renown. Maddie could already envision *Princess Beatrice's Favorite Tea Cake* or *The Perfume Noted by Princess Beatrice* on placards in shop windows after she departed. As coleader of the Royal Visit Committee, Maddie was tasked with overseeing every detail of making the event a success, but it was the princess's favor at the botanical exhibition that might change Maddie's stars.

Maddie had always preferred flowers to the trees and shrubs her father believed would be more profitable for the nursery. The previous year, she'd begun planting perennial flowers in the Ravenwood fields, and roses quickly became her passion. They were reputed to be too fragile for Cornwall's wild weather, but Maddie had experimented with crossing a hardy old rose her mother had grown with a daintier tea-rose variety in the prettiest pink-peach shades. More hybrid varieties had followed. And as soon as she'd learned that Queen Victoria's daughter would honor Haven Cove with a visit, she began working on a special bloom to be named in honor of the princess.

Whether she would see fit to favor Maddie's rose was the question that would gnaw at her for another fortnight.

"James, I don't have time to go back to the tree fields. But if you see Mr. Eames, tell him I'm beginning preparations for the storm."

The young man nodded and looked up nervously at the leaden sky. He looked dubious, but Maddie knew from experience how damaging one good windstorm could be. Their greenhouses still needed repairs after sustaining damage two months past.

With the death of her parents and a decrease in revenues, she'd added those repairs to the list of things that needed to be taken care of when sales were booming again.

And they would thrive again. She believed in the quality of their plants and, most of all, her roses. Now, if she could only get a princess's seal of approval, she might be able to sell them as far as Europe.

As Maddie made her way toward the greenhouses, Alice Eames stepped out of the cozy little structure Maddie's parents had built as an office from which to manage the nursery.

"Are you not to be advising the Countess of Trenmere about her garden today?" Alice was Cedric's clever daughter, and Maddie had been happy to employ her to maintain the accounts and process orders in the office.

"Good grief, what day is it?" Maddie swallowed against the fluttering in her chest to hold back the panic building there.

"Tuesday, Miss Ravenwood." Not only did the young woman keep the nursery's administrative matters in good order, she kept everyone else organized too.

Maddie closed her eyes and ground her teeth. She'd been busy of late and had perhaps taken too much on, but it wasn't like her to lose an entire day of the week.

"Shall I have a note sent to her ladyship letting her know you were unavoidably detained?" Alice spoke matter-of-factly but offered a sympathetic smile.

Not only was it mortifying to let a day slip away, but Maddie valued her relationship with Lady Trenmere and didn't wish to disappoint her. This visit was a special one too. Maddie hadn't seen the noblewoman since her trip to London and the encounter with an engagement-breaking gentleman in the countess's conservatory.

"Please do send her a note, Alice. That would be most helpful. Tell her I'll call on her tomorrow." Maddie started striding away again. The wind had picked up, and she had no idea how long she'd have before the storm hit.

"Doesn't the committee meet tomorrow?" Alice shouted over a whistling gust that kicked up a little cloud of raked shrubbery trimmings and dead-headed spring flowers.

Maddie slowed and called over her shoulder, "We've moved our meetings to Thursdays." Her weeks were always busy, and it made the time fly. She liked it that way.

Inside the greenhouse, she used a crank to close the panes that opened in the roof, secured the two exits that led out into the flower fields, and started pulling out the boards they'd used during previous storms to shore up the strength of the greenhouse walls.

Maddie wasn't dainty by any means. She'd grown taller than most men by her sixteenth year, but the boards were wide and unwieldy. A quarter of an hour later, sweaty and covered in dust, she'd done the best she could. There was only one more board to place. While trying to maneuver it, she bumped against a table of rose cuttings and a few pots of tender hybridized blooms began to wobble. Pivoting quickly, she pressed herself against the table to steady it and reached out to secure the pots. The new growth was a vivid bright green, and she smiled as she sat them gently in a wood box cushioned with straw, and then set the box on the greenhouse floor. She couldn't afford for an unstable table to cost her months of work.

A few of the more mature blooms were still too close to the greenhouse wall for her to feel comfortable, so she began the process of lifting and moving the pots to a more central area. Even if they lost a few panes of glass as they had in previous storms, she could be sure her hybrid roses were safe.

As she worked, she navigated around the crates she'd filled, and the low rumble of distant thunder spurred her to work faster. Placing the final potted plant far from the edge of the greenhouse walls, she cocked her head to listen to another sound.

A man's angry voice. She dusted off her work gloves and stepped outside.

"Where is she?" A gray-haired man had entered the nursery grounds and was shouting at Alice.

"Mr. Longford, kindly stop screaming at Miss Eames." Maddie hadn't recognized the voice, but now she could clearly see the uninvited visitor. "I presume you're looking for me."

As a child, she'd known Eli Longford as someone her parents had once called a friend, though they'd soon grown to loathe him. She wasn't certain why their friendship had soured, but over the years they'd become bitter business rivals. Maddie's father had warned her that Longford was as rude as he was avaricious.

He hadn't visited Ravenwood Nursery in years, not even after the death of her father nearly two years past. Maddie couldn't imagine his arrival now was a sign of anything but trouble.

"Miss Ravenwood." At least he possessed manners enough to doff his hat in greeting. "It is indeed you that I've come to see."

"You're a long way from home, sir." Maddie tried for a civil tone, aware that Alice and possibly other staff were watching warily to see how their interaction would unfold.

A single raindrop slid down her forehead. Maddie prayed that, whatever had caused Longford to call, she could resolve it and send him on his way quickly.

Yet the old man seemed in no hurry. He clenched his hat in his fist and took his time scanning the nursery as if inventorying their stock in his mind. He looked much the same as she recalled him from a visit to the nursery many years before, though perhaps more tired. His perpetually stern expression was still firmly in place.

"The place has grown since I last visited years ago. A great deal for a mere girl to manage on her own."

"She's not on her own." Eames had come in from the back fields and stood over Maddie's shoulder.

Maddie counted on Eames, just as her father and mother had for years, and he never disappointed her.

"My staff is more than competent, and I'm no longer a child, Mr. Longford. Now, what can I do for you?" Maddie gestured over her head. "As you see, there's a storm coming, and you've caught me in the middle of preparations."

"Let's talk alone." The old man gestured to the office building.

"No," Eames answered before Maddie had a chance to speak.

She turned back to her trusted foreman. "It's all right." If she didn't deal with Longford now, he'd no doubt be back, and she wanted rid of him as soon as possible.

"Follow me." Maddie slid her watch out of her pocket and noted the time. She'd spare the man five minutes and no more.

Swiping at the dampness on her forehead, she took up a spot behind her father's desk—now her desk. It was clear that Longford didn't respect her, and she doubted any show of authority would impress him, but she'd worked hard to maintain the nursery over the past year, even if they'd lost clients and income.

"How is business nowadays?"

The man seemed to read her thoughts, or perhaps he noticed the patched windows in the greenhouse or the fallow fields they'd not planted for lack of demand. Maddie intended to turn all of that around with the unique hybrid roses she had spent a year learning how to propagate and perfect. But that wasn't a plan she'd divulged to anyone, let alone a rival.

"Business is fine. I'm sorry, but I really have very little time. What brings you to Haven Cove?"

"Longford Farms is growing." His voice changed, warming with a sense of genuine pride. "We've bought land in St. Austell, and we had the prospect of working with a client nearby." His gaze narrowed to a glower. "But you've seen fit to interfere."

Maddie felt the crease of frustration deepen between her brows. "I'm afraid I don't know what you're talking about. I'm much too busy with my own business to interfere in yours." News that he was spreading his endeavors closer to her own made her stomach wobble. Perhaps *he* was the reason some of Ravenwood's established clients had fallen away.

"Viscount Prestwick."

"I know of him but have never met him." Lady Trenmere had mentioned him in passing—a longtime friend of hers who also owned a holiday home in Cornwall. Both were proud of their gardens and competitive with each other but only in the most amicable of ways, as far as Maddie knew. Prestwick had never come to her for plants or supplies. She assumed the viscount had hired a groundskeeper to live on his lands and acquired his plants elsewhere.

"That's well and good, but your patroness, Lady Trenmere, has advised Prestwick to hire you to redesign his garden instead of us."

Maddie tried to hold back a smile. She hadn't expected such loyalty from the countess, but she was grateful for it.

Longford inspected her office much as he had the fields of Ravenwood. He'd always seemed to look down on her father, though she wasn't certain why. His farm in Devon was certainly larger than theirs, but they served a much larger population than she could reach from Haven Cove.

Rain began a steady patter on the roof above their heads.

"I know nothing of Viscount Prestwick, Mr. Longford, but perhaps we should let him decide who to hire." Maddie found herself clasping the dirty work gloves in her hand tighter.

"Perhaps you could call off your patroness."

"If you think I can control anything Lady Trenmere wishes to do, then you've never met her. Why are you really here, Mr. Longford? Surely it can't be to accuse me of encroaching on your business interests when you are, in fact, eighty miles from Longford Farms. It seems as if you're in my town to encroach on *my* business prospects."

Under his overlong white mustache, his lips twitched. Maddie couldn't tell whether it was the start of a smile or a villain-style sneer.

"How is Ravenwood Nursery faring, miss?" he repeated.

"We're quite busy, and there's much to do. I don't wish to be rude, but if you'll excuse me—"

"I know your man out there defended you as a good employee should, but all of this must be a challenge. Your parents worked together." For a moment, he looked almost sympathetic. "My condolences to you, Miss Ravenwood, but it's a great deal on one young lady's shoulders."

It was. The truth was she was bone-tired, and her days were so long they had begun to meld together, but she would never admit it to a man who'd come to lay some nonsensical claim at her feet.

When she didn't say more, he reacted as if he'd gotten whatever it was that he'd come for—intimidation or to take the measure of the competition, she wasn't sure which. He lifted his hat as if he was going to place it on his head, but instead his hand dipped inside his coat, and he pulled out a card.

"Consider this. I would like to expand my business into Cornwall, and I'd pay you a fair price for Ravenwood's. Enough for you to live quite independently." His mouth twitched, causing his whiskers to wiggle. He looked gleeful at the prospect that what had belonged to her parents and was now her responsibility might one day be his. "Unmarried young women seek independence above all else nowadays, do they not?"

The storm clouds rolling into Haven Cove were nothing to the tempest building inside of Maddie. She could feel her cheeks flaming and sensed her heart beating wildly. Awful words perched on the tip of her tongue. For a supremely satisfying flash in her mind, she imagined telling the man exactly what she thought of his implications and his crass offer.

But Mama had taught her to be kind. She could not control the behavior and choices of others; she was only responsible for her reaction to them. So she sifted her thoughts, moderated her words, and did her best to make herself unmistakably clear.

"I have independence, Mr. Longford, and a business that was left to me. Ravenwood's is not for sale. My parents . . ." Her voice broke on the word.

The loneliness and uncertainty that had persisted for months after she'd lost them both welled up whenever they came to mind. "I won't let everything they worked for fall apart or be sold off to the highest bidder."

He stared at her as if testing her resolve, waiting for her to change her mind right there and then. She had a notion of how she looked. Tired and grime-covered and worried. But Maddie held still, trying to keep her expression free of all the thoughts whirring in her mind. No one would ever know of her moments of doubt and frustration.

Finally, Longford lifted his hat and settled it on his balding head. Then he laid his calling card on her desk. "Consider it, Miss Ravenwood. Imagine a different kind of life. My offer remains in case you change your mind."

He didn't wait for any kind of leave-taking and merely stepped out of her office, letting the wind slam the door shut behind him.

For a moment, she stood as if caught in the web a little spider had spun in the corner of her office. She glanced at the card he'd left behind, then lifted her gaze to look through the curtains and out onto all the acres of land her parents had labored over for years.

"I won't change my mind," she said, her whisper barely audible over the patter of rain above her head.

Then she stepped from behind her desk, pulled open the office door, and spotted Longford approaching the one-horse cart he'd driven to Ravenwood's.

"I won't change my mind, Mr. Longford," she shouted into the wind.

And she wouldn't. She couldn't. That would be giving up in a way her parents never would have and never would have wished her to.

Nothing would deter her from making Ravenwood's successful again.

Eames approached and stood under the awning of the office building, just out of the rain that had begun to come down steadily. "I've double-checked the greenhouse and cold frames and done everything I can to secure the stock that's not in the ground."

"We should send the staff home early," Maddie told him as she gathered her bag. "It's almost closing time anyway." She pulled the office door shut and stopped beside him. "Thank you, Eames."

"I hope he didn't trouble you much." He looked in the direction Longford had departed.

"If anything, he hardened my resolve."

Eames offered her an encouraging smile and headed toward a few staff members who were putting away tools and equipment. Maddie started on the path that led out of the nursery grounds. But she didn't head up the hill toward the small stone house on the edge of Ravenwood land that her parents had left her. Instead, she turned toward the sea.

There was a spot that called to her on days like this—the modest groundskeeper's cottage that sat on the seaside estate where she'd spent her childhood. Her mother's roses were there. Roses she'd used to create some of her hybrid strains. She felt a soothing closeness to her mother there. And visiting strengthened her resolve in another way, forcing her to recall a time when a nursery of their own was still just a dream for her parents.

She couldn't think about how far they'd come and not want to keep their dream alive. No more distractions and daydreams. Ravenwood's would be a success again.

Nothing would keep her from it.

Chapter Five

"Dear traveler, beware, the roads across Cornwall are changeable. While some will carry you smoothly to your destination, others may jar you out of your wandering reveries."

—*The Merry Wanderer*

*W*ill tipped one irritated brow up at the menacing sky. In reply, a raindrop struck him right between the eyes. Within minutes, cool rain pelted him from every side. He brushed a hand against his stubbled jaw and his glove came away soaked. *Wonderful*.

Soon every stitch of clothing he wore was sodden. A few icy drops had slid inside his collar, his gloves, and, judging by the squish as he trudged, his boots too.

Blasted Cornish weather.

A sun-soaked holiday, Cora had said as she'd bid him goodbye this morning. *A pleasant change from London's rain clouds*.

He'd have to remember to never take his sister's travel advice again.

All he truly wished was to get dry. As he walked, he kept his gaze focused on the lane that lay ahead.

The coachman had vowed that if he continued in an arrow-straight path, he'd soon reach his destination.

Even with moody skies and a slanting downpour of frigid rain, green enveloped him on every side. This piece of England was undeniably beautiful. If one liked wild, endlessly verdant swaths of windswept land. The very air felt different here. Fog, soot, and the rusty tang of industry laced every breath in London. But the Cornish breeze filling his lungs felt refreshing, crisp, and clean. Shapes were different too. Unlike London's squares and sharp corners, this slice of land at the underbelly of Cornwall was all curves.

Squinting, he could perceive no end to the road he traveled. Glancing behind him, he could no longer see the driver and team that had broken down just within the limits of the town of Haven Cove. He hoped both man and beasts had taken cover from the rain. Cold and wet and cross himself, he had half a mind to duck into the next obliging doorway he passed.

According to chatter on the train, there was a gleaming new hotel nearby, but now that he'd started on this journey, he was determined to reach the manor his father had purchased. Considering the old man's reputation and the spectacle Carnwyth must have been in its heyday, he wished to conduct himself quietly and keep to the property as much as possible.

Even if it rained throughout the fortnight, quiet

and solitude sounded appealing. And since Carn-wyth sat perched atop a cove, he could probably manage visits down to the waterside without draw-ing much notice too. What good was a tucked-away seaside cove if not to afford some privacy?

His mind persisted in seeing this trip as a series of tasks. It started with every instruction Cora had given: *Have fun. Get some sun. Relax.* But his prac-tical nature had to have a say too. What was to be done with the property itself? He'd been remiss and avoided everything to do with his father's pleasure palace.

When he allowed himself to consider its fate at all, he longed to do away with the house entirely. The manor was a part of his father's infamy and the disgrace he'd brought on the family, especially their mother. Selling the land would bring the ducal cof-fers a tidy influx of cash, but if repairs were needed, they'd require attention before a profit could ever come. His one certainty was that after his so-called holiday, the house needed to be dealt with. It had sat crumbling and unused for too long.

According to Cora, the staff had whittled down to a butler, a housekeeper, a few maids, and a foot-man. He would offer them work at another prop-erty, if nothing else. No reason they should suffer simply because he wasn't his father and didn't intend to invite a string of aristocratic friends to Cornwall for weekends of debauchery.

The sky cracked with a roll of thunder overhead, and his body tensed at the sound. If he died on this stony path in Cornwall, it would be a fitting epitaph. *He died while seeking a relaxing holiday.*

If Cora was right—and she *usually* was—most of their acquaintances had decided he was as stuffy and exciting as a dry biscuit anyway.

Still, Carnwyth's fate wasn't his most pressing practical concern at the moment. First, he needed to reach the damn place and get dry.

Squinting into the distance, he spotted something promising.

A small structure—a gate or carriage house, perhaps?—was the first sign he'd truly entered the grounds of Carnwyth. He picked up his pace and sprinted toward the door. There were no lamps lit inside, but he knocked anyway and wasn't surprised to receive no answer.

One twist of the latch and the door gave way with only a slight protest of aged hinges. Inside he found a spartanly furnished space that didn't look nearly as abandoned as he'd expected.

"Hello," he called, but only his echo came in reply, bouncing off the empty confines of the room.

"Thank god." A dry cushioned chair beckoned from a spot in front of an unlit hearth. Will peeled off his sodden overcoat, suit coat, and cravat before lowering himself onto the dusty cushion with a groaning sigh.

A few moments to rest and dry off, and he'd make his way up to the house and face the mausoleum formerly dedicated to his father's mischief.

He'd only sit long enough to get warm. He

couldn't tarry. The letter Cora had sent ahead of his visit would mean the staff was expecting him.

The truth was he hoped nothing would extend his stay in Cornwall. There was too much requiring his attention back in London. His sisters might want him gone to make their grand engagement party easier, and to that he had agreed. But abandoning his family to the games of the ton was exactly what their father had done, and he would never be like him. Let society think him dour and joyless. What mattered was that none could call him a liar, a lecher, a man who gave in to his passions no matter the consequences.

Whatever else he might be, he would never be the irresponsible man his father had been.

MADDIE PULLED THE hood of her cloak down farther, but it did little to keep the rain from her face. She didn't care about soaking her work dress, but the chill in the air cut straight through her cloak.

She dodged ruts in the road and jumped across the span of one large puddle without losing her stride. Even with her head tucked down to avoid the rain, she knew the way. The path to her first home was long and stony and wound through wild greenery, but she could walk it in her sleep.

Within minutes, she spied the boundary line of the estate. Though she hadn't visited the grand house since childhood, when her father had served as the Duke of Ashmore's groundskeeper, this patch of Carnwyth land would always have her heart.

Today, after her run-in with Longford, she yearned for the modest cottage where she'd grown up.

Her father had been responsible for all of Carnwyth's landscaping—trees, hedge maze, row after row of shrubs, and endless greens of grass and ground cover. But her mother had a talent for tending the flowers, especially the old roses like those her family had grown.

Maddie stroked the fat green bud of a cabbage rose, its pink and peach petals already pushing through the cocoon of green.

"I considered it for a moment, Mama," she whispered. Longford's offer. The prospect of leaving her responsibilities behind.

It wasn't that she hated running Ravenwood's. It just wasn't what she'd ever imagined for her future, and she wasn't doing it well enough to be successful. Her passion for flowers and garden design were what she'd always hoped to pursue. Perhaps training in art and botany and then designing gardens and decorating spaces with plants and flowers. That's what she did best.

The worst part was that everyone expected her to fail. The villagers who recalled her as a fanciful girl, even her father who'd never believed a daughter could run the family business and longed for a son until the day he died. No one had ever imagined she was as capable as she knew herself to be.

None but her mother.

"Thank you for believing in me." Swiping at the raindrops dripping down her cheeks, Maddie bent to check the other rosebushes. She was pleased to see that the mulch she'd laid a few weeks ago was keeping them safe from garden scavengers. The rest of Carnwyth's grounds might be gone to seed, but she made sure to tend her mother's roses.

If the irresponsible new Duke of Ashmore ever deigned to repair the crumbling estate, she'd consider asking him for permission to remove the roses to Ravenwood Nursery. Then she'd visit the dilapidated estate less often. Something about the half-ruined stone facade of Carnwyth made her uneasy. Gossip in Haven Cove indicated that the old duke had left the manor in a state of disrepair, and the family had shown no interest in the property since his death. Tales of the estate were colorful, and the way villagers spoke of its history, one might think it was the abode of the devil himself. But the old duke was gone, and his heir seemed quite as bad since he'd shirked his duty to care for the house and grounds.

The manor had become an eyesore, and as leader of the Royal Visit Committee, she'd led several discussions about what could be done to block the view of the manor from the hotel. Haven Cove Hotel and Carnwyth sat on opposite sides of the white cliffs of the cove, and none wanted the coming visit of Princess Beatrice to be marred by talk of the infamous ruin.

Maddie closed her eyes and took a deep breath, listening to the gentle patter of soft rain against the hood of her cloak and letting worries quiet in her mind. She focused on a memory of her mother, of her encouraging smiles and warm, tight hugs. *You can do whatever you set your mind to, my love.*

Perhaps Mama was right. She'd created a rose to catch the eye of a princess and would soon oversee what she was determined would be a successful royal visit. She could certainly figure out a way to put off Longford's machinations.

The rain had let up, so Maddie lowered her hood as she stood. She immediately tipped her head toward a sound coming from the cottage.

No one should be inside. She'd entered herself only rarely in the past months, just to ensure no animals had made their way in to wreak havoc. Creeping toward the steps, she lifted onto her toes, looked inside, and gasped.

It wasn't a squirrel or stray mouse. A man sat slumped on her father's old wooden chair, though his body was far too large for the modest piece of furniture. Based on the uncomfortable tilt of his head—neck bent and chin tucked against his chest—and the steady rise and fall of his shoulders, he seemed to be sleeping.

She should go. Leave the man to rest.

But something about him held her in place, and she was far too curious to walk away.

Chapter Six

*M*addie stepped inside the cottage as noiselessly as she could manage, then moved closer and studied the stranger. Judging by the length of his outstretched legs, the man was tall. Though the light in the room was low, she made out dark, disheveled hair, black brows, and a full mouth.

Her breath tangled in her throat. She recognized those lips.

Maddie stumbled back so quickly her shoulder bumped the mantel.

It couldn't be. Impossible. She blinked, but he was still there. Wet and apparently tired. In Cornwall. In her family's cottage.

The man from Lady Trenmere's party.

As she had that night, she had a flash of wondering whether he'd come here seeking her out. But, of course, that was nonsense. Why would he?

But it still begged the question of what a nobleman was doing in an old groundskeeper's cottage . . .

Oh no. Was he *the* duke? The heir of the infamous one? The irresponsible cad who'd let Carnwyth and its grounds fall into disrepair?

Maddie took a step closer and bent her head to get a better look. Maybe it wasn't him. The light was dim, and she'd been imagining the gentleman she'd met in London far too often of late.

Extending one finger, she gently swept the fall of dark hair off his face. She was undoubtedly the silliest woman in England, because even one quick touch sent her pulse racing.

And there was no doubt. The Duke of Ashmore had come to Carnwyth.

Blast it all.

Over the months since her visit to London, not knowing his name had allowed her to think of their unintended encounter in the conservatory with a secret wistfulness. It had been hard to forget the mysterious, jilted, handsome nobleman who'd seemed oddly disturbed that she might leave London and never return. Too many times, she'd replayed the memory, sometimes allowing herself to imagine his mind teasing over thoughts of her too.

Maddie crossed her arms and tapped a foot against the bare wood floor.

This was all very vexing. Yes, she'd thought fondly of this man and those few moments at Lady Trenmere's party. But she'd also spent a year and a half increasingly resentful of the new Duke of Ashmore. And all of Haven Cove felt the same. They'd watched the manor house diminish as it sat empty for nearly two years. No lights ever glowed in the long windows of its ballroom. No music or parties or wild midnight dances as there had once been to make the house seem alive.

Maddie knew the old duke's reputation was black as sin, but he'd been viewed as a kind of pillar, if a tarnished one, of their little town's economy.

Now the new duke had finally arrived, and he was *her* nobleman.

Why on earth was he here? In her parents' old cottage? From what she'd heard, there were a dozen beds in Carnwyth. Huge, gilded four-post beds with nymphs and satyrs carved into the wood. Or so they said. He could be reclining on a velvet settee instead of slumping before a dusty, unlit hearth.

He wore no gloves or coat, not even a waistcoat. Just black trousers and a white shirt. A partially unbuttoned shirt. Maddie told herself not to gape, but his neck was exposed in a V of open fabric, and she could see the shadow of his pulse jumping against his skin.

Her own pulse quickened. One step closer and she could see the high cut of his cheeks, the sharp peaks of his upper lip and generous swell of his lower. For a grumpy man, he had a very inviting mouth.

Even in repose, he looked formidable. Standing over her that night in February, she hadn't been disturbed by his height, only her reaction to him. Never in her life had she felt attraction spark so quickly and intensely.

He shifted, and Maddie nearly jumped out of her boots.

He crossed his arms, and his biceps bulged beneath the fabric of his shirt. His shirt was dirtied at the cuffs and torn near one wrist. The wet fabric clung to his skin.

With his tousled hair, drenched clothes, and stubbled jaw, he looked like he'd just washed up on the coast.

"You almost look like a pirate," she breathed as she leaned closer.

His eyelids slid open, and he lifted his head. For a moment, he simply stared at her. Then he blinked as she had, as if trying to determine whether she was a mirage.

He shot to his feet, tipping the chair onto its back, and squinted at her in the dim light filtering in through the windows.

"You." He scrubbed a hand across his face and looked around the cottage, then back at her. "What the devil are you doing here?"

"You remember me." Her heartbeat fluttered in her throat, making her voice wobble.

He stood and took a step closer. "Of course I do. That hair."

Maddie raised a hand self-consciously. She had been teased about her red hair often during her childhood, and between a day's work and being caught in the rain—

"It's lovely."

"Oh." No one had ever said such a thing to her. Not about her hair or anything else.

"If your memorable hair wasn't enough, I'd recall you as a lady with an extraordinary talent for sneaking up on me."

"I wasn't sneaking. I heard a noise." Her explanation sounded silly, and his arched brow indicated how dubious he found it. "I live but a few miles away."

That detail seemed to intrigue him. Something in his expression softened, and the tension in his jaw eased.

"How did *you* end up here?"

"The storm." He gestured toward the cottage windows where dark clouds were rimmed with the amber glow of dusk. "I ducked inside to get out of the rain."

Maddie noticed his sodden, discarded clothing and that the small space was full of the scent of damp leather and something deeper. His scent. Verdant, like crushed juniper needles.

"If you're who I think you are, then I suppose it's your cottage."

He dipped his head, staring at the dusty wood floor, and gripped the back of his neck. "We were never formally introduced, were we?"

"You're the Duke of Ashmore."

"I am." His gaze had turned surprisingly bleak. "So much for my plan to remain inconspicuous."

"Arriving in Haven Cove unnoticed never would have worked." Maddie found it was hard to keep her gaze on his face. She feared some of the silly quivering she felt inside must be reflected in her expression. "News travels fast here. And you're . . . noticeable."

He narrowed his gaze at that. "In the spirit of fairness, shouldn't I know your name?"

They couldn't very well stand on formality when everything about their acquaintance was already so unusual.

"Madeline Ravenwood." She held out her hand. It's what she would do when meeting a new client, no matter their rank.

He stared at her outstretched hand a moment as if trying to decide how to respond. Then a smile hitched up the corner of his mouth, and he responded with one brief, firm clasp of her hand. "A pleasure, Miss Ravenwood."

The gesture was simple but felt important. Not just mere politeness or civility. The start of an acquaintance with a man she'd never expected to meet again.

A man who all of Haven Cove thought of as irresponsible and an absentee landowner. Thinking of the list of complaints the townspeople had for the man, Maddie barely stifled a groan.

"Why are you here?"

"As I said, I live in Haven Cove."

"No, the cottage. Why did you come to the cottage?"

She glanced through the dusty window at the darkening sky. "The storm drove me inside, just like you. Though I suspect Carnwyth would be much more comfortable."

"I don't know about that." He worked his jaw, seeming to chew on whatever words he wished to say. "This is my first visit. I only know a little of its history and, of course, what sort of man my father was."

"I've heard the stories."

He quirked a brow. "Likewise."

Something hung over him, and she sensed he wasn't looking forward to stepping inside Carnwyth. Or perhaps this strange encounter was delaying him. Suddenly, she felt a fool for entering the cottage. Once he entered the manor, he could at least sit before a fire and have a meal.

"I shouldn't keep you, Your Grace. I should let you get up to the house and bid you good evening."

"I suppose I must." He let out a sigh. "It has to be more comfortable than that chair. I suspect an iron maiden would be more comfortable than that chair."

Maddie burst into laughter and then chuckled at the duke's perplexed expression.

"You have opinions on the chair, Miss Ravenwood?"

"My father built it."

"Did he?"

"This was my home. My childhood home. We left when I was ten years old. You see, my father had saved for years and purchased land to start his own business." She was rambling and forced herself to stop and take a breath.

What was it about this man? He was a duke. Conversation with him shouldn't be this easy.

Silly to worry over it, but she suspected her next words would change the rapport that came as easy as breathing between them. "My father was your father's groundskeeper. At least until he and my mother established their own nursery. Ravenwood Nursery, which is now mine to manage."

"Your parents?"

"Both are gone."

"I'm sorry."

Speaking of her parents, especially today, wasn't something she wished to do, but she nodded to acknowledge his kindness.

Silence loomed between them, and he seemed to be pondering all that she'd blurted about her history. But despite her expectations, nothing in his manner toward her changed.

"Miss Ravenwood, I'm already indebted to you for your discretion after our encounter in London. May I call on it again?" There was nothing of command in his tone as there had been when they'd met. "I don't wish to cause a stir. I came here to be quiet. For relaxation, whatever that means."

He had no idea what was waiting for him and what would be expected of him, it seemed.

"I'm afraid that even if I agreed not to tell anyone, the news will be out quickly."

"How quickly?"

"Tomorrow."

"Good grief, it's as bad as London."

"I'm afraid so. You've asked a favor of me twice, Your Grace. Shall we even that score?" Perhaps repairing a crumbling manor wasn't quite the same as discretion. But if she could get him to make modifications prior to the princess's visit, it would be one significant item to tick off her list.

"What might I do for you?" His tone was warm and his voice far too deep.

Maddie's mind went immediately *there*. To a kiss in a conservatory that had never happened and never would. *No*. One handsome duke would not distract her. Let him hole up in Carnwyth if he liked. She had too much to accomplish, and everything depended on her doing it well.

What she needed from him had nothing to do with his lips or his hands running through her hair or his chest pressed against—

Stop. Heavens, why was she overheating?

"I believe in fairness, Miss Ravenwood. So tell me. How can I repay you?"

He was standing close. As close as he had in the conservatory.

"It's not just one thing."

He frowned at that.

"There are several things I'd like to ask of you."

Those words made his frown deepen to a scowl. Perhaps it wasn't the night to tell him all that the citizens of Haven Cove would expect of him or to petition him for what mattered to her most.

"How about I write it all up and come visit you at Carnwyth?"

"Write it *all* up?"

Oh my, he was as grumpy as he was handsome.

"Yes, just a short list to organize things." Maddie tried to keep her tone cheerful, light. She even attempted a smile, but it wobbled the longer his dark gaze watched her. "I'll call on you tomorrow."

She backed away as she spoke and finally turned for the door. At the threshold, she hesitated, wondering if she should offer him a *good evening* or *farewell*.

Glancing behind her, she found him closer. As if he intended to exit when she did.

"Goodbye," she said on a breathy whisper, realizing she sounded like a foolish, awestruck ninny.

He frowned, glowered at her a moment, and then murmured, "I look forward to your visit, Miss Ravenwood."

Chapter Seven

*W*ill bolted out of bed, his mind still convinced by a nightmare that he was late for some crucial appointment. He stopped in his tracks at the gilded guest-room door, realized where he was, and scrubbed a hand across his jaw.

The previous day played through his mind. Cornwall. The trip, the broken coach, the lovely Miss Ravenwood threatening him with a list.

The notion that she would be visiting today gave him something most of his days lacked: a sense of anticipation.

If only she wouldn't be walking into this gaudy house.

Turning around, he assessed the chamber the staff had prepared for him. Not his father's, he'd made sure of that. Something serviceable was all he'd requested. The most understated room.

If this was understated, he shuddered to imagine the rest of the rooms.

An overwrought tapestry dominated one wall, and a suit of armor stood sentry in a corner, both giving the space a medieval feel. But all the rest—the reds and golds, the chips of mirror embedded artfully in the wallpaper, the gold leaf adorning every surface—made him feel as if he'd slept in an expensive brothel.

A few photograph cards were propped above the fireplace, and he drew close to examine them. Jubilant couples garbed as if for a costume party laughed and reclined in each other's arms or on each other's laps. They exuded a kind of frivolous carnality he hadn't allowed himself in too many years. A strip of velvet lay atop the mantel, and he reached out to stroke the soft fabric.

Scents rose from it—faded perfume, spice, wood smoke. Memories came to him of the one time he'd visited an infamous London brothel. Pleasure had been plentiful, but he'd found no true satisfaction.

Maybe satisfaction wasn't to be his fate.

He stalked across the room, pushed the crimson drapery aside, and lifted the window. Sea breeze rushed into his lungs. Something about watching the low, undulating waves rolling toward the cove eased the tension in his shoulders. The sky was a striking, cloudless blue. He could hardly believe he'd awakened in the same place that had welcomed him with mud and pelting rain the day before.

Flexing his foot, he felt a twinge of pain in his ankle. So the walk down the rain-inundated lane had been more than a bad dream. Which meant the red-haired beauty was real too. *Madeline*. Remembering her brought on an ache of a different sort. He'd almost forgotten how the heated rush of attraction felt.

She'd sparked something in him. Those eyes. Clear and incisive, almost demanding, and as blue as the sky above the cove. The way she'd looked at him with that penetrating gaze had kept him awake despite his exhaustion.

Ladies didn't generally stare at him with naked interest. They side-eyed him in ballrooms, whispered about him behind their fans, or maneuvered to sit near him at soirees. Even then, the glances shot his way were generally furtive.

But the night he'd first met her in London, she'd known nothing of his reputation or his family's infamy. She'd assessed him simply as a man and seemed to like what she saw.

As did he. She was an astonishing beauty with those loose red curls, pretty eyes, and freckled cheeks. The dimple in her left cheek fascinated him.

He replayed the moments in the cottage with her in his mind. The sound of her voice, the flash of curiosity in her gaze, and the way she'd drawn close to see him in the dim light. He'd caught her floral scent heightened by her rain-soaked clothes. Then he winced, recalling the moment she'd realized who he was. Something in her expression told him she wasn't terribly pleased to learn he was the Duke of Ashmore.

What would be on her list?

That fizz of anticipation came again, but it had less to do with her list and more to do with her.

He heard the sounds of the staff going about their duties downstairs and took one last long breath of sea air before preparing to meet them all. There'd been no time for it the previous night. He'd encountered only Bly, the butler, come upstairs, stripped off his dripping clothes, and fallen into bed. And, oddly enough, he'd slept rather soundly.

The pure exhaustion of travel, mostly likely.

He washed quickly, dressed in his traveling shirt and trousers, put on his boots, and made his way downstairs. Bly appeared as if he'd been listening for footfalls on the stairs, and Will asked him to assemble the house's staff. It wasn't long before four of them filed into a drawing room—did the manor even have a study?—filled with chaise lounges and papered in gold and plum stripes.

"You are the only remaining staff at Carnwyth?" Will met the gaze of each in turn.

"Besides Magda and Kate here, there is another maid and a footman called Mitchum, Your Grace." The butler, Mr. Bly, seemed a decent man and a bit jollier than Will would have expected of anyone who'd served the late duke for years. But he exuded a sincerity that made Will inclined to trust him. "He's in the stable at the moment."

"Serves as stable master and driver and manages one boy who works the grounds as well." Mrs. Haskell, the housekeeper, stretched a little taller when she addressed him. The petite older woman eyed him suspiciously and spoke with a nervous tremor in her voice. There was a defensiveness in her tone that Will understood.

"Maintaining this house must be a great deal of work for so few of you. What happened to the other servants?" Will realized he'd failed to learn much about Carnwyth and had come filled with mostly questions and uncertainty about its current state.

No one replied, but Mrs. Haskell's cheeks pinked, and Bly's white brows slid heavenward. "Some were let go, Your Grace. Others chose to go when it all came to an end."

The soirees, he meant. The wild house parties.

"We've closed up most rooms," Mrs. Haskell added. "Maintained only what was necessary. Repaired what we could but—"

"Things will change now, won't they? Return to as they were," Bly inquired. "Now that you've come, Your Grace. New staff will no doubt need to be hired on, especially while you're in residence."

Will squared his shoulders and crossed his arms. "I won't be remaining at Carnwyth long enough for that."

They glanced at each other, and one of the maid's expressions shifted into a worried frown.

Mrs. Haskell seemed particularly displeased. "Many in Haven Cove have been waiting for your arrival for some time, Your Grace."

"Have they?" This wasn't a ducal estate. As far as Will knew, his father had never established himself as a true member of Haven Cove society.

"The preparations for the visit, Your Grace." Bly spoke the words as if there was no doubt Will would understand.

When he made no reply, the maids and senior staff

exchanged another round of conspiratorial glances.

"Are you not here now because of Princess Beatrice's visit?" The younger maid spoke for the first time, her voice soft and almost reverent.

A muscle in Will's jaw began to twitch. "A royal visit." If he'd known, he never would have agreed to come to Cornwall. Though his immediate reaction to Cora's suggestion of a holiday had been resistance, some part of him was looking forward to a few days away from London's social scene, and certainly from any of the machinations at court.

From all accounts, Princess Beatrice was amiable and kind, but if this was to be a true holiday away from the weight of his duties, then it couldn't include a member of the royal family.

"When does this visit commence?"

"In a little less than a fortnight, Your Grace. Barely time for what will be required. But we will do all we can."

Will rose from the desk he'd been leaning against.

"Let me be clear. I do not intend to remain in Cornwall long, and I will most definitely depart before the princess and her entourage arrive. My main goal is to hire a land manager who can see to the sale of the estate."

One young maid gasped, and the other reached for her hand. Mrs. Haskell bristled but said nothing, and Mr. Bly couldn't disguise his shock.

"None will like that, if I may say so, Your Grace." The man started quietly, but his voice took on volume as he continued. "When word came that you were visiting, everyone in the town assumed it was to be here for the princess's vis—"

"Wait. Stop. Did you just say *everyone in the town*?"

The same maid let out a pained squeak, and her eyes went wide.

"A duke's arrival can't be a secret for long. Haven Cove is a small town but quite lively. No new arrival goes unnoticed." Mrs. Haskell stepped forward, positioning herself so that the maid was out of Will's line of sight.

"Of course." Clearly this journey wasn't going to go the way he'd imagined. "I'm used to being an object of gossip. But any expectation that I've come to revive Carnwyth or entertain as my father used to do is wrong. There will be no parties. No visits with the princess's entourage."

Bly strode forward to stand beside Mrs. Haskell, and they nodded at each other, almost as if they'd learned some sort of silent style of communication over the years.

"If I may ask, Your Grace, what is it that you do plan to do while you're at Carnwyth?"

Will saw Daisy's sweet, concerned face in his mind's eye. But the next thought was of all he had left behind to pile up in London—work he could be getting on with, duties he had agreed to abandon for a fortnight. Finally, he heard Cora's voice in his head.

"I plan . . ." Will tried for even a semblance of enthusiasm ". . . to enjoy myself."

Chapter Eight

*M*addie walked with a determined stride.

Starting up the drive toward the front doors of Carnwyth, she went over what she planned to say to Ashmore.

As long as she focused on what needed to be done and convinced him to undertake even a little of what she'd written on her list, it would be less worry for herself and more likelihood of a successful royal visit. Then he could return to London leaving a less dilapidated property behind.

It was all rather simple, if he would just agree.

On the front steps, Maddie reached up to knock on the oddly carved door and then stopped and stared. It always sparked this same reaction whenever she'd been admitted to the manor. Painted in vivid colors—lots of red and purple and a great deal of gold leaf—the carving portrayed a lavish feast with nude figures sitting, standing, and embracing one another. As a child, she'd known only that it was naughty and recalled her mother insisting she avert her gaze. Now she could see the joy and frivolity in the scene.

What would it be like to be so carefree, even for a moment?

A sound drew her notice. Someone was humming. A male someone with a lovely baritone voice. It was the duke. She'd only spoken to the man on two occasions, yet the timbre of his voice was unmistakable. The sound was coming from somewhere nearby, but she refused to sneak up on him again.

Two knocks on the front door brought a nervous young woman to answer. She peered at Maddie through the half-open door, and recognition bloomed between them.

"Kate, I didn't realize you worked at Carnwyth."

She was the haberdasher's daughter, and while they weren't well acquainted, Maddie was used to seeing her at work in her father's shop.

"Haven't been here long, Miss Ravenwood."

"I hope you're enjoying your new post." Maddie tried for her warmest smile. "I'm here to see the Duke of Ashmore."

"His Grace is seeing no visitors. I'm very sorry, Miss Ravenw—"

Maddie slammed her boot into the opening Kate was trying to close, forcing the door to remain open. "He'll see me. Ask him. He knows I'm coming."

Kate shook her head. Firmly. "Master was quite clear in his instructions." With that, she pushed the toe of her boot against Maddie's until she relented and then slammed the risqué door in her face.

Good grief. She understood the duke wanting solitude on his seaside holiday, but banning all visitors seemed extreme. Knocking again was useless. Kate, wishing to keep her post, would no doubt remain stubbornly resolute.

Planting her hands on her hips, Maddie assessed the windows on the ground floor. She'd almost consider climbing inside if she had to. It'd taken enough to convince herself to come at all. She wasn't turning back now.

The humming had stopped sometime between knocking and having the door shut on her. Maddie made her way around the side of the house where the sound seemed to be coming from. Overgrown juniper bushes lined the front of the house, giving off a lovely scent but making maneuvering difficult, especially if she wanted to avoid the neglected flower beds that lined the shrubs. Daylily stems were already up, preparing for a summer bloom.

Without a gardener at the manor, no one had removed the desiccated autumn leaves or thinned out the perennial beds for the flowering that would come whether they were pruned or not. Her mother would be aghast to see the untamed state of the flowers she'd planted.

Rounding the edge of the house, Maddie found herself staring at a hedgerow of hawthorn almost as tall as she was. It was too old and unmanicured for her to consider squeezing through, and she knew it wrapped around the entire back area of the house, a secluded terrace that had always seemed to her very in keeping with Carnwyth's history and purpose.

There was, of course, no helpful stool or ladder

nearby. Shouting seemed a bit too much in terms of decorum, though none of her encounters with the duke had been in any sense keeping with the strictures of propriety so far.

She started walking along the curved length of the hedge, looking to see if she could get a glimpse through the green border. That's when she noticed the empty trellis. It clung to the house at the juncture of a corner and the hedge. The flowering vine that had once climbed there had withered long ago.

Climbing up and getting past the hedge would get her as far as the terrace. Dare she?

Thinking too much would cause her to change her mind. Maddie rushed toward the trellis, hitched up her skirt, and placed her boot on the first wooden slat. It seemed to take her weight all right, so she reached up and stepped onto the next rung. Now that she was aloft, the hedge seemed taller, requiring her to climb higher. She inched up to the third slat of wood, and it wobbled. She clung tighter to the trellis frame. What she hadn't considered was how she might descend from this rickety wooden ladder. Scramble over a spiky, unkempt hedge?

The view over the bushes was clear now, and she could see the wide stone expanse of the terrace. The area was more spacious and inviting than she remembered. The sun lit up the stones, causing flecks of mica to glint in the warm glow. A single table and chair sat in the light, covered with pencils and papers filled with sketches. If it was the duke who'd been out of doors humming merrily, he was gone now.

She let out a sigh and leaned her forehead against the trellis. This wasn't a promising start to an endeavor that *had* to succeed.

"I appreciate how determined you are to see me, but I would have expected you to find an easier way."

Maddie gritted her teeth and tightened her grip on the worn wood of the trellis.

One look revealed the duke standing below her, squinting up into the bright sky, his hands resting on his hips. A mischievous grin made his already attractive face far more appealing than it had any right to be. He seemed to be enjoying her predicament.

"May I assist you?" Stepping closer, he lifted his hand.

Maddie stared at his broad open palm. "Do you intend to catch me with one hand?"

"Do you plan to jump?"

"No."

"I could climb up and get you, if you prefer."

"No. Thank you very much." Maddie huffed out a chuckle and a bit of tension seeped from her muscles. "You're too heavy. I climb ladders at the nursery all the time. I'll be fine." Of course, those ladders were sturdy, strategically placed as to be stable, and not as dry as driftwood—

"Oh!" Her foot slipped.

"Hold still."

"No, if I just . . ." She swung her foot and felt around for the bottom rung. "I'm close." She stepped down to the lowest level, then cast him a glance over her shoulder. "I'm not moving again until you get out of the way." If her landing wasn't graceful, she could at least avoid ending up splayed on top of a duke.

He took a single step back and cast her a look she could only interpret as doubtful.

To prove him wrong, she took the final step down with care, gripping the frame and praying it would hold her for a few more seconds. When she touched the ground with the toe of one boot, she slid her hands down the trellis and lowered her other foot.

"There, you see." She spun to face him and only made it halfway. Her scarf had gotten caught on the structure and tugged her off balance.

He caught her with one warm, heavy hand gripped against her arm. "I do see."

The amused glint in his dark eyes made her pulse dance and jitter under her skin.

"You're quite a determined young woman." In one sweeping glance, he took in the hedge and the trellis and then rested his gaze on her face again. "But what the hell were you doing scaling the side of the house? I am truly beginning to believe you're in the employ of Her Majesty's spy service."

Maddie tugged at her scarf to free it from the split wood and then pulled at her arm to get free of his grip. He released her, but slowly.

"Your maid refused me."

"Ah. That's my doing. Forgive me. I didn't expect you so early."

Early had seemed best when deciding on this plan. Especially today. The weather promised rain again in the afternoon, and if she was to convince him, she needed clear views across the cove.

"Perhaps I should have sent a note first."

"Not at all. We agreed to not rest on formalities. Though, I do wonder how others might view you coming to visit on your own."

This Duke of Ashmore seemed much more concerned with propriety than his father had been. But she'd carved out an independent life for herself and rarely worried about her reputation overmuch.

"No one minds where I go or who I see. I run Ravenwood's on my own, and I'm a spinster."

"A spinster?" He gave her a long side glance, his mouth twisted into something between a smirk and grimace.

"That's what people say." She'd accepted that marriage and a family wouldn't be her future. Not anytime soon anyway. *Spinster* was such a loathsome word and brought all sorts of assumptions from those in the village. But it also brought autonomy, the freedom to go where she wished and speak to whoever she needed to in order to conduct her business.

"I'll inform the staff that you should be admitted the next time you call."

"Is that an invitation to visit again in future?"

"Yes." The word came so quickly and his gaze held on hers so boldly that Maddie was tempted to look away. She sensed a familiar heat rising in her cheeks. Never before had she begun an acquaintance that lacked pretense, and she found that she quite liked not needing to pretend with him.

"Then, I will."

He offered her something like a smile, a softening of his face that tipped his mouth and drew lines at the corners of his eyes. "Excellent."

"So . . ."

"Shall we have a look at your list?"

Yes, of course, the lack of pretense also meant he'd expect to get to the point of her visit immediately. And, of course, she wished to get it over with as soon as possible and get back to all that needed doing at the nursery.

So why did she feel disappointment at his suddenly businesslike manner?

"Was that you I heard humming earlier?"

He looked as shocked as the maid had when Maddie asked to enter Carnwyth.

"It was, but I didn't realize anyone was listening."

"I thought it was you. It's why I was determined to get past the hedge."

"Spying on me again, Miss Ravenwood."

"In this instance, you gave me little choice."

"Fair enough."

"Those drawings on the table. Are they yours?"

He let out a breath, and it turned into a chuckle, a lovely, low-pitched rumbling sound. "You don't miss much of anything, do you? That keen perception does nothing to dissuade me from my theory."

"Could I see them? Your sketches?" An idea had

begun to bloom in her mind. If he was the sort who appreciated a fine view enough to capture it in a sketch, perhaps he'd understand why the eyesore of Carnwyth would put a damper on the royal visit.

"They're a few scribbles I got out this morning." He glanced down and then up at her again. "I'm no artist. I enjoyed drawing in school, but it wasn't a proper pursuit."

"For an heir to a dukedom."

"Precisely." He drew in a sharp breath as if preparing himself for what came next. "Come." Though he'd just grabbed her underneath the trellis, he now seemed unsure what to do with his hands. He reached out as if to escort her, then simply turned, waiting for her to join him.

As they walked to the front door of the manor, Maddie sensed the easiness between them ebb. He clenched his hands into fists. On the front steps, he stopped her with the touch of his hand. "Prepare yourself, Miss Ravenwood."

Maddie couldn't help but glance at the door again where voluptuous and generously shaped bodies writhed and embraced.

He noticed her examination of the door and nodded. "That's just the start." Then he pushed the doors open and gestured for her to step in ahead of him.

The day was sunny and warm, and the house felt like a respite. Its foyer was entirely marble—walls, floor, ceiling—and the cool, clean stillness of the space made Maddie let out a deep exhale. As a child, Carnwyth had seemed grand and intimidating, and she hadn't expected the infamous house to feel welcoming today.

"Just through here." Ashmore stood in the doorway of what she assumed was a sitting room.

Stepping inside, she realized it was a good deal more. "Oh my."

"Mmm. My reaction too, though I expressed it a bit less politely." He arched both brows and took in the room in one all-encompassing glance. Brow furrowed, mouth tense, he looked as if he wished to rip everything from the walls and throw the rest on the fire.

It was . . . a lot. Furnishings cluttered every inch of space and none of it was unassuming. Purples, every shade of it, dominated the room. Except for the parts that were gold.

"In exploring the house this morning, I found this room." He kept his back to her as he spoke and parted a pair of long gold drapes to reveal French doors. "Then I found these and realized it was a means of escape." Pushing them open with dramatic flair, he proceeded out onto the terrace and stood in a pool of sunlight.

Maddie was so enjoying the strangeness of the interior that she wanted to stay and explore, but he wore an impatient expression as if he was leading her to some discovery and couldn't imagine why she was dawdling.

"I might loathe every inch of the house, but no one could argue with this view."

Maddie joined him on the terrace, and her own breath hitched when she looked out on the cove and sea beyond. Even after living in Cornwall her entire life, she was always taken with its beauty. And she'd never seen the cliffs above the cove from quite this spot. Carnwyth was perched closer to the sea than Allswell, and its view was of the new hotel. Its gleaming white pillars and broad two-story balcony looked majestic and appealing in the morning light.

But as pretty as the view of the hotel was, his words hung in the air between them. Perhaps it was rude or too blunt, but she had to know.

"Why do you loathe every inch of the house?"

THE QUESTION WASN'T a surprise, but the answer led to places inside him that Will didn't wish to explore.

Still, she'd asked with such genuine curiosity—a curiosity he suspected was an inherent part of her nature—that he had to give her something.

"What do you know of Carnwyth?"

He turned to look at her, but she only offered him one sidelong glance. "Mostly wild tales and exaggerated stories. I came inside a few times as a child when no one was in residence. The staff, including my parents, would sometimes share a meal belowstairs. But I never ventured out onto the terrace, and I wasn't allowed in any of the rooms." She offered him a rueful grin. "And for some reason, I never received an invitation to any of the parties."

He couldn't imagine her at one his father's raucous revels, lounging on the lumpy chaises or cavorting with the kind of company his father kept. Though, the thought of her dressed like the couples in the guest-room portraits, diaphanous silk hugging her body, her gorgeous hair unbound . . .

"The rumors are . . ." she started, then stopped and glanced at him as if to gauge his reaction. "They're colorful." Turning from the view to stare back into the overfurnished room, she smiled and added, "Like the house."

"And of my father? What do you know of him?"

He could only imagine what the people of this quaint little seaside cove thought of a man like Stanwick Hart.

"They say he was quite scandalous, threw the best parties of any host in England, and laughed so heartily you could hear it for miles." A wistful look came into her eyes, and her mouth tipped in the ghost of a smile. "I can attest to the laugh."

"Did you meet him?" Will couldn't quite imagine his father facing off with the perceptive woman at his side. He sensed she was too intelligent to ever fall for the man's false charm.

"No, not at all. I have a vague memory of him visiting Carnwyth when I was young, though I don't recall him coming often. There were sometimes visitors when he wasn't in residence."

Will had found notes to that effect in his father's paperwork. He'd gifted visits to the house to friends and loaned it out for exorbitant rates to those willing to pay. Turning every relationship into a commercial transaction would have made a scandal of most dukes, but somehow his father had emerged as a kind of folk hero—ostentatious, raucous, but rarely did anyone mention how dangerous he was to anyone who trusted him.

"He was loud. My mother and I were tending the flower beds once when he shouted orders at the house staff while descending from a carriage in front of Carnwyth. An entourage of other equally noisy, overdressed ladies and gentlemen tumbled out behind him."

"So you've always had a curious nature and a penchant for observation?" He'd spoken the words lightly, wishing for that ease that came so naturally between them. Something about her manner, her openness, made him want to converse more than was his tendency.

Exactly the sort of talent a lady spy would have, surely.

"My family and I were on the outside of that sort of life, and I suppose I did wonder about your father and all that went on in this grand house." A wash of pink swept across her cheeks.

Will turned to face her, though she kept her gaze on the view across the cove.

"I meant no offense, Miss Ravenwood." He waited, hoping she'd look at him again.

"I do have a curious nature." When she turned, the blue of her eyes shone bright and clear. If he'd angered her, she hid it well. "Anything colorful or appealing to look at will catch my eye." The pink seemed to deepen just under the smooth curve of her cheeks. He noticed the freckles he'd seen a hint of the night they'd met. They were darker now and had multiplied, and he had the fleeting thought that he wished to trace them with his finger as he had the constellations in the sky when he was a boy.

"You appreciate beauty too, I take it?" She glanced back at his drawings.

The lady was leading him. He could hear it in her voice, the way he could with Daisy when she was on the verge of asking him for funds for a new frock.

Will turned and rested his backside against the balustrade so that he was facing her and crossed his arms. "I appreciate beauty very much."

He wondered if she understood that, at this moment, he was referring to her beauty. Each time he was with Miss Ravenwood, despite the ease of conversing with her, he found there was more he wished to convey. She intrigued him. And even after that first meeting in London, when he'd had no reason to expect he'd ever see her again, he'd thought of her. Often. Looked for her in the bloody ballroom in his own house.

"Is it the view across the cove that you were sketching earlier?" She glanced once more at the table where he'd taken his morning tea and breakfast.

"It is an undeniably appealing view."

Her eyes widened, and she came another step closer, a sort of breathless eagerness causing her to practically vibrate. "Yes, that is exactly it. From Carnwyth, the view is lovely. The hotel looks like an alabaster jewel atop the cove. But from the new hotel, Carnwyth looks rather . . ." She furrowed her brow as if taking care to find the perfect word. "Unkempt."

Without even turning to look behind him, Will cataloged the failings of the house at his back. The facade had begun to crumble on the seaside edge, mostly because a sort of buttress structure had been ruined in a storm, according to the staff. To call the grounds *unkempt* was an understatement.

"The house has been—"

"Abandoned?"

"Avoided." Will ground his teeth and considered how much he deserved the accusation implied in her tone and arched brow.

"But now you're here."

"I am." The same kind of chill when Daisy and Cora joined forces against him began to work its way up his spine.

"And you can begin to undertake repairs."

"Uh—"

"Soon. Now. So that progress can be made within the next fortnight?"

His breathing hitched, and that feeling of panic that greeted him upon waking was back again. He hadn't come to Cornwall to repair his father's den of debauchery. Cora insisted he needed the exact opposite of a new project. No projects. No worries. *Enjoy your time away.*

"No." The word came out of him almost unbidden and much louder than he'd intended. Like a refusal welling straight up from the core of his being.

Miss Ravenwood let out a little breath of shock, but whatever surprise she felt was immediately swept away by a look of what he could only call consternation. Her nostrils flared, her forehead between her pretty reddish brows crimped, and her lush mouth turned down at the edges. She was the very personification of a teapot about to boil over.

"I don't understand." She turned away from him and walked a few feet farther down the terrace. The area was shaded and covered in moss, and wild ground cover had crept up between the stones.

"Take care," he called to her. "Some of the stones are crumbling."

She spun toward him and planted her hands on her hips. "Then, you should have them fixed. And if you start with the paving stones, why not fix all of it?"

Will swallowed hard. It was precisely the wrong moment to notice, but standing with the sun at her back, the light gave her hair a fiery glow, and her skin flushed, not with embarrassment but determination. She was without a doubt the most appealing woman he'd ever seen.

She was lovely. Cornwall was lovely. But despite her expectations or those of his staff, he wouldn't be here long. And for however many days he stayed, he would not devote his time to refurbishing a house built to host his father's misdeeds.

"No." He spoke the word softly this time but felt it just as emphatically.

"You did say you owed me a favor."

"I did, but surely your favor cannot be that I undertake the renovation of a crumbling manor house and complete it in two weeks."

"Not the whole house. Only what's visible from the hotel." She gestured toward the seaside edge of the manor. "This bit back here."

"So you're an architect and a nursery owner?"

"Not at all, but I know an appealing view when I see one." There was a bit of playful impertinence in her tone that Will found himself wanting to spark again. "Perhaps if you visited the hotel, you could take in the view from there and see the problem."

Will let out a sigh. He didn't know how to make her understand. Just as he hadn't known how to make Davina understand.

"What else is on your list?"

She stuck a hand in a pocket hidden in the folds of her skirt and approached. Pulling a piece of paper out, she thrust it toward him.

It was a surprisingly short list. Two items. The first was *See about repairs*, and below that only two other words were written on the scrap of paper: *Mother's roses*.

"The roses I refer to are planted near the grounds-keeper's cottage. My mother planted them and tended them for years. It will only take me a day, depending on weather, to remove them."

"They are of sentimental value to you?"

"Yes, of course, but also practical value. They're a very hardy type of old rose, and I've used some blooms in my experiments."

"An experimenter too?" Where did one young lady find the time to do so much?

That excited glint came into her eyes again. "I create roses."

He'd never given a single thought to where roses came from or how they were grown, but he had never imagined one lovely businesswoman in Cornwall creating them. "How does one create a rose?"

She laughed, and the sound was sweet and slightly husky, and he felt it all the way to his boots. "Not from scratch, mind you. I take a rose of one type and cross it with another, and a new bloom emerges."

Her passion was contagious. Will found that he wanted to know more or, even better, watch how she performed this floral alchemy. Good god, when had he ever cared about gardening?

"Why have you never taken them?"

She shrugged as if the answer must be obvious to him. "They belonged to the house, to your father. Now to you. But if you mean to sell the house or destroy it, I'd like them. There are several varieties in the beds my mother tended, and I've used two of them in my hybridization experiments."

"Spy, nursery owner, rose creator. I'm beginning to wonder what you don't do."

He quite liked watching all the frustration he'd sparked a few moments ago give way to a hint of pride.

"I try to keep busy." Her jaw firmed, and she squared her shoulders before taking a step toward him. "Today I'm here in another role. As a leader of the Royal Visit Committee. Everyone on that committee and, I suspect, many in Haven Cove are hoping you can be convinced to repair Carnwyth. The royal visit could change everything for our town, so I must convince you." She notched her chin up and looked steadily into his eyes. "I'm determined."

"Of that I have no doubt." She was possibly the most determined woman he'd ever met in his life. And he understood determination. He felt that same fiery compulsion in himself—the drive to secure his sisters' futures and make the Ashmore dukedom respectable again. But that work did not involve making immediate repairs to the temple to his father's infamy.

"So you're convinced?"

"If I could be, you'd be the one to do it. But my answer remains the same. I can assure you that I'll bring no more scandal to this house, but I'm not inclined to spend time or money on repairs for purely aesthetic reasons."

Anger swept across her face, and her cheeks reddened.

He expected her anger and probably deserved a bit of it for inviting her to bring her list and then disappointing her.

But instead of unleashing her frustration with words, she turned and strode toward the table where he'd taken his morning meal. She scooped up a couple of his sketches before he could stop her. "These are quite good," she said tightly. "A man who can capture the beauty of a view like this should understand the importance of aesthetics." She laid down his sketches and turned to face him again. "And a duke should do better for the staff he employs and the properties he owns."

Without allowing him a single moment to respond, she started toward the doors that led from the terrace back into the house.

"Wait." The sight of her walking away put a bite of command in his tone that he hadn't truly intended. She wasn't the sort of young woman to be commanded by anyone.

But when she did stop, relief rushed through him.

"What is it, Your Grace?"

"I don't wish to disappoint you entirely, Miss Ravenwood."

She kept her expression cool, but one red brow arched in curiosity.

"The roses. You may take them whenever you wish. As far as I'm concerned, they're yours."

In her blue eyes, he watched a minor skirmish unfold. As if she was deciding whether to offer him gratitude or more anger. "Thank you, Your Grace. I will return for them with one of the workmen from the nursery."

"Very good."

"Good day to you." The words of polite leave-taking didn't soften her expression or the tightness in her tone. Without a glance back, she entered the house, no doubt beelining for the front door.

Her frustration with him disturbed him more than it should. But he felt something else too: that new sense of anticipation. She had to return for her mother's roses, and he quite liked the guarantee that he would get to see her again.

Chapter Nine

The next afternoon, Bly caught Will in the hallway. The staff had a habit of seeking him out and checking on him often, as if they feared he might depart at any moment.

"May I help you find anything, Your Grace?"

"My coat. The one I wore to Cornwall. Have you seen it? It's not in my bedchamber."

"I shall bring it to you straightaway, Your Grace. You're on your way out?"

"I am."

The man's face remained placid except for the slightest twitch of his mustache. "Shall we delay the midday meal, Your Grace?"

"No midday meal needed, Bly. I overheard the footman mention a local pub."

"If you prefer that, sir." The old man managed to look disgusted, shocked, and utterly offended in one single expression. When he finally collected himself, he gave one firm nod. "The Black Anchor. Next to the coaching inn. Shall I have Mitchum prepare a conveyance?"

"Not necessary. I walked by on my way into town, and I can walk that way again." The formality of the staff shocked him, considering how laissez-faire his father had been about everything. "Bly, the staff need not make a fuss on my account. There is nothing formal about this visit. I intend to leave aside all the trappings for these few days." He could hardly explain to the man that he wished to forget his duties, his title, and most of all his reputation as a joyless wretch.

The butler shook his head. Whether in denial or disgust, Will couldn't tell. But then he offered a tight-lipped look of begrudging acquiescence. "As you wish, Your Grace."

Will's traveling trunk had finally been retrieved from the coachman who'd conveyed him to Haven Cove, but every item of clothing in it was rumpled or waterlogged, according to Bly. Except, it seemed, his overcoat. The butler presented him with the freshly laundered garment, and Will slipped it on as he headed for Carnwyth's front door.

The housekeeper emerged from a darkened corner like a watchful wraith. "May I have a word, Your Grace?"

He bit back the urge to snap at the woman. It wasn't her fault that he'd slept miserably and had been out of sorts since Miss Ravenwood's visit the previous day.

"What is it, Mrs. Haskell?"

"Visitors, sir. I noted that Miss Ravenwood called yesterday morning. Should visitors be welcomed in future?" A little, hopeful smile lit the housekeeper's face.

"No, most definitely not." However much they might wish for the house to be bustling again, he had no interest in entertaining.

"But should we admit Miss Ravenwood if she calls again?"

Well, perhaps there was one person he *did* wish to see again.

"Yes, please make an exception for her when she visits in future."

If she wanted her roses, she'd come. And beyond the plants, he had the sense she wasn't quite done with him.

He was definitely not done with her. Coming to Cornwall may not have been his idea, but the prospect held more appeal with Miss Ravenwood nearby.

Her frankness, curiosity, and the very perceptive way her bright gaze ate up everything around her were reason enough to think his time in Cornwall might be bearable.

The moment he descended the steps of Carnwyth and had escaped its cloying excessiveness and decaying walls, he felt lighter. Freer. He wore no hat, no gloves, and no cravat and was pleased to feel the wind buffeting skin that would normally be covered when going about his very proper days in London.

Good god, he *was* painfully proper if shedding a tailored suit and gloves made him this giddy. Maybe he was a bore. Or worse than a bore. *Heartless.*

It had been easy to deny the accusation when Davina threw it at him in anger. Easier to believe she simply didn't understand how essential it was for him to set things right. But now he'd seen that same flare of anger in another woman's eyes. She hadn't called him heartless, but seeing the disappointment in her bright blue gaze made him feel as if he was.

Never before had his reputation as an implacable man bothered him. He liked the fact that when he said no, everyone knew he meant it. Of course, Cora maneuvered her way past his disagreement most of the time, but no one else did. Even Daisy understood that when he refused an invitation or a petition, he was unlikely to change his mind.

He meant what he said, and his steadiness was why others trusted him. Friends he'd never made easily, but of the schoolmates he'd maintained association with and noblemen he worked with in the House of Lords, he was relied upon because he kept his word.

Which made the present circumstances quite extraordinary. His steadiness had apparently turned him into a curmudgeon.

As he walked toward the town's public house, his eyes cataloged the windswept beauty of the sea view, and his mind churned over the matter of how he might redeem himself with Miss Ravenwood.

That disappointed look in her eyes. How could he dispel it?

He didn't wish to analyze why he cared so much. Yes, he intended this visit to be free of worry, but surely he could devote himself to this single concern.

Back in London, he fretted constantly over the way society viewed his family—his sisters, his mother's memory, the dukedom that would continue on when all of them were gone.

But here, now, he wanted *her* esteem. For himself. Not for his family or his name.

The area outside the coaching inn was much busier than it had been the day he arrived. Almost twice the number of carriages were gathered outside, and he wondered if that meant the pub would be crowded too.

When he stopped to make an assessment through the pub windows, an older man approached to stand beside him. He crossed his arms to match Will's stance.

"Busier than usual."

"Is it?"

"Oh aye. The royal visit, you see."

"But it's not for weeks, as I understand."

"Precisely, sir. Many holidaymakers getting their seaside time in now before the real crowds come."

Wonderful. He'd come to the soon-to-be most crowded seaside town in England to get away from the bustling London scene. The most shocking part was that Cora had missed this snag. His sister usually thought of every possibility when she plotted.

"Still some open tables," the man called as he pushed the door of the public house open and made his way inside.

"Very good," Will answered and waited a moment before following behind him.

The frisson of anxiety he usually felt when entering a drawing room or salon in London was noticeably absent as he stepped into the pub. No one would recognize him here. They wouldn't recognize his face or know him by name, and, perhaps most satisfyingly, not a single person in the room would know of his reputation as a too-proper grouch.

It seemed he could be anonymous, and he'd never imagined how good it would feel.

No, that wasn't true. He'd liked the anonymity of his first encounter with Miss Ravenwood too.

After the fresh air and bright skies of his walk, the heat and low ceiling of the pub felt confining. Though others might think it cozy, scents and sounds assailed him. Laughter, the clink of utensils on plates, and the smell of food and drink. It made his stomach rumble, if nothing else.

The old man he'd spoken to outside made his way to a booth near the back as if it was his own. Will stopped just inside the door and surveyed the crowded space for an available chair.

But the longer he looked, the quieter the interior became. Two ladies dining alone watched him with the same kind of curiosity he recognized from London ballrooms. Gentlemen nearby assessed him more warily.

He spotted an empty chair and claimed it.

"Welcome to Haven Cove, sir." The barmaid looked as tired as he felt, but she put on a welcoming smile that seemed warm and genuine. She assessed him as boldly as the ladies near the hearth had. More so. "How long do you plan to stay in our lovely town?"

"Not long, I'm afraid." He spoke the words in a low tone but felt as if everyone in the pub heard his answer. More gazes had turned his way.

"They're just curious about newcomers." She smiled and winked at him. "Especially one as handsome as yourself." After positioning her body to block the gawping ladies at a table nearby, she leaned in. "If it bothers you, I can find you another table. But shall I bring you something to drink and eat in the meanwhile?"

"Thank you, yes."

After his food had come—an unexpectedly tasty pocket of pastry filled with meat, potatoes, and onion for seasoning—and he'd downed one glass of ale, the whispers and looks eased. Now he was among the watchful, and he realized that everyone who entered the pub was subjected to the same perusal.

He opted for coffee after his meal, and the barmaid arrived with a steaming cup as dark and rich as the finest coffeehouses in the city. The sounds of the pub, its crowded tables, the clink of dishes all became almost soothing.

A word of conversation here and there told him that nearly everyone in town was consumed with plans for the royal visit. They expected the princess to "put Haven Cove on the map." She would shop at one lady's haberdasher and soon "everyone in England will want our goods." Will wondered if

Princess Beatrice knew of all the hopes hanging on her brief presence in this corner of Cornwall.

As he took a sip of searing hot coffee and relished the smoky flavor, a name floated above the din of conversation.

Ravenwood.

Will scanned the pub surreptitiously, trying to find the speaker. A white-haired man sat in the far corner conversing with the barmaid.

"Wouldn't know . . ." the barmaid told him, though whatever else she said got lost among the voices in the pub.

The older man seemed to sense Will's regard and offered him a swift, assessing glance.

". . . only a matter of time . . ." He spoke with a tangible arrogance.

After the barmaid departed, the man swigged down several gulps of his drink, sat his glass on the table, and began tucking into a bowl of stew.

Another gent stopped next to the snow-haired man on his way to the pub's door. He chatted with him briefly, then offered a pat on the shoulder in parting. Will heard him call the white-haired man *Longford.*

Will left coins on his table and made his way to the bar of the public house. Longford's booth was nearby, and he was gulping down another glass of ale as if it might be his last.

"Pardon me, sir." Will remained at the bar but turned in Longford's direction. "I heard you mention Ravenwood Nursery." Will spoke the name with special emphasis and a little louder than necessary.

Out of the corner of his eye, he saw Longford pause in lifting his glass and look his way. "I did, sir."

"What do you know of it?" Will moved to take a seat across the booth from Longford as if he'd been invited.

Longford's only response was a brief lift of his bushy brows. "Who am I addressing? I'm Eli Longford of Longford Farms."

Will had no notion what or where Longford Farms might be, but the man spoke the name with obvious pride.

"Good to meet you, Longford. William Hart." Will stretched out a hand, and the older man took it in a firm, brief shake.

"What is it you'd like to know about Ravenwood's?"

"Anything you can tell me."

"Planning to do business with them, are you, Mr. Hart?"

"I'm considering my options." Will offered a nod of thanks to the barmaid who approached with a pot to refill his coffee.

"I knew Ravenwood who started the business. He and his missus. A duke's groundskeeper, he was. Then gave it all up to tend his own land." Longford gave Will an assessing once-over. He wasn't dressed as he would be in London, but his clothes were pressed and clean. Still, he wore little that would indicate either profession or rank. "Are you looking for plants and such?"

"Perhaps." Will loathed offering up all-out falsehoods, but the question of who this man was in relation to Miss Ravenwood and her business intrigued him. "How did you know Ravenwood?"

"As a fellow nurseryman. Struck up a conversation with him when he traveled to Devon for a few of our trees. That's where you'll find Longford Farms. Our nursery is far more extensive than Ravenwood's, sir. And we can construct whatever your garden might require. Hothouses, cold frames, greenhouses, trellises."

The mention of a trellis brought a sharp memory of Maddie clinging to the rickety one at Carnwyth to mind.

"Is Mr. Ravenwood still the proprietor, then?"

Longford grimaced. "He's not. God rest him, he passed a couple of years ago. His daughter took it all on, silly girl. I visited not long ago and must say the business has declined since she took over the running of it."

"Has it, indeed?"

"How could it not? One girl with more interest in drawing up fancy garden designs and puttering with flowers could have no notion what it takes to run a business meant to supply landscaping stock for the entire county."

"She designs gardens, then?" Will recalled something Davina had told him about Lady Trenmere having her garden redesigned by a young woman.

Calculating that Maddie had been that designer and it had been the cause of her visit to London wasn't much of a leap. "Actually, I believe she may have designed a garden for an acquaintance. I thought she might do the same for me."

It wasn't entirely true. At least not in regard to Carnwyth. Though he quite liked the idea of getting her down to Sussex to the Ashmore estate one day and letting her redesign the gardens there.

One day.

No. That was a ridiculous notion. There would be no continued association with Miss Ravenwood once he returned to London.

"Do you have property here, Mr. Hart?"

"I do," he admitted, though he wasn't about to mention the name of the manor house and forfeit the bit of anonymity he had within the confines of the pub.

"Then, perhaps you'll wish to speak to her." Longford shoved a beefy hand inside his coat and offered Will a slightly bent calling card. "Though, if you're looking for a full-service provider of landscape stock and supplies, we'll soon have a nursery established not far from Haven Cove." He took another long sip of his drink, enough to drain the tankard.

"Perhaps I'll venture there tomorrow." Will understood a little better now. Mr. Longford, it seemed, wasn't expressing true concern about Miss Ravenwood's handling of her family's business. He had the distinct impression the man wanted to see her fail. And if he was establishing his own business nearby, that made sense.

"Suit yourself, sir." Longford used the table to anchor himself as he stood, then he burped and ambled toward the door.

Will waited until he'd departed, then headed back to his abandoned table. He wasn't quite ready to return to Carnwyth, and perhaps he'd stumble upon some other local who'd divulge more about Miss Ravenwood.

As he crossed the pub, he heard a name that stopped him short.

This time it wasn't her name but his.

Ashmore.

Will held his breath but realized the two women speaking about him were utterly engrossed in their gossip. They'd heard the new duke had arrived at Carnwyth, but they cast him only a passing glance as he continued to his table. Blessedly, they didn't recognize him as the topic of their tongue-wagging.

A sigh rushed from his lungs when he took a seat again. But the relief was short-lived.

"There she is," one of the gossiping ladies shouted.

Will turned, and his relief of a moment before became something much more potent.

"Miss Ravenwood!" one of the women called.

She entered the pub on a powerful gust that whipped at her gown and hair as she tugged the door shut behind her. After several moments of righting her scarf and skirt and running her fingers through her mussed hair, she heard the ladies calling to her and cast a gaze across the crowded pub.

When her hand came up to wave at the ladies, her gaze flitted momentarily toward him. It was the merest brushing glance, but he felt it like the cool breeze that had followed her inside.

"Come, Maddie, tell us all you know," one of the ladies said, urging her over.

Maddie. Will tested the name on his tongue. He liked it and immediately envied the ladies who knew her well enough to use it so freely.

"We've heard you paid call at the infamous house." On a breathy, eager whisper, the second lady asked, "What was it like? What was *he* like?"

She hadn't moved closer to the women but neither had she acknowledged him. One surreptitious glance in his direction and she told the ladies, "I didn't see much of the house. Mostly, I spoke to the duke out of doors."

"Will you be reviving his garden? Was he awful or charming?"

"Eleanor, we've not even given her a moment to get off her feet. We would ask you to join us, but we've just finished and have an appointment with the dressmaker." The older of the two adjusted a beribboned hat on her head. "We've been waiting for weeks. Everyone must have something new for the princess's visit."

"Of course," Miss Ravenwood said with a genuine smile. "I look forward to seeing your gowns."

Only after the ladies had made their way out of the pub did she truly look Will's way.

"Thank you." Will stood to greet her. "Yet again, I'm in your debt."

"It seemed unfair to launch them on you." She offered a hint of a smile.

Will didn't even try to temper the smile he offered in reply. In fact, he gestured toward the empty chair at his table, hoping she'd join him.

"I have a very practical suggestion for how you could repay me," she said pointedly, though there was none of the tension in her voice as there had been the day before.

"Lunch?"

She laughed, and it was a sound he immediately wanted to hear again.

"Looks as if you've already had yours."

"Some bread. A drink. I had considered heading out, but you're a good reason to stay." He meant it. If he could be guaranteed to stumble upon her at the pub each day during his stay, he might consider extending his holiday.

She seemed to sense his sincerity. Her gaze held on his, and her cheeks turned the lightest shade of pink. Then she held up her hand to the barmaid, who seemed to know what the signal meant. "I don't have much time, but it's nice to have company."

"And the opportunity to represent the Royal Visit Committee again?"

She assessed him and the same spark of determination he'd come to expect from her flashed in her gaze. "I would if I thought I had any chance of persuading you."

Will sipped his now-cool coffee to stop his mind from straying to means of persuasion he knew she didn't intend but that his head seemed determined to conjure.

"Do I?" she pressed.

"Possibly," he told her.

Did she know what he was thinking? She tugged gently at the high neck of her gown as if she too felt the urges that had begun to plague his thoughts whenever they were close to each other.

"I'm sure we could come up with solutions," Maddie told him earnestly. "I have lots of ideas."

"I'm certain you do." He had ideas too, but all of them involved being alone with her. Her hair freed of pins and cascading over his fingers, or splayed out on his bed as she lay . . .

Good god, what was the matter with him?

One lovely red brow winged up as if she could see every inappropriate thought in his head.

The barmaid cut through the tension between them when she arrived with a cup of tea and bowl of soup for Maddie. *Miss Ravenwood*. She picked up her spoon, slid it into the thick stew, and then gave him a guilty look. "I'm famished. This won't be dainty."

Will laughed. The easiness of it felt good. "Eat and enjoy it."

She took her first bite, closed her eyes as if it was bliss, and then let out a contented sigh.

Will glanced at her lips and at the long stray curl that bounced at the edge of her cheek, then forced himself to focus on the dregs of coffee in his cup before he made an utterly boorish fool of himself.

"Has it been a busy morning?" he asked to keep himself from staring hungrily at her.

She swiped at her cheek, then ran her hand through her wind-tousled hair. "I must look a fright."

"The very opposite, I assure you." Will circled his cup in his palm. His hands had grown warm, awkward, as if he suddenly had no idea how to be across the table from a woman who affected him so much. "But you must work very hard at the nursery."

"There is satisfaction in hard work." Her tone had an edge of defensiveness.

"I admire you for it. For running a business on your own. And taking on so many other roles in Haven Cove."

"I like being busy." Still the defensiveness, and he hated himself for making her feel that she needed to justify herself to anyone.

"May I visit the nursery?" He changed tack, not only because he no longer wanted to tread any ground that made her uncomfortable but because he truly did wish to see the place that carried her name and that she devoted so much time and effort to.

"Of course you may." But she poked nervously at her soup as she answered. "When?"

She didn't look eager, more like wary.

"Tell me a day and time, and I'll be there. I'm conspicuously without a social calendar at the moment."

"A social call." After assessing him over a long sip of tea, she sat the cup down and said, "And here I thought perhaps you were considering hiring us to revive the garden at Carnwyth."

He had considered it. For entirely mercenary reasons. Not because he gave a whit about improving the grounds of that infernal house but because it would give him a reason to see her.

In that moment, it became blazingly clear that he wanted to see her as much as he could reasonably manage. The prospect of any day of his Cornish holiday not including time spent with her was suddenly unthinkable.

She tightened her hold on her teacup and then set it down so quickly it nearly toppled. When she reached out to stop it from spilling, Will extended his hand to do the same. Their fingers clashed, and Will drew back slowly.

"You really won't relent, will you?" That same frustration he'd sensed from her at Carnwyth was simmering just below the surface now.

"Repairing the house holds no appeal, but I *am* willing to hear your ideas. Perhaps we could find a compromise."

"Truly?"

If only this wasn't about the damned house. He'd be willing to agree to a great deal to spark that hopeful look in her gaze.

Leaning forward, he rested his elbows on the table and whispered, "I'm not actually heartless, you know."

At least that's what he told himself, despite what everyone seemed to think.

"Oh no." Eyes wide, she hurriedly tipped back the remainder of her tea and then wrapped her scarf over her hair. "I must go. I'm going to be late."

"For what?"

"A committee meeting."

Will wished he'd come in a carriage or could offer her a conveyance of some sort, but she was already out of her chair. He wanted to know about her committee too, but she was already standing, clearly eager to get out the door. When she lifted coins from her pocket, Will stopped her with a hand up.

"I did say I'd buy your lunch."

"Thank you." She stilled her anxious movement and turned her full attention his way. "I'll come for the roses this weekend and present you with some ideas."

"I look forward to it, Miss Ravenwood." His voice emerged huskier than he'd intended. He was beginning to mark his time in Cornwall by the next opportunity to see her. He couldn't resist adding, "I promise to be in a relenting mood."

Chapter Ten

"I hereby call this meeting of the Royal Visit Committee to order." Jane Reeve stood at the head of the long oval table and nodded at Maddie. They worked in tandem almost seamlessly and had formed a bond over their shared goals. Maddie respected her and felt that respect was returned.

"Miss Ravenwood, would you please read the agenda?"

The request shouldn't have surprised her. They'd had dozens of meetings, and they all began in just this way. But Maddie didn't have her folder open and didn't have her neatly written agenda in front of her. She'd felt out of sorts since speaking with the Duke of Ashmore yesterday, as if the path she'd been on had taken an unexpected turn.

And today, when her path had led her to the pub, she'd been pleasantly surprised to find him there. So pleased that she'd almost wished there wasn't a need to convince him of anything and they could just enjoy a lunchtime conversation.

"Is everything all right?" Mrs. Reeve whispered out of the corner of her mouth. "I can improvise if you wish."

"No, I have it here." Maddie shuffled through the documents in her folio and finally found the agenda she'd written up early this morning. "First, we shall have a status update from all parties on their preparations for the visit. Mrs. Reeve plans to tell us about the features that they're adding to the hotel grounds, and Miss Caldecott—"

"May we add an agenda item?" Mrs. Pendenning interrupted, her cheeks flushed, eyes bright as if she was bursting to share some bit of news.

"What is it, Mrs. Pendenning?" Maddie couldn't temper her curiosity. The agenda could wait, since whatever Agatha had to impart seemed much more intriguing.

She turned in her chair so that she was facing Maddie and cupped her hand around her mouth as if the entire table of committee members weren't listening with anticipation.

"The duke," she breathed. "The Duke of Ashmore has returned to Haven Cove."

"The *new* duke," a committee member down the table from Agatha corrected.

"Yes, of course the new one, Beth. The old one is dead."

Each committee member leaned in, and they pitched questions at one another like they were conducting a tennis match.

"Have you seen him?"

"Why is he here?"

"How long will he stay?"

Their exuberance was long on curiosity but few

of them seemed to have answers. Maddie held her tongue and wondered if she should divulge her acquaintance—it was that, now, wasn't it?—with the duke.

But as she often did, Mrs. Hobbs cut across the excitement and focused them once again on the practical matters at hand. "Most importantly, what will he do about that infamous eyesore of Carnwyth?"

"Oh, I think we should consider more than repairs at Carnwyth." Mrs. Reeve remained standing, and all eyes turned her way. "The house is a bit of a ruin, but we could cover it with trees." She gave Maddie a questioning glance. "Couldn't we?"

"We could devise something—"

"Or you could simply build some trellises to block the view."

Maddie nodded, though she didn't mention that Ravenwood's wasn't in the business of building garden structures. Plants and trees were their specialty. However, there was one company not too far away that did specialize in buildings for gardens— Longford Farms.

Bracing her palms on the tabletop, Mrs. Reeve leaned forward. Eyes glowing, voice low and intense, she said, "Imagine if we could get him to help with the visit. With entertaining the princess or drawing more guests to Carnwyth. He could host a party at the manor. It's infamous. Many would come, and we could induce them to attend the events during the princess's visit, buy souvenirs at local shops, eat at the hotel."

"I don't think he'll agree to any of that," Maddie said with quiet certainty. "He doesn't seem particularly amenable."

"You've spoken to him?" Miss Dixon looked thrilled at the news, and though she sat two chairs down, she leaned aggressively past the young woman next to her. "What is he like?"

The eagerness at the table was palpable. Ladies held their breath. Others were breathing hard. They were interested in *him*. And not in a practical way. Miss Merrick, who had characterized herself as a spinster for years, looked downright mesmerized.

"Well, Miss Ravenwood," Mrs. Hobbs prompted, "it's clear we won't get to any of the business at hand until you satisfy the ladies with any tittle-tattle you might have about the new Duke of Ashmore."

Maddie felt the weight of twelve curious gazes turned her way. Her mind spun through what she knew and what he would probably prefer she not divulge.

"We met by happenstance." It was the truth, though she wasn't certain it would satisfy any of the townspeople present. "He's come to Carnwyth on holiday. To rest and rejuvenate." The wording was straight off one of the pamphlets she'd seen at the hotel's front counter and echoed well enough what he'd told her.

"What does he need rest from?" Mr. Peregrine put in. "Is being a nobleman so very wearying?"

A few of the ladies tittered.

"He's run away from all the whispers about him in London," Mrs. Hobbs said with her chin notched a little higher than need be. "A fine young lady jilted him, and they say it's because he's a bit of an ogre. I hear he's quite a nasty piece of work."

Maddie let out a little guffaw she couldn't restrain, and then a giggle almost chased its way up her throat. "He doesn't seem the villainous sort." Not with those sad amber-tinged eyes and laugh lines that softened the edges of his perfectly carved mouth, even if they didn't seem to get much use nowadays.

"Is he as handsome as they say?"

"Yes." The word came out breathily, almost unbidden. There was no concealing that fact. Anyone who set eyes on him would agree.

Miss Merrick cleared her throat, drawing Maddie's gaze. "Does he seem keen to marry?"

"I certainly never asked him that."

"An eligible duke. In Haven Cove. My goodness, what a boon," Miss Dixon said in a dreamy tone. "We must take advantage of this fortuitous turn of circumstance. Why don't we auction him off?"

When she was met with stunned silence, she added, "At the dance, of course. We could promote the event to all the best families in Cornwall. Or even further. Contribute to the visit committee and you could win a dance with a duke."

"Like a raffle," Miss Merrick put in quite unhelpfully.

"You can't be serious." Maddie ran a finger along

the inside of her gown's collar because it seemed to be suffocating her. Air tangled in her lungs, and a flare of irritation made her cheeks burn. "He's not ours to auction off or to dance with. He came for a quiet fortnight away from London. He didn't even wish to have his presence here known."

"Whyever not?" Mr. Peregrine grumbled.

Maddie gestured around the table. "I imagine this is the reason. Requests, demands, expectations." She understood now in a way she hadn't before why he'd wish for a solitary sojourn. There were no tenants here or social acquaintances who could expect anything from him, and yet the whole of Haven Cove seemed to think he owed them a great deal.

"As the highest-ranking noble landowner in a town on the cusp of a royal visit, you'd think he'd wish to do his part."

"He must know the princess," a committee member said emphatically.

"Did he know about the princess's arrival?" Miss Merrick asked. "Is that why he came?"

"Not at all."

Peregrine let out a grunt of ire. "Means to hie off before she arrives, I suspect."

"Well, that won't do." Mrs. Reeve had taken her seat, but she held a pen in her hand that was perched over a clean sheet of paper. Clearly, she was prepared to list all the ways the Duke of Ashmore must do his part in making the visit he'd not even known about a success. "We need him, and we must persuade him of that." Her gaze locked on Maddie's. "Did you ask for his assistance with preparations for the visit?"

"I encouraged him to make repairs to Carnwyth." None needed to know that by *encouraged* she meant that she'd become frustrated with him and stalked off. Simply being in his presence disturbed her peace of mind. And yet she'd taken lunch with him today because she was ridiculously pleased to see him every time they crossed paths.

Her thoughts about the man were all a most distracting jumble.

"I take it your petition was not favorably received?" Mrs. Reeve said pointedly.

Brows inched up foreheads. Committee members craned their necks to cast her expectant looks.

"He does not wish to undertake repairs." Whatever his reasons, he'd made his lack of interest in Carnwyth perfectly clear. "I don't think he wishes to keep the property."

"Then, we should find a buyer immediately," Mrs. Reeve pronounced, as if undertaking the transfer of land and property that didn't belong to her was a simple matter, "so that the house can be returned to its former glory."

A few ladies averted their gazes.

Few in Haven Cove ever spoke of Carnwyth in glowing terms. Not only because of whatever had gone on there when the previous duke lived but because it had always been a bit of a ruin.

"I'm not sure *glory* is the correct term," Mrs. Hobbs

said dubiously. "The old duke was a scoundrel, and this one sounds like quite a worthless rogue."

"What if he tries to tear it down?" Miss Dixon sounded genuinely curious rather than concerned.

"Wouldn't mind the old duke returning, if you ask me." Mr. Peregrine crossed his arms as he met the gazes of the ladies seated across from him and then glanced up at Mrs. Reeve. "Might have been a bounder, but he brought visitors to our town. Spent money. He was good for Haven Cove. Not like this rotter."

"He's dead, Mr. Peregrine. He won't be returning." Mrs. Reeve spoke the words in a long-suffering tone, as if she had the duty of convincing a child to accept reality as it is. "So the new duke is who we must contend with, and we cannot accept his refusal. I shall pay the duke a visit myself." Following the pronouncement, she shot Maddie a look of challenge.

Six and twenty years of stubbornness fired Maddie's blood. The two of them usually got on quite well. They shared a common goal: making the visit the most successful event in Haven Cove history. But Mrs. Reeve didn't know the Duke of Ashmore. Maddie did.

Sort of.

"I think it best if *I* try again."

"But you've already failed."

Failed. Maddie clenched her jaw. What an awful word. Fear of failure had hung over her like a summer storm cloud since the death of her father. She'd heard the whispers of townspeople. They harbored the same doubts about her ability to keep Raven-wood Nursery afloat as he had.

Eli Longford wasn't the only person in Cornwall who wondered if she'd taken on too much.

But it was her nature to do too much, and it was also her stubborn nature not to give up.

Maddie tamped down her frustration. *You're too emotional*, her father had often told her. Perhaps she was, but she needed her wits about her now more than ever.

"I believe that with another visit, I can convince him. My understanding is that the duke was un-aware of the state of the manor house. He'd never seen Carnwyth before this week."

"And didn't care to." Mr. Peregrine *really* didn't like the current Duke of Ashmore.

"Whatever his reasons for staying away, he has no reason to respond to the demands of the committee now." Maddie waited a beat but then quickly added, "But my acquaintance with him is established."

"And will your acquaintance be enough to con-vince him?" Mrs. Reeve shot Maddie an unblinking stare.

Why was the hotelier challenging Maddie so fiercely? They weren't adversaries. The survival of both of their businesses depended on the success of the royal visit.

"I won't fail." Maddie held Mrs. Reeve's gaze, willing the older woman to relent. She could do this, and he'd already said he'd welcome more visits from her. Mrs. Reeve had no such standing invitation.

"Very well." The hotelier nodded and offered Maddie a smile. "I trust your judgment, Miss Ravenwood."

Maddie let out a relieved sigh. She had no wish to bicker with her committee coleader in front of the others. Keeping everyone dedicated to the weekly meetings and the preparatory work for the upcoming event was difficult enough.

Mrs. Reeve seemed lost in thought, which was entirely unlike her. Then she squared her gaze on Maddie again. "Do let him know he's welcome at the hotel. He can sample our rooms, or a meal in the dining room. Or even make use of our tennis courts or pool."

Her establishment featured more amenities than some of the most famous hotels in London. She and her late husband had made maximum use of the land they'd purchased and spared no expense, ensuring every aspect of the hotel was grand. It made sense that she was anxious for the duke to help make the upcoming event a success. Maddie understood, and she was more determined than ever.

"I'll tell him. And perhaps he'll see the value in assisting with the visit."

"We shall see, Miss Ravenwood. Let's continue." Mrs. Reeve proceeded to update the committee on the status of her own preparations for the visit, and every lady and gentleman present followed suit.

After the meeting adjourned, Maddie moved quickly to file out among the first to leave. She was to meet with a client back at the nursery before closing time.

The hotel was busy, and getting back into the main hall and through the front doors proved more difficult than expected. After trying to squeeze past a large party of ladies who'd taken over one of the main gathering spaces, Maddie tried a shortcut she knew that led her past the hotel's enormous balcony. Elegantly appointed tables for two or four filled the space, but along the edge of the balcony, there was an open path for promenading or stopping to look out onto the hotel's exquisite sea view.

Maddie couldn't resist glancing out toward the water. The cliffs of the cove looked extraordinary in the afternoon light.

She slowed her steps. A man stood at the edge of the promenade silhouetted against the bright sky. He stood with his back to her and looked out onto the view of the cove and the sea beyond and, just on the opposite cliff, Carnwyth and its crumbled, dilapidated facade.

There was no mistaking the width of those shoulders or the wavy jet-black hair.

Ashmore's gaze seemed to be locked on the view of Carnwyth across the cove. Good. Excellent, in fact. He seemed a man who needed to see things himself to believe them, and he'd said he might be persuadable.

Was he convinced?

Maddie glanced at her watch and knew she should go. She didn't have many minutes to spare if she was to reach the nursery in time for the meeting with a potential client.

And yet impulse carried her toward him. Something always seemed to pull her in his direction.

"Are you convinced?" she asked softly as she approached.

He glanced back and looked momentarily surprised to see her. Then he offered her a smile. She could get quite used to how easily he smiled at her now.

"It does look dreadful. Unless the princess is fond of ruins. Then one could almost argue that it has a kind of Gothic appeal."

Maddie stood next to him, her elbow a few inches from his. "Except that the style of Carnwyth isn't Gothic, and it's less of a ruin and more of an eyesore."

He huffed out a chuckle and quirked one dark brow. "It's refreshing to find someone who dislikes it as much as I do."

"Oh, but I don't dislike the house. Seems unfair for me to when I've seen so little of it."

"You're not put off by what you have seen?"

"No." Maddie thought of the explicit carvings on the front door, the mural she'd spied in the hallway, and the statues of scantily clad goddesses in the abandoned gardens. "It simply lives up to my expectations, and I'm fond of things that are colorful and ornate."

He turned away from the view of the cove to face her. She half expected him to snap some reply about how much he loathed the house, but his entire manner seemed more relaxed. He seemed more at ease each time she encountered him.

"Then, when you come for your roses, I'll give you a more thorough tour."

"I'd like that very—"

Maddie heard the voice of Miss Dixon and froze. Then she heard Miss Merrick reply. The two women were taking a stroll down the promenade, heading in Maddie's direction.

"What is it?" He brushed a hand against Maddie's arm in concern.

"The ladies approaching on my right. If they see me with you, they'll probably conclude you're the Duke of Ashmore."

He looked over her head directly at the two women and took a step away from her. "I'd love to avoid that discovery, but I suppose my anonymity can't last forever." His brow knitted into a frown when he turned toward her again. "Or is it that you wouldn't wish to be seen with me and are concerned for your reputation?" He pitched his voice low. "I'd never wish to do anything to risk your good standing in Haven Cove. I have a notion of how important one's reputation is."

It touched her that he seemed sincerely concerned for her well-being.

"No, I told you. No one thinks of me as anything but a spinster and local business owner."

"Then, will it seem so strange to see you conversing with a gentleman?"

"You don't look like most gentlemen."

Maddie just resisted pushing him in the opposite direction of the approaching committee members. "You should go if you don't wish me to be forced to introduce you."

"Will you come to the house? I could offer you dinner. Believe me, the cook is eager to show off her culinary skills to more than an audience of one."

Dinner at Carnwyth. She never could have imagined she'd be invited to dine with a duke. Part of her wanted to accept, but she could sense Miss Merrick and Miss Dixon drawing closer. Their voices grew louder and, of course, they were talking about the new duke.

"I have an appointment back at the nursery," Maddie told him with a glance.

"You keep busier than I did back in London. If my sister knew you, she'd send you on holiday."

Maddie was too distracted to reply.

"Miss Ravenwood, I thought you'd departed." Miss Merrick had spotted her.

"Come soon." He'd drawn close, and Maddie felt the heat of his breath against her ear, but when she turned, he'd gone.

Maddie offered the ladies a wave. "Sorry, I'm just on my way back to work." She immediately headed in the opposite direction and had just reached the far end of the balcony when the women's conversation carried across the distance.

She rather expected to see the duke waiting for her at the hotel's entrance, but he wasn't there, and, foolishly, that made her heart sink.

Heading toward the exit, she heard Miss Merrick mention her by name.

"Do you think that gentleman is courting Miss Ravenwood?"

"He might have been a customer, for all we know."

Maddie picked up her pace and left the hotel. She didn't have time to eavesdrop on gossips.

The Duke of Ashmore—though they didn't know that's who he was—courting her? Maddie let out a gusty laugh. What a silly, nonsensical notion. An impossible notion.

And one that, suddenly, she couldn't stop herself from imagining.

Chapter Eleven

Avoiding a house while living in it was rather difficult to pull off.

Will tried to be out of doors as much as possible, having no desire to be stuck in the single guest room where he slept. But whether the skies were a vivid cloudless blue or storm-swept and menacing, the wind off the sea remained a constant.

Hair tangled, skin buffeted, fingers numb, he'd sit in the gusts on cloudy days as long as he could. Sunny days made the wind far more bearable. Today had dawned like a cerulean dream, and he'd looked forward to walking down to the seaside, but soot-gray clouds had barreled in by the time he'd taken his first sip of coffee.

He sighed, scooped up his drawings, and headed for the dining room, where the staff always laid out something for his breakfast.

Art had become his refuge since arriving at Carnwyth. If one could call it art. He'd sketched often as a boy, dabbled in paints at university while making a serious study of architecture, and then stopped after being chastised by tutors who insisted it was not a worthwhile endeavor for a ducal heir. He hadn't sketched since, but he'd found a cache of drawing paper and pencils left by a previous visitor to the house and had covered half the pages in the stack within days. Clouds, the hotel across the cove, the cliffs leading down to the beach—the view inspired him.

But he took inspiration from elsewhere too.

The lovely Miss Ravenwood, who found him as frustrating as everyone else did, appeared on his pages too.

He'd seen her only a handful of times, yet he'd memorized little details. The way a few curls always seemed to slip her pins and frame her face. The little notch in the center of her chin. And those eyes. Even the brightest day he'd seen in Cornwall didn't match the blue of her eyes.

Every day, he debated whether to seek her out. It had been three days since their encounter at the hotel. She'd said she would come for the roses at the weekend and today was Sunday. He was usually a patient man, but letting his days in Cornwall slip by without seeing her was proving as miserable as he'd suspected it would be.

And who could blame him for the desire to spend time with her? Other than Carnwyth's staff, she was the only person he knew in Cornwall. No, that wasn't true, was it? The butler mentioned that Lady Trenmere's holiday house wasn't far from Carnwyth. Though, he wasn't sure where he stood with the countess anymore. He hadn't seen the noblewoman since the night his engagement ended.

Lifting the silver dome over the tray the staff had left for him, Will found poached eggs and kippers, and his stomach lurched at the smell. Thankfully, there was an urn with more coffee too, and he took solace in another cup.

Then he strode toward the window to check on the changeable weather. He passed near a candle sconce that projected from the wall like the masthead on a ship and featured a curvaceous female form painted in chipped gilt. As he passed, the sconce tipped sideways, and one of the arms fell off, as if it had been waiting for a witness before self-destructing.

He groaned. Every day the house reminded him of its need for restoration. Each morning he awoke to find plaster dust on his bedside table, as the fresco on the guest-room ceiling sifted off. Mr. Bly reported that he'd spoken to Will's father several times about restoring or replacing the painted ceiling, but his requests had gone unheeded. It seemed his father had simply allowed his friends and cronies to use and abuse the property, and it had never properly recovered from some of the wilder parties. Then several fierce Cornish storms had taken their toll on the exterior too. Every time the wind made the eastern side of the house creak, Will recalled the broken stones Miss Ravenwood had pointed out and wondered if that side of the house was on the verge of collapse.

A whine sounded somewhere in the house.

The wind, no doubt, slipping past sundry holes in the walls.

He took another bracing sip of coffee and turned his mind to escape. Perhaps it was time to pay a visit to Miss Ravenwood's nursery.

Then the sound came again. Louder and longer than before.

"Did you hear that?" Will strode toward the open dining-room door and called to a young maid carrying a tray in the hallway.

The girl whipped around to face him, eyes wide and worried. "Hear what, Your Grace?"

Will held a finger up. "There. That sound." It was muffled but distinct. "A whining sort of cry, almost a wail. As if someone is in distress. Is a staff member ill?"

"Not to my knowledge, sir."

Will didn't believe the girl. Her eyes shifted as she spoke, as if she feared his scrutiny. He strode from the dining room and headed toward the sound. Then it stopped for a moment, and he stopped too, waiting, hoping to hear it again.

Mrs. Haskell's voice echoed from the back of the house. She wasn't happy, but he couldn't make out her words. As he continued down the hall, the noise came again. A bleating cry that sounded more like an animal.

His mind spun with terrible scenarios. He'd heard of some wealthy Londoners keeping wild beasts in their homes as pets, mostly to show off to shocked and amazed guests. His father had never allowed anyone in the family to keep a pet—too much work and upkeep for very little payoff, he'd said—but he'd seemed just the sort to use creatures as props for entertainment.

Had he inherited a menagerie no one had thought to mention?

The housekeeper emerged from a room near the far end of the hall, slamming the door behind her. She jolted at the sight of him.

"Your Grace, was your morning meal not to your liking?"

"Never mind breakfast. I've come to investigate a noise. Did you hear it? Something like an animal cry."

"No." She shook her head slowly and twisted her mouth as if she was seriously pondering the possibility. "No animal sounds here, sir."

The mewling sounded again. Louder and coming, it seemed, from the room at her back.

Will stared the older woman down, but she didn't say a word.

"What's in this room, Mrs. Haskell?"

"This room? Used it as a ballroom, your father did. But we've . . ." She drew in a breath before continuing and straightened her spine as she did. "We use it as storage, Your Grace."

"Storage? Why on earth would anyone use a ballroom?"

"I suppose it was nearest."

"I'd like to see."

The housekeeper looked at him a long, silent moment, as if willing him to change his mind, then finally stepped aside and turned the latch on the door.

"Suit yourself, Your Grace."

Will stepped across the threshold and immediately had the urge to sneeze. "Good god."

"It happened over time," Mrs. Haskell explained weakly. "One thing and then another."

Furnishings were haphazardly placed within the high-ceilinged room. Piled like a barricade. A listing, dusty barricade. Chairs were stacked on sofas. A table with a broken leg leaned against a bookcase that had a warped back, as if it had sustained water damage. In fact, the entire space smelled musty.

"Is the roof leaking?"

"Not in here, no."

Will quirked a brow at her. Her reply implied other rooms did have leaks. He had seen the damage to the sea-facing side of the house, and since water fell from the skies with shocking regularity here, he assumed some got inside.

"I still contend this is an odd place to store furniture." Will took a few steps, glanced up, slid his gaze around the space, and grimaced at the odor, a mix of dust and earth and musty fabric.

"When something broke, we'd put it in here." The housekeeper spoke slowly, as if she was taking care with each word. "Always expected we'd eventually get it all fixed. But then there was a fierce storm not six months past that broke windows on the east side of the house and soaked much of the furniture. We thought to let it dry here while the windows were repaired."

Will hadn't been in many of the rooms on the

east side of the house. He'd been wary of exploring the house much at all and had spent his time in the chamber he'd been sleeping in or outdoors on the back terrace or in the neglected gardens.

Guilt came down on him like ballast on his shoulders. He might loathe his father's behavior and see the house as a temple to the man's debauchery, but it *was* Will's responsibility now and had been from the moment he'd inherited the title. Avoiding unpleasantness was his father's way, and Will had always believed it was not his.

But Maddie had been right that day on the terrace. A nobleman did have a duty to those in his employ. And apparently, he, and his father before him, had left the staff of Carnwyth to persist in a manor house that was falling into shambles around them.

"Why was the furniture not moved back after the windows were repaired?"

The older woman ducked her head and then eyed him warily. "Not all the windows have been repaired. We were short on funds, Your Grace."

Will frowned. "Were no funds sent to maintain the house?"

Admittedly, he was guilty of putting off dealing with his father's various pleasure retreats, but he had directed his estate agent in London to send funds as needed.

"To maintain, Your Grace, not to repair." She worried the keys pinned to the belt of her dress and turned her gaze down again, but before Will could press her, he heard the sound again. Not the insistent cry, but one small quiet mewl.

"A cat?" They were keeping a feline among stacks of broken and ruined furnishings?

"Mrs. Haskell, I got the milk." Kate entered the ballroom and then immediately stopped on the threshold. "Oh, I didn't realize . . ."

Meow. Will looked down to find a kitten on his boot, staring up at him and rubbing against his trouser leg. Then another emerged from the dusty shadows, and two more, and then a fifth. The last was smaller than the rest and unsteady on its tiny paws.

"We have a kitten infestation," Will said wryly. The one that perched on his foot sat down, as if it had found the perfect spot to relax.

"A stray mama came up through a hole in the floor."

Will grimaced. "How many holes does the floor have?"

"Just the one that's cat-size," Kate said cheerfully.

"Oh good." Will glanced at the piles of furniture, then knelt to scoop up the orange and white kitten from his boot. The tiny thing stared at him curiously but seemed content to be held. "Why were you trying to hide them and all of this from me?"

Mrs. Haskell cast a quick look at Kate. "You did say you were here for a short time and seemed to want to avoid worries." Her face softened as she watched the kitten he held bat a paw at his chin. "Your father didn't care for animals, and especially not in the house, but it's clear you're not like him in that regard."

"I'm not," Will assured her emphatically.

They'd all asked for a pet at some point as children. Will had wanted a dog. Cora had asked for a parrot. Daisy had petitioned the most vehemently, and she'd wanted a kitten. She would adore the little beasts mewing at his feet.

He tried not to think about his father and worked hard not to be anything like the man. But one of his father's chief characteristics was a tendency to shirk responsibilities and commitments, and wasn't that what he had done to Carnwyth?

"We should move them to a safer spot." The stack of furniture looked precarious, to say the least.

"There's a sunroom near the kitchen. Would it be all right to move them there, Your Grace?"

"That sounds like just the thing."

"Excellent." Mrs. Haskell's eyes widened, then she nodded and allowed herself a tremulous smile. "We'll go and begin preparing a space for them. Thank you, Your Grace."

Was he truly such an ogre that any agreeableness on his part was met with such surprise?

"Oh, you're absolutely gorgeous." Maddie rushed through the greenhouse, careful not to brush her best dress against any of the dirty tables or gardening tools, and bent to take a closer look at her Victoria rose. The bloom was an extraordinary shade of peach darkening to a lush coral at the petal edges.

Maddie had propagated the bloom with one of her mother's old sunny yellow roses and another red tea-rose variety.

She'd debated whether naming the rose after the monarch was too much, but it was the name of Princess Beatrice's daughter too, and she wanted the princess to know this particular bloom was created with her visit in mind. Even if Maddie's flowers didn't take first place in the competition, she hoped to at least catch the princess's notice.

Since the first hybrid tea rose had been created in France in 1867, they had become quite the rage among gardeners and those who appreciated roses. If a cultivar was hardy and featured unique coloring, it might become popular and sell well to nurseries and gardeners across the country. But if such a rose was shown favor by a princess of the realm, it would become an unmitigated success. Maddie collected magazines where gardens and nurseries advertised their various hybrid roses. She wanted to see hers there with the words *Favored by Princess Beatrice during a Visit to Cornwall*.

"I knew you'd be in here," Alice called from the greenhouse door, startling Maddie out of her daydreams. "I've a message for you. A note from Mrs. Reeve."

Maddie stiffened. Today was the day she planned to visit the duke. The hotelier wouldn't go ahead of her, would she? The woman's lack of trust in her was new and unpleasant. She wanted to dispel Mrs. Reeve's doubts as well as her own.

"What does she say?" Maddie had slipped on her gardening gloves and had one potted rose in her hands. It needed more light, and she planned to move it closer to the greenhouse wall.

Alice unfolded the note, scanned the contents, and looked up at Maddie with a crimped brow. "It's cryptic, but perhaps you'll understand. She says, *Tell him that I will name a suite after him if he wishes to stay at the hotel. It's an honor I am offering to only the most notable visitors.*"

"Thank you, Alice. She's referring to the Duke of Ashmore."

"You're going to see him today, aren't you?"

Maddie tipped a glance over her shoulder. "How did you know?"

Alice grinned broadly. "That's the prettiest dress I've ever seen you wear."

"It's old," Maddie protested, though the truth was that all of her best dresses were. They'd been purchased when business had been flush and her parents—especially her mother—had expected her to go away to a ladies' finishing school or make a promising match with a young man in town.

"It's lovely. The blue suits you. The same shade as your eyes, just darker."

Maddie settled the potted rose on a table in the sun and stripped off her gloves. She pressed the back of her hand to her cheek and wasn't surprised to find it flaming hot. A ridiculous bout of nerves had been with her all morning, but Alice's compliments only served to heighten her anxiety. And make her feel like a bit of a fool. She had chosen her best dress and taken special care with her hair.

"I need to persuade him, so I want to feel confident when I go to see him." Though she'd originally expected to retrieve the roses today, that plan had changed after the committee meeting. Before she worried about her own needs, she needed to resolve matters regarding the royal visit.

"You should feel confident. You go as a leader of Haven Cove."

"I'm not a leader."

Alice's eyes lit with amusement, and she let out a quiet chuckle. "You're head of the Royal Visit Committee—"

"Coleader." Maddie knew that Mrs. Reeve would be the first to offer that reminder.

"And founding member of the Horticultural Society of Haven Cove, treasurer of the Historical Society, president of the Ladies' Library Council." Alice drew in a deep breath and laughed. "Mercy, I'm tired just listing them all."

Maddie couldn't help but offer a lopsided grin in reply. She did take on too much, and yet it never satisfied the sense that she wasn't doing enough. That there was something more that would make her feel fulfilled. She just hadn't found it yet. "I keep busy."

"You do, and you manage it all so well."

"I'm not sure that's true." She was more exhausted than she was willing to admit, and lately she'd endured too many sleepless nights because she'd allowed thoughts of the duke to distract her. It had been a long time since she'd had a day to herself to simply be at ease.

"You're quite accomplished, whether you're willing to admit it or not." Alice offered her the note from Mrs. Reeve. "I've no doubt you'll bend the duke to your will in no time."

Maddie choked, coughed to cover it, and accepted the piece of paper. What Maddie saw was a vivid image of the Duke of Ashmore on bent knee in front of her and her body warmed from her cheeks all the way down to her toes.

Quite inappropriately, that image played in her mind as she drove the pony cart all the way to Carnwyth. Her horse took the journey too slowly, and Maddie urged her on. Perhaps once she got the duke to agree, that anxious quivering in her stomach would finally ease.

The day had turned sunny, and there was an undeniable charm to Carnwyth's facade. The diamond-shaped panes of the upstairs windows glinted in the afternoon light.

She approached the door as she had the first time, determined to get inside no matter what opposition she encountered.

But there wasn't any opposition. In fact, the large carved front door stood ajar. Maddie peeked through the opening, saw a rush of movement in the long marble hall, then pushed her way inside.

"Hello?"

One maid exited and passed another who was entering a room at the far end of the hall. The one going in shouted behind her.

"Kate, we're going to need more milk."

Maddie started down the hall and nearly collided with a footman coming from the door near the stairwell that led belowstairs. Arms filled with linens, he stopped just short of bumping into her.

"Pardon me, miss," he said abruptly and then continued quickly down to the same room the maid had entered.

"I'm looking for the Duke of Ashmore," Maddie said quickly, but the young man seemed focused on his destination.

What had everyone so fretful? As she made her way down the hall, she glanced into each room but didn't see the duke in any of them.

"Ow!"

The single cry emerged in a familiar male voice and from the room that seemed to be the center of some crisis in the house.

"Little blighter," his deep voice offered sweetly.

Near the threshold, Maddie spotted Kate emerging, carrying a little bundle in her arms.

"Oh," the girl said when she spotted Maddie. "Hello, Miss Ravenwood. His Grace is in the ballroom." She tipped her head to indicate the room she'd just exited.

Maddie stepped into the doorway and gasped. The room was full of towering piles of discarded furnishings.

Then she spotted the man she'd come to see. He was crouched in a far corner of the room, and when he sensed her presence and turned, a tiny tabby kitten scrambled off his thigh.

"You've come." He rose in one graceful movement and revealed a white kitten cradled in one of his arms. "May I interest you in a kitten?"

A chuckle burst from Maddie, and she knelt to meet the orange and white kitten who was making her wobbly way toward her.

"As you see, we have a plethora of them." He crossed the dusty ballroom floor, and Maddie stood to pet the kitten cradled against his chest.

"What happened to this ballroom, and how did it sprout kittens?"

His gaze held on her face a moment before he replied. "Apparently the staff was hiding this away from me. The mother cat found her way in somehow."

"I suppose it's warmer than outdoors, and few people would disturb her."

"Until the maids found them this morning, and I uncovered this debacle of a room."

"It's quite a collection."

Will handed the kitten over, carefully releasing its little claws from his shirt sleeve. He was dressed as he had been the last time she visited, in a loose dress shirt, unbuttoned at the throat, no cravat, and a half-unbuttoned waistcoat.

Maddie suddenly felt far too proper in her best tailored day dress.

The duke noticed her perusal, and his brow drew tight in a frown. "Forgive me. I walked this morning and meant to change before your arrival."

"I don't mind the pirate look."

A little smile teased at the corners of his mouth. "Perhaps I should acquire a sword and eyepatch to perfect it."

Maddie grinned, imagining him walking the deck of a ship. Yes, she could see it quite easily.

"It's too dusty in here. Let's try the sitting room." He gestured toward a room across the hall and waited for Maddie to precede him.

He considered the furnishings in the ornate room. Gesturing toward two gold velvet chairs, he said, "Shall we sit?" Glancing back at her he added, "I know you've come on official business."

"I'd planned to come for the roses, but this seems more important. And you did say you wished to hear my ideas." Maddie sensed he was cutting across the lightness of the moment before and wondered why. But she took a seat, reminding herself she wasn't here so they could enjoy each other's company.

He sat too, but only perching at the edge of the plush chair. "Good grief, is there another list?" he asked as she pulled a piece of folded foolscap from her pocket.

"I like to be organized." As she reached out to stroke the kitten that had happily settled in her lap and begun to doze off, she reassured him. "Truly. This isn't a list of demands. Just notes so that I don't forget anything."

"That implies there's quite a lot."

"You might like some of it."

He rushed his fingers through his black waves. "I should tell you that I've already decided to make some repairs to the house."

Maddie swallowed hard at his words. Had he truly decided to relent?

"Starting with the pile of dilapidated furniture in the ballroom?" Maddie spoke lightly, afraid of seeming too pleased. It was imprudent to count one's bulbs before they bloomed. But she still hoped to draw that tiny, begrudging smile from him again.

But he didn't smile. His jaw tensed, and his gaze turned serious. "That's a good place to start. I understand there are windows in need of repair, a ceiling to be replastered, and at least one hole in the ballroom floor."

"You've truly decided to repair the house?"

"Yes, it's my responsibility, precisely as you said."

Maddie saw the sincerity in his gaze, and excitement made her pulse thud loudly in her ears. This might actually work.

"I have several ideas about how we might repair or at least block off the view of the east facade in time for the princess's visit. We could use tall potted shrubs or trees. Another option would be to build some kind of trellis structure that could be adorned with some of the more mature vines we have at the nursery."

He allowed her to finish and then offered her his steady gaze. "My priority is to see about securing the

inside of the house. The damage must be repaired."
With a quick sweeping glance, he took in the room
and then looked at her again. "I still struggle to give
a damn about any of it. But they do." He tipped his
head toward the sitting-room doorway. "My father
left them with a pile of broken furnishings, and I've
done nothing to act as steward of this property."

Maddie could almost see the guilt and weariness
begin to bend his broad shoulders. And it was more
than simply Carnwyth. "You carry a great deal of
worry."

"I'm quite capable of bearing my duties, I assure
you." The words seemed to offend him. He immediately straightened his back and settled back in the
chair, his long legs still higher than they should be,
as the chair wasn't made for men built like he was.
With his hands perched on the edge of the armrests,
he looked like a regent on a throne.

"I meant no judgment. Only observation."

"You are a most observant young woman. Isn't
that how we met? You were watching me from behind a palm tree."

"I wasn't looking at you."

"Mmm. But I was looking at you." He smiled and
then let out a long sigh. "To tell you the truth, I fear
that if I repair the ballroom, someone will want me
to hold a ball."

Maddie's eyes must have widened, because he
looked horrified.

"Oh no. Please tell me that's not on your list."

"There are other options."

"Wonderful."

"You could either host a ball—"

"Out of the question."

"Or . . . attend a dance at the hotel."

"I can't express how thoroughly I dislike balls." Though there was misery written in every tense line of his body, he nodded. "But if I don't have to host one, I would consider attending a dance." He rolled his hand. "What else?"

"Mrs. Reeve, the owner of the hotel, would like you to host an event with the princess. It could be as simple as a small luncheon or—"

"I don't plan to be here when the royal entourage arrives."

"That's on the list too. Staying through the visit."

"I have a great deal to attend to in London."

"You did say you planned to stay for a fortnight. The princess's visit is within that frame of time."

"What else?"

"Well, now we come to the easiest part. Deciding how to block the view of the damaged side of the house. We have some potted sycamores at the nursery that are mature enough to form a quite appealing cover for the damage to the seaside wall of the manor."

"And you think that will look good enough to satisfy the princess and all the visitors the hotel will host?"

"I do. Plus, with the round of events we've planned,

she and everyone else will be quite busy. When she does look toward Carnwyth, I suspect she'll mainly focus on the sea."

"But you also want me to invite her for lunch?"

"You could always host her at the hotel. They can provide a room for a private event."

He tapped his fingers against the chair arm. "I'd prefer not to, but I agree to all the rest."

"You do?" Maddie's heart did a little flip-flop in her chest. "Truly? That's wonderful." Maddie was so thrilled she dropped her list, and the kitten jumped down to bat at it.

"But . . ." He paused after the single word.

When Maddie lifted her gaze to the duke, the flutter of relief she'd felt in her chest a moment before plummeted to the pit of her stomach. He was watching her. Thoughtfully. Intensely. In that way that made her feel as if her thoughts were transparent.

"I have a request of my own."

Maddie hadn't expected this, but it wasn't unreasonable. Though, she couldn't imagine what Haven Cove had to offer that a duke of the realm might require.

He looked away, then steepled his fingers under his chin contemplatively.

"I came here for respite. And, per my sister's orders, to have . . . fun." He spoke the word as if it wasn't just rare on his tongue but also irritating to say aloud. "So I would ask you, as someone familiar with the area, to inform me of places of interest. Enjoyable activities I might engage in."

He was so serious as he asked her to be his guide. A man had never looked at her as if she alone could lead him to everything he sought.

"Enjoyable activities." Unbidden, her mind went to scandalous places. To sharing with him those things she'd known so briefly but remained so curious about. How would it feel to be held by him? To kiss those lips that turned down grimly but then occasionally stunned her by curving into a smile?

"Have I asked too much?"

"No." Her voice betrayed her by emerging huskier than she intended. "Not at all. I can make you a list."

"You could, but I'd prefer you tell me."

"The quickest and easiest might be a short boating trip. I suspect there are boats here at Carnwyth, perhaps stored in an outbuilding. Or you could rent one. I can give you the name of a man who rents boats. The weather is to be mild and clear tomorrow. You might consider going then."

"Perfect." He nodded as if the decision was made, then his gaze held on her again. "And of course you'll join me."

"No." Maddie's heart was thumping that wild way again. Why did he wield such power over her heartbeat? "I have a great deal to do before the princess arrives."

"Surely a short boating trip can't take terribly

long." He gestured casually toward the seaside window. "We're surrounded by water. We could probably go down and secure a boat now."

There was absolutely no doubt in Maddie's mind that spending more time with him was a distraction she did not need. The man already occupied too many of her thoughts, and those thoughts seemed determined to take the most fanciful turns. But what other choice did she have? The prospect of returning to Mrs. Reeve having failed again to secure his agreement was impossible.

"I'll go with you." It was the only way to do her duty to the Royal Visit Committee, and she'd make it a short outing. "Tomorrow."

"Then it's settled."

"I'll arrange the boat." Maddie reasoned that the more of the plans she managed, the quicker the venture could be over and done.

"As you wish."

"I should be on my way." Maddie offered a final stroke of her fingers against the kitten's soft fur. When she stood, he did too.

"Another appointment?"

"A meeting of the Historical Society."

His mouth pursed in an amused smirk. "Of course. The busy Miss Ravenwood."

Maddie was used to his teasing about her busyness, though she knew he must, in some way, be deriding himself. After all, hadn't his sisters compelled him to go on holiday for a respite from too much work?

"You needn't look so miserable about our boat excursion," he said quietly. "You might enjoy yourself." There was an enticing glint of mischief in his dark gaze.

She hadn't a single doubt she would enjoy her time in his company. That's what scared her most.

Chapter Twelve

Bly? Is that you?" Will heard the faint sound of footsteps in the hall outside his open bedroom door.

Somehow in the course of a week of freedom from his fastidious valet, he'd forgotten how to fasten a tie. He'd found a linen suit among his packed clothing and it was blessedly light but still made him feel overly formal. What did one wear on a boat?

And why the hell had he suggested a boating excursion at all?

He'd never been sailing in his life, not even on one of the paddleboats people loved to rent to navigate the Serpentine. Before this journey, his experience at the seaside consisted of a few visits with his mother and sisters to Brighton. And that had always been more about socializing and promenading than being on the sea.

"Bly?" The soft footfalls had stopped, but the butler never appeared. Will slid the twisted fabric at his throat free and balled the tie in his hands.

"Shall I send Mr. Bly up to assist you, Your Grace?" Mrs. Haskell stood on the threshold of the guest room where he slept. The housekeeper had a habit of approaching with the sort of stealth a cat burglar would envy. She was a curious woman, ever watchful.

"No need. I've managed to dress myself." Will looked back and found the woman assessing him with a knowing look.

"I'm going boating with Miss Ravenwood." Might as well confess rather than have his comings and goings whispered about by the staff.

"Thought you might be seeing the young lady again, Your Grace."

"You're a perceptive woman, Mrs. Haskell."

She bowed her head to hide a smile. "Doesn't take much cleverness to see that you two get on well."

"What do you know of her?" Why bother questioning gruff old men in pubs when the watchful and knowing Mrs. Haskell was at hand?

"Oh, a good deal. Known her since she was a child. Now there's a clever young woman if I've ever seen one. Useful too. The lass never misses an opportunity to pitch in and help where she can."

"Who does she help?" Of course Maddie's busyness and commitments would have a purpose.

"Societies, committees, groups, and clubs of all kinds. Might be easier to list what she doesn't do," Mrs. Haskell said in an almost prideful tone. "Her mother was the same—accomplished and charitable. With her upbringing, that only follows."

Will straightened his tie and considered trying to noose himself into the thing again. "Did her mother have a notable upbringing?"

"Mrs. Ravenwood was a proper lady, Your Grace.

A viscount's daughter, though she was estranged from her family after marrying Ravenwood. Her daughter quite took after her mother's kind heart. But she does work herself too hard, if you ask me."

Apparently, they had that in common.

"What say you?" Will turned to his housekeeper with the tie around his neck, not fully tied but in place.

The older woman tipped her head, crinkled her brow, and let out a gusty chuckle. "I don't think you should wear it if you plan to look that miserable while you do."

Will couldn't argue with that advice. He whipped the tie off again just as the elaborate gilded clock in the corner chimed ten.

"Thank you, Mrs. Haskell. I must be on my way." He bounded down the stairs, unable to slow once anxiousness fueled his momentum.

The sun was up, the weather was warm, and Miss Ravenwood had sent a note the night before letting him know she'd be waiting at the edge of the cove at ten o'clock. There was a path just below the broken wall that led down to the beach. As he walked, the sea air and gentle breeze loosened some of the tension humming in his body.

The prospect of seeing her again pleased him. If he was meant to enjoy his time in Cornwall, she seemed an essential part of that equation.

Her perceptive, guileless nature put him at ease. Which made no sense at all since no one in his life had seen him in so many awkward circumstances in such a short acquaintance. Yet, somehow, however awkward and unexpected, he recalled every encounter with her fondly.

She had the strangest ability to make him forget all the rest—London, his endless lists of things to be done, and the realization that everyone thought him a curmudgeon.

And wasn't an escape from all that exactly why he'd come to Cornwall?

As soon as he reached the switchback in the path's descent that pointed him away from the house toward the other side of the cliff hugging the cove, he saw her there.

The sea was calm, and she stood with her back to him. She'd pulled her hair into a thick auburn braid and held an enormous straw hat in her hand. Her light, gauzy dress billowed in the breeze. She looked serene, but selfishly he longed for her to look back at him. Instead, she reached into the pocket of her skirt and pulled out a fob watch.

Was she anxious for his arrival?

"I hope I'm not late," he called to her.

Her lips parted a moment in surprise as she swung to face him. "Only by four minutes."

"So, forgiveness is possible?"

MADDIE HADN'T MOVED from the moment she spotted him descending the beach path. In a week's time, he seemed to have grown more comfortable.

His shoulders weren't squared, his brow wasn't furrowed, and the grim set of his mouth had softened into the slightest of smiles.

But when she didn't answer, his frown quickly made its return.

"I'll consider forgiving you, but only if you help me get the boat launched."

His gaze swung to Eames's rowboat, and the confidence of his swagger down the hill evaporated. Was he expecting something grander?

"We're going out straight away, then?"

His first look at her had been the same intense sort he'd given her the night they'd met. The kind of look that set her nerves on fire. Now he looked distinctly wary.

"Yes, of course." If the man could pin her in place with a single gaze, spending any more time in his company than necessary was utter folly. "The wind isn't due to pick up for a few hours. We should seize the calm."

Maddie put on her hat and tied the ribbons as she watched him.

He looked helplessly at the boat as if he'd never seen one before. Maddie grabbed the tow line on one side and loosed it from the stone Eames had lashed it to. As she'd hoped, he'd been happy to lend her his boat, and, blessedly, with very few questions as to why she needed it.

The duke copied her movement on the opposite side, and soon the starboard edge was bobbing in the shallow water.

"I'm afraid both of us are going to get wet in this process." Water was already rushing up her calves and making the bottom of her light skirt heavy.

"I'm sensing that." He glanced down at his sodden boots and trouser legs.

"Get in," she told him, "and I'll push us out farther."

He frowned at her. "Isn't that what the oars are for?"

"Once we're a bit farther out." Maddie pointed at the center of the boat. "Please, Your Grace. Get in."

"If we're going to be risking our lives in that tiny thing, you should at least call me Will."

Will. The name fit this easygoing, playful version of the duke. She liked it, and she wanted him to speak her name too.

"Will, please get in."

"And what shall I call you?" Hopefulness laced his tone.

"You may call me Captain." *Good grief, stop flirting, girl.* "Maddie. Everyone calls me Maddie."

"You're certain it's seaworthy?"

"I'm certain." The rowboat was solidly made but terribly small compared to some, and she knew Eames took his boat out regularly.

The duke stared at the humble rowboat, drew in a sharp breath, and nodded once. Then he stepped in.

"Toward the middle," she shouted as the boat started to dip low enough to slosh water inside. He glanced at her but obeyed, somehow folding his long legs and broad frame onto the center thwart. As the hull dipped with his weight, some water got inside but not enough to cause concern. The slight current was already making her job easier. She walked deeper into the water and gave a forceful shove, and the boat began to bob farther out into the cove.

Walking behind it, she let out a little gasp as the water rushed up her legs toward her waist and her skirt billowed around her.

"Your plan isn't to set me afloat solo, is it?" There was real concern in his dark eyes.

He clearly wasn't used to the sea. Maddie wondered if he'd ever even learned to swim.

She waded to the boat's edge, gripped the side, and lifted one leg as she reached for the duke. He gripped her hand instantly, holding her steady. She tried to turn and pull the rest of her body in, but it was tricky with sodden skirts.

The duke seemed to recognize the problem. He reached down to her waist and moved his hand across her body as he searched for something to hold on to. Then his hand slid lower, over the curve of her backside, and he gave one strong tug that landed her quite clumsily inside the boat. The rest of her lower half came in, but the ribbon tied beneath her chin caught on his boot and her hat slid off her head.

"My hat!"

She felt the boat tip and heard sloshing and then his deep voice. "I have it. Don't worry."

As she got in and gingerly took the bow seat in

front of him, he tugged at her soaked skirt that had twisted around her legs.

When their gazes met, his glinted with amusement.

"As a gentleman, you shouldn't have enjoyed that," she told him, mostly to remind herself of propriety. It was a challenge when her skin felt warmer every place he'd touched her.

"I enjoyed making sure your skirt didn't pull you under," he told her with mock seriousness. "And I saved your hat." The straw was a bit mangled, and the ribbons were soaked, but she took it from him with a nod of gratitude.

"Thank you. It would be easier if we had a pier here." Maddie grabbed the fabric of her gown, bunched it, and held as much as she could over the side to wring the water out. "There was one once."

"For my father and his friends." When he spoke of his father, there was a bleakness in his eyes, and anger roughened his tone.

Despite her curiosity about what had stoked the ill will between them, his reaction made her wary of asking more. Was it only his father's scandalous reputation? It seemed to Maddie that nobles were often embroiled in some scandal or another, but this Duke of Ashmore—Will—did seem concerned about what others thought of him. That very first night they'd met, the one thing he'd asked of her was discretion.

"We should use the oars now to get us out of the cove," she told him as she reached for one.

"Since you've reminded me that I'm to act the

gentleman, I'll row." Even as he said the words, he looked dubious about the claim.

"You've never done this, have you?"

"Never."

"Have you been on many boats?"

"None." In only a few days' time, the sun had begun to give his skin an appealing sun-kissed glow, but under that, she noticed the heightened color of embarrassment. "Until today."

"Then, I'll do the rowing." She reached for both oars, but he already had his hands on them.

"Allow me," he said, gripping the wood more tightly.

"You're a stubborn man." Maddie held on as firmly as he did and tugged the oars toward her.

"Perhaps I'm trying to impress you."

"Having the good sense to allow the person with more experience to row might impress me more."

"You always make a good deal of sense." He smiled at her, let out a long, dramatic sigh, and released the oars. "Show me how it's done."

It wasn't a simple request for a lesson. It felt more like a challenge.

Maddie let the oars dip into the water as she leaned forward, then she pulled back as she scooped against the sea. From her position in the bow seat, it was much more difficult than it needed to be.

"We should switch places," she told him on another long pull of the oars.

The edges of his mouth tipped up slightly. Not an all-out smile but the promise of one to bloom.

"You could join me on this bench." He slid so that there was enough room. Almost. "Surely my weight is too much for that spot."

Maddie bit the inside of her cheek, and her heart thudded loudly in her ears. How many times had she imagined being that close to him?

"I can take one oar and you the other. Better to teach me how to do it by practice, don't you think?"

She almost couldn't reconcile that this charming, flirtatious man was the same one she'd seen that night in London. His voice, his eyes, the very way he held himself. If she didn't know better, she would think he was trying to woo her.

Somehow, she sensed that if she gave in now—if she took a seat on the bench beside him—they could never go back to any kind of unaffected propriety again.

And she found that with the one remaining logical part of herself that wasn't distracted by the way his mouth was inching up into a wicked smile, she didn't mind that they'd never go back. She wanted to be close to him, and this might be her only chance.

She offered him her hand, and he took it quickly, as if he was afraid she might change her mind. He pulled gently, and Maddie made sure to get her footing just right so that she could pivot and take a seat without rocking the boat too much.

The hand in hers slid around her waist, then grazed her hip as he helped steady her as she settled next to him.

Mercy, the man was warm. His hip fit against

hers, his arm brushed hers, and when he turned to look her way, she could see that his eyes weren't just a dark chocolate brown with hints of amber. There were flecks of green too, like the leaves of that *Ficus elastica* that had christened them in Lady Trenmere's conservatory.

"Shall we move as one?"

Maddie swallowed and fought hard to find the usually sensible voice inside her head. "Yes." She gripped her oar, and he held his. "You'll want to keep both hands at the top of the oar. Like this." In demonstrating, her body shifted against his.

He licked his lips and gave her a glance. "I think I've got it."

"Then we go forward and back."

"As one."

"Yes." Her voice was too soft, too breathy.

They moved forward, and he mimicked her movement when she pulled back. Then again. Maddie had to strain to pull with as much force as he managed, and he was quicker than she was, which made them out of sync.

"You must follow my lead," she said. His scent was making her mouth water, and the little glances he offered out of the corner of his eye were wreaking havoc with her composure.

"Like this?" He eased off on the power of his pull, and the boat sliced through the water like a warm knife in jelly. They were perfectly in sync as they repeated the motion again and again.

"This is likely far enough out." While boating with her father, they'd ventured much farther, but she didn't want to push her luck and end up with a seasick duke on her hands.

"We can't see much of the coast farther down past the cove. A bit farther, perhaps?" That mischievous sparkle that occasionally came into his eyes matched the challenge in the arch of his brow. "I think I'm quite getting the hang of this."

He was proud of himself, almost gleeful in an artless, boyish way, and she couldn't tell him no.

"A bit." Something about being out on the sea alone with him felt freeing. Free of propriety and the watchful eyes of Haven Cove.

As they continued to row toward the open sea, he asked quietly, "Do you come out on the water often?"

"No. Not anymore. My father was the one who loved to be out on the sea. He loved to fish or just sit and think. He said the land was too confining." The laughter that came surprised her. Most often when she thought of her father, she thought of duty, expectation.

"And your mother?"

"She loved looking at the sea." A sharp, vivid memory of her mother painting a sunset seascape flashed in her mind. The colors lingered in her mind's eye, and suddenly everything took on a golden hue. "Painted it too. Often. That seemed magical to me. I can draw a scheme for a garden, measuring out each square inch of space. She could capture what she saw in front of her." Maddie's gaze clashed with his. "Like you can."

"I only sketch, and not terribly well."

"Finally something about which you're humble."

"Stop or I'll be arrogant about it just to challenge you."

"You should be proud of your drawings. They're good."

"Are you trying to distract me with praise to keep me from getting seasick?"

"Is it working?"

"To dispel seasickness, perhaps, but it only gives me an opportunity to praise you in return. According to Mrs. Haskell, there is nothing you don't do around the town."

"That's an exaggeration."

"She says you're a member of a dozen clubs and societies and committees."

"Not a dozen."

He leaned toward her, then pulled back to give the oars a fulsome pull. "How many?"

"You're a nobleman. You must be involved in charities and committees too." Maddie watched the way the water sparkled in the sunlight to avoid his steady gaze. "How many estates do you have?"

"Excellent attempt, but you first."

"Ten." Maddie didn't count the Midwinter Decorating Committee since it only came once a year.

"Ten is a great deal of commitment."

Maddie couldn't tell if he was impressed or thought her a fool. There were moments when he could sweep emotion from his face like a slate washed clean. Only in his eyes did a hint of something warmer always flicker.

"There is only one Ashmore estate, in Sussex. But my father acquired or inherited other properties here and there."

Maddie glanced up but couldn't see the infamous manor high on the cliff above. "Carnwyth is likely the least of them."

"No. Not the least." The oars stilled, and he turned his head toward the cliff too. "Just the one I wished to avoid."

"Because of your father." Maddie spoke the words softly, aware she was likely treading on history he might wish to avoid.

"Because of what my father used the manor for."

"The parties? Assignations?"

His dark eyes widened, and the sun turned them a rich honeyed brown. "What do you know of assignations, Miss Ravenwood?"

"You assume I've never had any of my own?"

"Have you?"

Maddie bit her lip. Something about that crook of one brow did things to her insides. He might claim she had the observational skills of a spy, but he had an air about him that made her wish to confess. Perhaps it was that he truly seemed curious and was good at listening.

"Forgive me. That was terribly impertinent."

"There was a young man once. My parents didn't approve of him."

"So you met him in secret?"

"Not often. Just a few walks I never told my parents about."

"Did you love him? Did he offer for you?" He'd rested his arms on his knees, and his back was hunched as he leaned toward her. He was close enough for her to reach out and sweep away the fall of hair on his forehead, and she was distracted by the urge to touch him.

Memories came. Some good, some less so.

He mistook her silence for offense. "Forgive me. I'm being brutish."

"No, he didn't offer for me. And I'm not sure I did love him." Maddie rarely thought of Tom Hale or what might have been. "It was simply infatuation."

Somehow making that admission—to him—was the hardest part of all. Because whatever Tom had made her feel, it was nothing to her reaction to *Will*.

Peeking at him in her periphery, she found him squinting toward the sunlit sea, brow furrowed in contemplation.

"What of the lady in the conservatory?" she asked with as much nonchalance as she could manage. Which wasn't much at all.

"Davina?" The crease deepened between his brows. "You saw how that ended." The flash of a smile he offered was tight and held a tinge of embarrassment. So different from his anger that night.

"Yes, but I didn't see how it began."

"A negotiation." He tightened and loosened his grip on the oar. "We agreed on what we could offer each other. A dowry. A title. An exchange."

Maddie knew from her mother that aristocratic nuptials were often arranged in the way he described. And she couldn't forget the vehemence with which her mother always urged her away from such a marriage. *Marry for love, darling. Nothing else matters as much.*

All at once, she realized he was watching her.

"I couldn't imagine a match arranged so emotionlessly."

"Perhaps I am heartless."

Maddie pressed her lips together, then smiled. "That night you did say you were."

"And now?" He'd released his hand from the oar and swept his fingers lightly against her cheek.

Shivers chased down her spine, then a melting warmth pooled in her belly.

Turning her gaze to him, she found the same warmth reflected in his eyes. "What do you think about me now, Maddie?"

"I think . . ." If there were thoughts in her head, she couldn't find them. She could only feel and want, and acting on that seemed far better than words.

Reaching up, she traced the sharp stubbled edge of his jaw. Then she leaned closer. His breath was coming fast, tickling her skin. And his lips parted when she raised her head to skim her lips along the same hard line she'd touched. Then his cheek. Then she had to taste his lips. One gentle press, and he let out a little rumble in the back of his throat. Both hands came up, cradling her face. He offered her one searing look, and then his lips were on hers again. But he took the lead, deepening the kiss, stroking his fingers along her neck as he stroked his tongue against hers.

Maddie gasped and he drew back, resting his forehead against hers. They were both breathless, and she couldn't seem to stop touching him. One hand was still on his shoulder, and she ran her fingers along the buttons of his shirt. She liked being close to him, this man who claimed he was heartless but looked at her as if he truly wished to know all her thoughts.

When they stopped touching each other, it would be the start of going back. To even the minimum propriety they'd managed before this moment. To wanting to avoid the watchful and whispering. To their proper roles.

A swishing sounded. Then a metallic grinding. Maddie shifted her gaze in time to see his oar slip its mooring and plop into the water.

He released her instantly and lurched toward the oar. The boat tilted wildly, and Maddie grabbed the back of his shirt to keep him from diving in after it. The flat end floated, but the soft flowing current carried it farther. Maddie leaned across him to grab for it. He wrapped an arm around her waist, and she thought he was pulling her back. In reality, he was mooring her to stretch farther. The boat's edge tipped, and her upper body splashed into the water, but she was so close . . .

"I got it."

"Well done," he enthused and reached over her head to get a grip and pull the oar in.

Maddie grasped the edge of the boat to right herself at the same moment a gust of wind picked up her mangled hat and nearly swept it over the side. She lunged for it and caught it, but Will pulled her back sharply. Her back slammed against his chest.

"If you lose that one, I'll buy you a dozen bloody hats. Please stay in the boat."

Her chest was heaving, and her dress was soaked again, but she'd never felt warmer. Safer.

"Thank you for keeping me from falling in."

"I'm quite content to hold on to you as much as I can." He nuzzled his lips against her cheek, then whispered in her ear, "I want to kiss you again."

Maddie turned her head, and he took her lips. Soft and questioning at first, but she wanted the hungry kisses of a moment before. Reaching back, she wrapped a hand around his neck and gazed up into his eyes.

A flash of light caught her notice. Someone was up on the cliff near the hotel. A man with an apparatus in front of him that glinted in the sun.

"Is that a camera?"

Will snapped his gaze toward where she saw the man and instantly his hands fell away. "It is," he said, "but it doesn't seem to be pointed our way."

"No, it looks as if he's taking photographs of the sea. But we should go back."

"Should we?" He reached up and slid a wisp of hair behind her ear. "I wasn't entirely sure about boating, but this has been the best part of my holiday thus far."

"For me too." For a moment Maddie got lost in being close to him, the feel of his fingertip tracing softly down her cheek, and the heat in his gaze. Then she realized what she'd said and smiled. "Not that I'm on holiday. I had planned to devote only an hour to this excursion."

"And then I upended your plan by kissing you."

"As I recall, I kissed you."

He said nothing, but his gaze turned molten. "Yes, that was undoubtedly the best part of this outing."

The grin that came next was too much. Full of ease and warmth, but also tempting. A smile that tempted Maddie to believe this would continue. That they could spend day after day like this, happy just to be near each other.

But that was a daydream. His duties would soon call him back to London, and her duties were waiting for her the moment they returned to shore. She *had* only intended to devote an hour to their excursion.

"You have that look in your eye," he told her quietly, the joviality of a moment before still lightening his tone.

"What look is that?"

"As if you've just remembered something you

need to add to a list you're making. I know that look well because my mind is much the same. Especially when I'm enjoying myself." He laid a hand on hers where she held the oar. "Shall we go back?"

"I think perhaps we should."

"At least allow me to row. I promise not to let go of either oar until we're on land."

Maddie laughed and relented, but she missed his touch when he slid his hand from hers and onto the oar she held. If she'd disappointed him, there was no sign of it in his expression.

"I did enjoy today," she told him softly.

He flashed her a mischievous grin. "Which part did you find most enjoyable? Being soaking wet or nearly drowning?"

Maddie laughed because despite the wonder of those kisses, the whole brief excursion had been so ridiculously close to tragedy several times.

Before she could answer, he said, "Perhaps we can venture out again before the visit."

"Yes." The answer came quickly before she could talk herself out of her eagerness.

"And I suspect I'll be better with these." He pulled the oars back in a neat even stroke, and the boat cut through the water swiftly.

"You've taken to boating quite readily. I trust there's no chance you'll ever have to worry about losing an oar again."

"In fairness, I didn't *lose* the oar." He was unforgivably handsome as he shot her a look of mock offense.

Maddie enjoyed watching the muscles of his forearms shift and tense as he rowed them back into the cove. As they drifted in, he moved quickly to exit the boat first, then held the hull steady before offering her his hand to help her disembark.

"You know," he said as Maddie secured Eames's boat, "from a certain perspective, I saved the oar."

"And my hat."

"Exactly."

"So I should be thanking you?"

"I wouldn't object." He'd stepped closer. Near enough for her to smell his juniper-berry aftershave, now mixed with the scent of the sea.

His gaze fell to her lips. They still felt swollen and warm. He'd ignited every desire she'd thought she'd put away with his kisses. Maddie feared it would be all she would think about for a very long time. Even if it never happened again.

And it couldn't, of course. He had all the duties of a dukedom to return to, and she had responsibilities that kept her occupied night and day.

But she found herself staring at his lips, longing. Remembering.

He leaned forward and cupped her cheek in his palm. His skin was deliciously warm nestled up against hers.

"I have an idea of how you could thank me."

Maddie's eyes widened, and a pulsing began in her stomach, then lower, between her thighs. She wanted him. "Tell me." The whisper emerged husky and rough, and her pulse was racing so wildly she pressed a hand to his chest to feel his solidity and heat.

He reached up instantly and covered her hand with his. For a moment, he simply glanced at where they touched, then he looked at her from beneath sooty lashes.

"Give me a tour of Ravenwood Nursery tomorrow."

Maddie blinked up at him, and then laughter bubbled up in an unladylike burst. It wasn't at all what she'd expected him to say.

"You really want to see the nursery?"

"Of course, but only with a personal tour from the proprietress."

He still held her hand, and she forced her mind away from the warmth of his touch to the meeting she'd committed to in the morning and the other work she'd planned to accomplish.

Will noticed her distracted gaze. "Unless you can't spare the time. Perhaps another day."

"No. Come tomorrow." Sensible Maddie who had told herself she could spend an hour with him and go on with her duties was gone. Now she stood before a man whose juniper and spice scent she could smell on her clothes and whose kiss had kindled something deep inside her.

In that moment, more than anything, she craved the prospect of seeing him again so soon.

"I'll make the time."

Chapter Thirteen

*W*ill was winded and warm by the end of his walk to Ravenwood Nursery, but he didn't regret traveling by foot. There was a cool sea breeze at his back, and the air smelled fresh after an evening rain. He liked imagining that this was the path Maddie had taken on the night he'd arrived in Cornwall.

The final approach to the nursery was a bit of a climb, and by the time he could see an enormous stone carved with its name and pointing the way to the entrance, scents assailed him. Sweet, rich floral notes, but also the loamy smell of damp earth. As he crested the hill, the world bloomed with color—reds, yellows, peach and lavender hues, all pillowed in shades of green.

Then he spotted her. A tall, flame-haired beauty standing in a sea of flowers and wearing the enormous straw hat that had nearly floated away the previous day. For a moment he saw only Maddie, and then he noticed the movement around her. An older gentleman in a tailored black suit followed close behind her, his hands clasped behind his back as he surveyed whatever she was pointing out to him. And farther away, nursery employees worked in the fields, tending the flowers, shrubs, and a stand of sapling trees.

As he approached, Will could make out snippets of their conversation. The gentleman was clearly a client or a potential one.

"The viscount will want something bold," the man said.

Maddie turned to face him with a confident smile on her face. "We can do bold, Mr. Beale." She scanned the field to her left and gestured to a tall man in the distance. When she turned back, Will knew the moment she spotted him.

Her pretty eyes widened, and a warmer, sweeter smile lit up her face. But the moment the man from far back in the field approached with a cart weighed down with several small fiery-red trees, she turned back to her client.

"Now, that's more like it," Beale said, scooting his wire-rimmed glasses farther up his nose.

"Japanese maples," Maddie said as she gestured toward the diminutive, red-leafed tree. "I think with the ground-cover options we discussed and the perennials as accents, the approach to the viscount's estate will be bold."

"Very good, Miss Ravenwood," Beale said, as he scribbled information in a pocket notebook. "Send your design plan along once you've added these, and I shall take all of this information back to Lord Prestwick and be in touch with his decision."

"Thank you, Mr. Beale."

Will waited until the man departed before he approached. "You won him over, I think."

"We shall see," Maddie said as she nodded to the gentleman with the cart, apparently indicating he could retreat with the colorful trees.

"I came too early." Will had been unable to sit still most of the morning and headed out as soon as he could.

"Not at all." She stripped off her gloves and stepped closer. The sun turned her eyes a clearer blue, and Will loved the way her gaze roved over his face and dipped down to the open neck of his shirt before she smiled at him again. "Shall we start in the greenhouses?"

"Lead the way."

She did, pointing out that the flower fields they'd passed through contained mostly perennials, though annual varieties were planted near the front too.

"The tree fields are farther back, and we have a whole section beyond the stable that's devoted to shrubs." She glanced back as if to gauge whether he was still listening. "Flowering shrubs and more ornamental ones, like boxwoods."

As they entered the enormous greenhouse, Maddie seemed to relax. She removed her hat and unbuttoned her cuffs and rolled them up. Captured under glass and the heat of the sun, the air inside the greenhouse was warmer, and the scent of roses sweetened the air.

Will looked around the tidy but packed space and

imagined her here day after day, experimenting, planting, nurturing.

"Would you like to see the princess's rose?" He heard a nervous wobble in her voice and wondered how many people she'd shown the new rose to.

"Of course." He stepped closer, and she led him to a table covered with pots near the back wall of the greenhouse. Some contained only a stem with a single bud. Others contained flowers just starting to bloom, and a few pots were full of plump, colorful roses in their full glory.

"This combination, one of my mother's roses from Carnwyth and a new tea-rose variety, resulted in the prettiest shade of peach." She glanced at him with a question in her gaze. "Do you like the color?"

"I do," Will told her immediately. And he did. The rose itself was lovely, delicate, a lighter peach that darkened at the edges. But he liked the color- fulness of Maddie's world too. She had an energy about her that made everything around her seem more vivid.

"I think it could win." More quietly, she added, "I hope. A year of trying and failing went into this bloom."

"So this is where you spend your days experiment- ing?" He noticed a chair and desk in the corner, and tools and a magnifying glass and microscope that made the space look like a laboratory.

"Many of them." She glanced around as if assess- ing how it must look to him. Dust motes danced in the sunlight, and Will followed her gaze to a spider-web high in a corner of the glass roof. "It's cozier than it looks."

Will chuckled. "It does look cozy. More so than my study." That space was lavishly furnished but still smelled of his father's wretched cigars, and everything about it reminded Will of him.

She assessed him a moment and then asked, "And what do you spend your days doing in your study?"

Will's heartbeat seemed to slow in his chest. He enjoyed asking her questions, learning about her. How did he confess that he was loathed by much of good society and spent his days uncovering his father's sins?

"Running a dukedom, I suppose," he said a bit too blithely to be the least bit believable.

"You suppose?" The edge of her mouth kicked up in a mischievous grin. "Tell me what running a dukedom entails."

"Ledgers. Many ledgers. Also correspondence. Signing lots of documents."

"Parties like the one at Lady Trenmere's?"

"Sometimes," he agreed, recalling that night and the unexpected moment when he'd met her. "I go to as few as possible."

Maddie laughed. "Why?"

"I'm not terribly good at dancing, and I'm even worse at conversing." He examined a few seedlings pushing up through the dirt in a rectangular pot. "Like now."

"You're doing fine," she said in a reassuring tone. "But you're being awfully mysterious."

"Perhaps I am mysterious." He added a tinge of bravado to his tone, but Maddie seemed thoroughly unimpressed. She crossed her arms, and one coppery brow arched up her forehead.

Will let out a sigh. "We've already spoken of my father's reputation."

"I know of the gossip in town, mostly. My parents never spoke of him after they left his employ."

"He was a scoundrel." Will frowned. "No, that sounds too appealing. He was a liar, a cheat, a swindler, and I have yet to discover a relationship of his that didn't end in betrayal."

"I'm sorry." She unfolded her arms and began to take a step toward him when the light above their heads shifted.

They both looked up at the high glass panes that had been warmed by sunlight a moment before. Now dark clouds crowded the sky, and the breeze kicked up to rattle against the greenhouse walls.

"I'd almost forgotten that rain was due." She started toward the center of the greenhouse as she spoke. "If we close the upper windows, everything inside should be safe." She pointed to a metal crank against one wall and strode to one on the opposite wall. "If you turn that one, I'll take this one."

Will twisted the crank quickly, and the window above soon snicked into place.

"I can do this one too," he said as he approached to help with the crank she had her hand wrapped around.

"It's rusty and uncooperative."

Like my heart. The thought came unbidden, but then Maddie blew at a stray hair that had fallen onto her forehead, and he couldn't hold back a grin.

"Let me." He remembered their little skirmish over the oars.

He'd relented then, and she relented now, letting go of the crank and allowing him to get close enough to put his weight against it. It wouldn't budge, and a few cool raindrops fell from the open window.

One plopped onto Maddie's cheek, and she swiped it away. Another landed on Will's forehead, and she reached out to run her finger across the drop before it could fall into his eye.

"Thank you."

"The least I could do." She glanced at where he strained against the lever for the crank.

After a few attempts, the crank gave way, and the pane gave a metallic groan as it slid into place.

"You did it." The beaming smile she gave him made Will wish there were more stubborn cranks to conquer.

Maddie immediately turned to shift pots, moving some off the table and others away from the greenhouse walls.

"I spend my days running a dukedom, yes, but since his death I have devoted myself to discovering all that my father did. Every lie he told, every rule he broke, every person he swindled."

Maddie paused and then turned toward him, holding still as if waiting for him to say more.

"I've repaid those he stole from, apologized to

those he betrayed, and tried to make some of his wrongs right. I needed to restore the Ashmore title to some shadow of respectability for my sisters' sakes."

"How many sisters?"

"Two. Cora is in the middle and Daisy is the youngest." He scraped a hand through his hair. "She's to marry soon. Her engagement party was to be this week." Each day he'd spared a thought to how the preparations were coming and wondered how the whole thing would come off, but he trusted that Cora would let him know if she ran into trouble.

"They're very lucky to have you working so hard to restore the family's reputation."

Rather than respond, Will stared up at the high ceiling when thunder rumbled overhead. His eyes had taken on a bleakness Maddie hadn't expected. She'd meant to compliment him. Wishing to undo his father's wrongs was honorable, but it was clearly a topic he found hard to discuss.

"I don't think they see it that way," he finally said. His tone was rueful. Maybe even bitter.

"Why not?"

He stepped closer. "You remember the night we met?"

"I do." She'd never forget it, even when he walked out of her life and returned to his own.

"As you probably recall, my fiancée was quite angry with me."

"She said awful things."

His lips began to curve, but no smile ever came. "Her anger was personal. I discovered something about a family member of hers during my inquiries regarding my father. That family member was quite embarrassed and fearful of being exposed."

"Did you expose them?"

"No. Not at all." He dipped his head before looking at her again. "But fear is powerful, and even the thought that a nobleman's deeds might be exposed creates a certain enmity."

"So you're feared among London's nobles?"

"More like loathed." This did bring a smile to his face, and, as always, his smile did odd things to her insides. "It's why I'm here."

Maddie listened to the patter of raindrops on the greenhouse roof and tried to summon the equation that would explain why coming to Cornwall on a holiday had anything to do with being loathed in London.

"Are you hiding out?"

He flicked his gaze up to hers and burst into all-out laughter. The sound reverberated off the glass walls, rich and warm and deep enough that Maddie felt the rumble of it in her chest.

"That's the story I should have told you to begin with." His laughter quieted to a little chuckle of consternation. "And it's not far from the truth. But it's more that I was banished in the most loving of ways. My sisters wanted me away for Daisy's party, and Cora insisted that I needed to enjoy myself."

He gazed at her steadily.

Maddie found herself fiddling with the buttons on her cuff, rebuttoning them and missing some of the loops. She'd lost track of time. That happened when she was with him. She wasn't certain how long they'd been in the greenhouse together. Eames would be wondering where she was, and though she didn't have any more meetings, there was plenty of work to be done.

But first she needed to know.

"And are you enjoying yourself?"

He took another step closer, then another. They were as close as they'd been that night in London when he'd reached for a leaf in her hair.

"When I'm with you, I am."

They were the words she'd wanted to hear but hadn't expected him to say. She'd sensed it. Felt certain that what had happened on the boat the day before had been mutual and true. But his honesty and willingness to say so put a lump in her throat.

"Me too," she whispered.

"Then that brings a question to mind."

Maddie tipped her head and waited for him to ask.

"I heard Carnwyth's housekeeper mention a summer festival in Bodmin. Would you accompany me?"

Her immediate impulse was to agree, but then guilt and a sense of responsibility swept in. She thought of Mrs. Reeve, the committee, all that was yet to do.

"I shouldn't."

"Are you concerned about what people will say about us going together?"

"No, not that. I quite like my independence."

"So, we'll go?"

"There is a princess arriving in seven days. We've called for an extra committee planning meeting in two days."

"What about tomorrow?"

"Such tenacity."

"I have been called single-minded. But am I persuasive?" He took her hand. Gently. As if he was touching something quite precious to him. "You've done something to me, Miss Rav—Maddie. And I'm not sure I should like it as much as I do." Then he bent his head and touched his lips to the back of her hand.

The brush of his mouth on her skin sent a spiral of heat through her body. Persuasive, indeed.

"Shall I collect you? Apparently, there is a serviceable carriage in the stables."

Maddie bit her lower lip and calculated in her mind what she could shift and how much time she would truly need to prepare for the committee meeting. "Early?"

"If you like."

"Tomorrow, then. Will," she added, enjoying the sound of his name on her lips.

He flashed an artless, crooked smile in surprise. "Thank you, Maddie."

Goodness, was it possible a duke of the realm hiding out in Cornwall truly had decided to woo her?

Chapter Fourteen

As he explored the house a bit more, Will discovered that a dusty second-floor room decorated in shades of pink and gold with satyr murals on the ceiling had the perfect light for drawing in the morning. He retreated there two days after his boat excursion with Maddie.

Most conveniently, the room also offered a gorgeous view of the sea. Though, it wasn't the sea that filled his sketchbook. A rowboat featured prominently. As well as the profile of a lady with a delicate nose and a stubborn chin.

He chuckled remembering her stubbornness and recognizing that he was very much the same. That moment when he'd asked her to accompany him to the festival in Bodmin, he'd held his breath until she answered. He had some sense of how tenacious Miss Maddie Ravenwood was about keeping her commitments.

And he knew how lucky he was to get more of her time.

In truth, he admired her independent nature. She seemed so certain of herself, of her plans and desires. He understood having a sense of purpose, but not necessarily one that he'd carved out for himself.

What struck him as most impressive was that despite her duties to her business endeavor, she sought to help others too. What could such a woman do in London where there were needs to be met on every corner? She'd have all of London's aristocrats organized into committees within a month's time. And while she won over every one of his acquaintances with her beauty and determination, he'd want to steal her away for activities that had nothing to do with duty.

Maybe he'd finally have a reason to rent one of those silly boats on the Serpentine.

Will shook his head and stood to stretch. Good grief, this was beyond woolgathering. His mind was weaving a future with her, and yet he had no reason to believe she could ever be persuaded to walk away from the life she'd made for herself in Haven Cove.

But as soon as he settled into his chair again, his thoughts raced ahead. What would his sisters make of Madeline Ravenwood?

That thought hung in his mind. Stopped him, in fact, with his pencil perched above his drawing paper.

Cora would adore her. They had competence and determination in common. She'd scare Daisy half to death. His little sister knew her duty and did it most of the time, but she didn't particularly like being dutiful, and she'd happily go off on a months-long holiday given half the chance.

That was where he and Maddie were different

too. He knew what was expected of him, but a part of him bristled at it of late. She seemed content in the life she'd made. Even the suitor she'd mentioned seemed an afterthought.

"Your Grace?" Bly cleared his throat after speaking.

Will dropped his pencil, then lowered his feet from the gilded table he'd propped them on. "Good grief, Bly! You're as stealthy as Mrs. Haskell."

"I did call out to you twice, Your Grace. You seemed deep in contemplation."

Lost in thoughts of the busiest woman he'd ever met.

"Concerns over the state of the manor, sir?" Hopefulness lit the older man's gaze.

Will now fully felt the weight of guilt about the state of the house. It was, without a doubt, a uniquely crafted place. Gaudily decorated, yes, but also perched above the loveliest view he'd ever seen. Anyone would call themselves lucky to live in such a spot. The Ashmore estate in Sussex was grand but landlocked and too big and often dreary. If only Carnwyth didn't remind him constantly of his father.

"We should find a time to discuss what might be done to repair the damage in the ballroom and the east side the house," Will finally told the older man. Even if he intended to sell or let the property, it would have to be in better condition than it was now. It had seemed appealing to ignore the house and send a land agent back after he'd returned to London. But he was here now, and he couldn't just go back to the city and leave Carnwyth to crumble into the sea.

"Very good, Your Grace." The older man's eyes bloomed with satisfaction. "Perhaps after your sister is settled."

"Pardon?" Will couldn't have heard the butler correctly. "My sisters are in London, Bly."

"Perhaps one of them is, sir. But the other is definitely here." He glanced back toward the open doorway. "She's rather . . . eager to see you."

It wasn't until then that Will noticed the noises coming from downstairs. Women's voices. One louder than the other. He knew that voice as well as his own. *Cora*.

Striding past the butler, Will took the staircase in long strides, his mind trying to formulate any set of facts that would explain his sister coming all the way from London. Worry made him take the lower stairs in an all-out sprint.

"Are you all right? Is Daisy?"

She turned to face him and ran her gloved hand gently over the kitten in her arms. "Good grief, Will, don't shout. You'll scare the little thing." Then, almost as an afterthought, she added, "I'm well, as you see, and Daisy is too. She's visiting with her betrothed's sister for a few days."

"Thank god." Will breathed out an enormous sigh of relief, but he still couldn't fathom why his sister had traveled to Cornwall in the middle of wedding preparations for their sister. "But why are you here and how?"

"I took the Cornishman. Brunel is so clever, isn't he?"

"Yes, exceedingly clever. I took the same train. But the trip was eight hours long, and that train doesn't leave Paddington until ten in the morning. It's not yet nine." No matter how he twisted the numbers, the math didn't make sense.

"Oh, I arrived last night. I stayed at the coaching inn."

"You stayed at the—"

"Have you been? It's rather charming. You should."

"Cora. The why. Get to the why."

"Oh very well." She nuzzled the kitten, looked around the oddly decorated sitting room, and decided on a royal blue settee. Gingerly, so as not to disturb the sleepy feline, she took a seat. "Please sit and I'll explain."

He didn't feel like sitting, but he did it anyway. Anything to expedite an explanation.

"I came out of worry for you. The stories I've heard didn't sound at all like you." Now that she had given him her full attention, her brow puckered in dissatisfaction. "And you do look quite transformed."

He sensed it himself. The band of tension that always rode his shoulders had eased a bit, and waking to the sounds of the sea was a balm he hadn't expected. He'd actually slept for long stints of uninterrupted hours. That alone had improved his mood.

But as she continued to study him—his face, his hair, his clothing—with a worried frown, Will was surprised to realize she didn't mean that he'd transformed for the better.

"You look dreadful."

Will glanced down at his freshly pressed linen trousers, white shirt, and gold waistcoat. He'd made an effort today in anticipation of his outing with Maddie.

"Clearly, you should have brought your valet. Did you not bring a razor? And where are your clothes? Please tell me you haven't been going round in shirt-sleeves for a week?"

"These are my clothes, Cora." Will swallowed down his irritation. "I'm on holiday, remember? It's not as if I'm entertaining guests or accepting invitations to dine with the locals."

"Except for one, or so I hear." She did that uniquely Cora thing of focusing her gaze so that it felt as if a searing light was searching every corner of his mind.

He rapped his fingers against the upholstery and ground his teeth together until his jaw ached.

"News of my time in Cornwall has traveled as far as London?" He was deflecting, mostly because her question made him wish to shout, and he didn't want to bicker with her. He was more than happy to tell her everything he'd done each day since arriving at Carnwyth.

Except for his time with Maddie. His instinct was to protect everything about his encounters with her and their connection, whatever it was or would become.

"You know how rapidly gossip spreads. Goodness,

shouldn't our whole family know that by now? And isn't it why you and I work so hard to do all that propriety requires?"

"I've done nothing improper." The memory of their kiss came vividly to mind. But they'd been in a boat, in a secluded cove, and not a soul had been nearby. "Certainly nothing gossip-worthy. And who would spread nonsense from as far as Cornwall?"

She tipped her head and examined him. A technique that usually wore at his conscience. "I understand Princess Beatrice is due to descend on this little seaside town in a week. Did you know Lord Esquith has been sent ahead to ensure accommodations are prepared for her?"

"I did not." The last time he'd seen the pinched-faced nobleman had been that night at Lady Trenmere's party. It was clear Esquith loathed him, but Will wasn't entirely certain why. Was it simply loyalty to Will's father? Then again, none of the noblemen he'd contacted in an attempt to right his father's wrongs had been thrilled about his inquiries.

Cora stared at him expectantly. When he said nothing, she huffed out, "He's staying at the hotel. He observed you kissing a young woman."

Will gripped the freshly knotted muscles at the back of his neck. "How did you come by this knowledge? Are you in the habit of corresponding with Lord Esquith?"

She was angry, her cheeks flaming. "You're more interested in how I found out than in explaining exactly what you were doing pulling a young woman into London's gossip mill."

"I don't want that. I'd never want that." He curled his hands into fists. God, what a careless ass he'd been. His stomach twisted at the thought that his desire for Maddie might cause her harm.

Cora took a deep breath, seeming to struggle for calm. Then she stood, taking care not to disturb the napping kitten, pulled a folded slip of paper from her reticule, and shoved it toward him.

"A telegram from Lady Trenmere. That's how I found out. She's friends with Esquith," Cora explained. "The countess seems to know everyone, and with a house in Haven Cove, of course Esquith would dine or take luncheon with her."

"She wrote to you?"

Cora nodded. "She also sent me this." She offered a smaller second piece of paper. "That is how I knew that I needed to come immediately."

It was a torn page from a tattle rag.

A Hart may have finally found a wanton filly to soothe his heart after his infamous break with Lady D. D. News has come from the Cornish seaside that the Duke of A— has picked up where his pater left off and is entertaining himself with a Miss R—, a commoner tradeswoman in a tiny haven town.

"Maddie." He breathed her name quietly and felt a crushing wash of guilt for being so reckless that he'd put her livelihood at risk. "I'm a bloody fool."

"Apparently Lady Trenmere is familiar with the young lady. She's worried for her reputation and her livelihood."

Crossing her arms, she let out a pained sigh. "Will, what have you done? You've only been here a week, and you're already having a dalliance. You've apparently compromised an innocent young wom—"

"That's not true." Will shot up from his chair and began pacing the overly gilded room.

He was not and never would be his father. He didn't engage in dalliances, and whatever this was with Maddie, it would never be that. She lit up something inside of him that he'd forgotten he could feel. He wanted her—mercy, how he wanted her—but it was more.

"What shall I say? If you'd behaved like this in a London drawing room, you'd be expected to marry her."

"Perhaps I should." The words slipped from his lips so easily, and he realized they were words he'd said to himself plenty of times but never aloud.

Cora's jaw dropped, and she blinked as if trying to determine whether she'd imagined the declaration. "Is that what you're planning?"

"I have no plan." It was odd for him to say those words. He was a man of strategies and forethought. But since his departure from London, he hadn't planned anything. He hadn't planned to ever see Maddie again, and he certainly hadn't planned how meeting her would make him feel alive again. Hell, he hadn't even planned this trip to Cornwall.

"Would she even wish to be a duchess?" Cora asked in a softer tone.

"I—" It was a question he'd asked himself and still had no answer to. "She has a full life here. And not just a life of genteel pursuits and seeking a good match. The lady has an entire business enterprise. I'm not certain she wishes to marry at all." Will looked at his sister, who looked less angry and merely listened with both dark brows arched curiously.

"Knowing how to run a business wouldn't be bad experience for being a duchess, I suppose. She'd know how to manage staff and oversee the running of a household and wouldn't be shy about all the people she'd meet."

Now it was Will's turn to be shocked. "You're amenable to this?"

"Lady Trenmere sent a letter after the telegram. She says the girl is a noblewoman's daughter and quite an accomplished young lady."

"She's all of that, and a great deal more."

"Goodness." His sister stripped off her gloves and slumped down on the chair nearest the one where he'd been sitting. "You care for her. Are you truly smitten?"

Was he? *Smitten* seemed a silly way to describe what he felt for Maddie. He hadn't thoroughly sorted what he felt for her. He was merely enjoying the fact that she made him feel something in a way he hadn't in years.

Perhaps ever. He cared for her, and that flicker of feeling that had come alive in him made him believe she cared for him too.

"I enjoy her company."

"Obviously you do." For the first time she seemed to truly examine her surroundings. She took in the room, and her expression shifted as she appraised the dramatic paint scheme, the now shabby but once opulent furniture, and the erotic art. "Perhaps it's this place that's caused you to forget yourself."

"Cora, you're the one who sent me here."

"I know." She nibbled at her lower lip and looked at him with guilt in her gaze. "I shouldn't have taken her advice."

"Whose advice?" But as soon as the question passed his lips, he knew the answer.

"Lady Trenmere," she told him. "I think she hoped you might like this place and revive it."

Good grief, was this entire trip a scheme to get him to fix Carnwyth in preparation for the royal visit? The blasted event was all anyone thought about, and it had brought Esquith here. Who knew the man was such a dreadful gossip?

Will continued pacing, sparing glances out the window at the sea. He longed to be out of doors as he never did in London. Most of all, he wished to see Maddie again, though the notion of someone seeing them and writing more specious drivel reminded him that he needed to be less careless with her reputation.

"You are the head of this family. We look to you in all things, and you've always been the one to take care of us."

"And I always will." Sadness and anger washed over him. Those feelings always came when they referred to anything involving their father. The man had been too preoccupied with the pursuit of pleasure to ever make any of them feel protected or cared for.

"Mama did her best too," Cora amended.

She didn't have to say the rest. They both remembered how their mother had struggled to ignore or accept the late duke's behavior.

Cora fell silent, and Will did too, both of them lost in memories they usually tried to leave in the past.

"I'm not like him. I will never be like him. A week in this house hasn't turned me into Father."

"Of course not, Will. I know who you are, and I'm sure this young woman is lovely."

"She is." He wondered if Cora could see the jumble of emotions that came whenever he thought about Maddie. His sister had always been able to read him more easily than anyone else.

The concern in her gaze eased, and she spoke more quietly. "I'm not going to remind you of your duty because we've both had those expectations on our minds for much of our lives. You most of all." She stood and joined him at the west window.

"It's good that you've enjoyed your time here, and perhaps you've found more in Cornwall than you bargained for. But decide what you truly wish to offer Miss Ravenwood, because your choices have consequences."

Will swallowed against a stony lump in his throat. She was right, as she usually was. Their whole lives had been altered by their father's choices and the subsequent loss of their mother.

"And don't forget that you'll be leaving soon." After giving the kitten's head a gentle stroke, Cora retrieved her gloves. "You could even come back with me. I'm departing this afternoon. The engagement party is over and was a grand success."

"I'm glad." The news brought relief for Daisy's sake but no accompanying desire to return to London. "I promise I will return soon. But not today. I've made commitments that I must keep."

"To the girl?"

"Yes."

She didn't look pleased by that news. "Will, it's fanciful to think—"

"I will take more care, Cora. I'm well aware of the need to protect our family's reputation, and I certainly wish to protect hers." He'd already resolved that he would be more controlled where Maddie was concerned, but he had to see her again. Leaving Cornwall now was unthinkable. They'd made plans, and he'd already become attached to the notion of seeing Maddie as often as he could during the coming week.

Cora stepped closer and placed a hand on his arm. They weren't a family of overt affection, so the gesture took him by surprise.

"I trust and believe you. But I needed to see you, to hear you reassure me. I felt it was my duty to come and tell you myself about the whispers. Lady Trenmere cares for the young woman. I can see that you do too. I should almost like to meet her."

He liked the idea too, but mentioning it now seemed pointless.

"It was good to see you, whatever the reason you came."

For the first time since he'd stepped into the room, she smiled. Then she tipped her head and assessed him again from head to toe. "You look like you just walked out of a Dumas novel."

"I only need a sword."

"And a mustache, a beard, and a heart full of vengeance."

"I'll consider acquiring them."

MADDIE HAD REORGANIZED the greenhouse and prepared a special order of primroses that Mrs. Reeve wished to have planted along the private promenade they'd built for the princess. Then she checked on the Victoria roses that she planned to display at the garden show but tried not to fuss over them too much.

The early-morning busyness was necessary if she was going to attend the outing to Bodmin with

Will. The thought of it brought a smile to her face and an odd flutter in her middle. But anticipation didn't fully stem the irritation she'd felt upon finding a letter from Longford in the morning post.

In an effort to persuade her to sell Ravenwood's, he'd spoken of how he might expand the business, how he understood her father's intentions for his nursery and would honor them. Then he'd included a list of all she could gain with the monies from the sale. Arrogant, self-important man.

She took in a deep breath, relishing the scent of her rose blooms. Longford and his pompous letter could not be allowed to ruin her day.

After ensuring the greenhouse was tidy, she made her way toward the office. Alice had Mondays off, so Maddie wanted to ensure there were no outstanding orders left to fill. A moment after stepping inside and beginning her perusal of the neat piles of paperwork on the desk, the door creaked open, and Alice let out a squeak of surprise.

"I didn't expect you to be in here, but I'm so glad you are."

"What is it?" Maddie came around from behind the desk.

The girl's face was splotchy, she was breathing heavy, and perspiration dotted her forehead. Maddie scanned her face and hands, praying she hadn't been injured somehow.

"The grandest news," she said on a breathless whisper. Then she nearly shouted, "Alan proposed."

The girl launched herself into Maddie's arms and pulled her into a laughter-filled hug. "Isn't it wonderful?"

"It is."

"Can you believe it?"

"Of course." Maddie laughed and released Alice, who held on for another minute. "He adores you."

The young grocer had been courting Alice off and on for the better part of a year. She'd shared details with Maddie because of her frustration over her father, who didn't like the young man.

"I truly believe he does love me."

"I'm sure he does. How could he not?" The young man had been persistent and devoted in his interest, even when Alice had tried to dissuade him to please her father.

Maddie feared tamping the girl's joy, but she had to ask. "Has your father come around to accepting Alan?"

Alice's broad grin wobbled, then her chin trembled. A moment later, she slumped into the visitor chair in the office, and tears slid down her cheeks. "Not entirely, no."

Maddie drew a chair around and sat down, covering Alice's hands with her own. "I'll help in any way I can."

"He's very stubborn, and he dismisses me when I try to speak to him about Alan. I'd be rich if I had a coin for each time he's called me a *lovesick girl*." Settling back against the chair, her expression grew serious. "Perhaps I am lovesick, but does that mean I can't decide what I want my future to be?"

Maddie gave Alice's hands a reassuring squeeze. "I don't think so. As much as we can, we should try to carve out the future we want for ourselves."

As soon as the words were out, Maddie's throat tightened, and she swallowed hard. It's what she believed, but she wasn't certain she was living the truth of it.

Alice misunderstood her reaction. "You mustn't worry, Maddie. I'm not going to leave you without finding someone to replace me. In fact, I'd like to stay as long as I can. Until we start a family, and we have no intention of doing that soon."

"That's not what I was thinking, and it's the last thing you should be concerned about. I could never *truly* find someone to replace you, but I'm not alone either."

"Of course." Alice smiled. "You have my father, and he's always told me he plans to stay forever."

"He's the most loyal of men."

"I know. He's always done everything well, and he's always expected a great deal of me."

Just like Maddie's father. No wonder the two men had gotten on so well. They were cut from the very same cloth.

"You know him well. Do you think I can convince him?"

"To accept your engagement? Yes. To ever believe Alan is good enough for you may take some time."

"I have plenty of time." She beamed a guileless smile that reminded Maddie how much younger she was. "My father is steady as a rock, but he can be worn down with good arguments and time."

Eames was steady, and Maddie had no doubt he would stay at Ravenwood's forever. Truth be told, he would do an excellent job as owner of the whole enterprise. Had her father ever considered passing it to his longtime manager? His heart had taken him so unexpectedly, there'd never even been time for a will.

"Plus," Alice added dreamily, "Alan and I will be together forever, so what's a few weeks to get Father's blessing?"

Forever. Maddie kept her focus so fixed on what needed to be done next that she never let herself think of forever. Or her near future, for that matter. Oh, she had pages of plans for her roses, and future garden designs, and ideas about how she might keep her parents' business afloat. But she'd once been as full of hopes for a romantic future as Alice was. Her parents had been a love match. Her mother had changed the whole course of her life when she met Maddie's father.

Maddie couldn't help but wonder if she would be willing to do the same. Not that Will would ever ask her to. Would he?

"What are you thinking?" Alice's question broke into her reverie.

The girl wore a knowing grin, and Maddie was glad to see her teary-eyed misery of moments before had eased.

"Your mention of forever got me thinking. Forgive me." Maddie tucked a stray curl behind her ear, as if she could as easily tuck her wayward thoughts away.

"Nothing to forgive. But you had the most wistful grin on your face. Does it have anything to do with a certain visitor to Haven Cove?"

Maddie said nothing, but Alice seemed to read her thoughts anyway.

"It does." Her eyes widened, and she looked almost as excited as when she'd burst into the office to announce her proposal. She leaned forward and lowered her voice to a whisper, though no one else could hear them. "Maddie, does he mean to offer for you?"

"No." A hundred reasons why he wouldn't rushed into her head, but she'd be lying if she told Alice she'd never considered it. "I don't think so."

"Oh my goodness. Who knew both of our fates were about to change so happily?"

"You're getting ahead of yourself where I'm concerned. Even if he did, how could I leave Cornwall and the nursery?"

"Your mother left an estate in Derbyshire and a whole other kind of life to marry your father."

Maddie narrowed an eye at Alice. It wasn't fair of her to use her parents against her. The memory of her mother's voice echoed in her head. *Marry for love, darling. Nothing else matters as much.*

"I have duties here. And what is a life as a duchess but one of more duties? Do I even want to consider exchanging one set of responsibilities for another?"

Alice pressed her lips together, but her mouth curved mischievously. "You've given this some thought."

"Not a great deal."

They both laughed, though the whole conversation made Maddie uneasy. She was being fanciful and debating a future that might never come, when she had very real concerns to face here and now.

The clock struck the hour, and she jolted in her chair.

"Do you have another commitment?" Alice laughed. "Of course you do. I know there is much to do before the flower show. If you need to pull me out of the office to help next week, please do."

Should she cancel her planned outing with the duke? *Yes.* The answer rushed into her mind. Clear. Practical. She had no business gallivanting around the countryside. She wasn't on holiday like he was. He should be carefree. She, on the other hand, had a great deal to do.

But another part of her, a deeper, more insistent part, told her to go with him. To grasp the opportunity to spend time with a handsome, kind man whose kisses ignited a longing inside her that she couldn't deny. He would soon depart. If her forever was to be the nursery, when would she ever have such a chance again?

"I do have an appointment, but if you need me, to listen or even to speak to your father on your behalf, I will."

Alice stood and offered a hand to pull Maddie up too. "You go to your appointment. I mostly wanted to tell you that Alan had proposed. I'll speak to my father again in due time."

Maddie's heartbeat sped. She wouldn't have to cancel. And foolishly, scandalously, all she could think about was kissing the duke again.

Alice stepped behind her desk. She ran her finger across the calendar she maintained for Ravenwood's. "You have no other appointments today, but there is a planning-meeting notation for tomorrow with Mrs. Reeve."

"Yes, a final meeting to make sure our checklists are complete."

"Then, it looks like you have nothing on your calendar to attend to except for preparations for your meeting."

Maddie had done that preparation before she got started in the greenhouse.

Alice smiled. "So enjoy yourself." Though she seemed less excited than when she'd told Maddie her news, her body still hummed with a kind of joyful energy. "I'm going to go and speak to Alan."

"Enjoy the rest of your day off," Maddie told her. "And try not to worry."

"I should be telling you that. You take so many responsibilities on your shoulders, but I *know* your roses will be a grand success."

Maddie gave in to the girl's enthusiasm and agreed. "I think so too."

Alice departed with a notable bounce in her step.

Maddie sifted through the pile of office mail after Alice left and read a short note from Mrs. Reeve reminding her of their upcoming meeting and dropping a not-so-subtle hint that the Duke of Ashmore would be welcome to join them if he was so inclined. Maddie drew in a deep breath and sighed. Eventually Mrs. Reeve would show up on his doorstep with her list of requests.

As Maddie locked up the office and prepared to leave, the sun turned the window into a looking glass, and she stopped to study her reflection. Disheveled hair, a cheek smeared with potting soil, and eyes full of worry.

In her mind's eye, she saw Will's dark gaze. The heated intensity of the way he'd looked at her on the boat took her breath away even now. Somehow, he saw past the busyness and worry that filled her days. He made her wish to slow down—and nothing ever made her wish for that—to savor each moment with him.

He spoke to her playfully and she loved it. Though he'd tried to turn their connection into some kind of bargain of her showing him Cornwall while he acceded to the committee's requests, when they were together he never seemed to expect anything of her in the way that everyone else did.

Though, he did want something. Her company. She found herself craving his too.

Soon he would be gone. She might never feel this sort of desire again for anyone.

She would enjoy their day together and then focus on all the rest.

Just one day. Surely, she could give herself a single day and then get back to all that needed to be done.

Chapter Fifteen

*W*ill feared she wouldn't come, and now that she sat a few feet away across the train carriage, he couldn't think of how to tell her he'd be departing Haven Cove earlier than he'd initially planned.

Hell, up until the moment he'd headed to Ravenwood's to pick her up and drive them to the train station, he'd considered sending a note to cancel their journey altogether. Not because he didn't wish to have her all to himself for a day, but because Cora's warnings echoed in his mind.

For years, he'd taken care to guard his reputation. If gossips chewed over his behavior, they only noted how it contrasted with his father's. And he'd reveled in being everything Stanwick Hart had not been.

But he didn't want a pristine reputation if it meant he couldn't spend time with a woman who heated his blood as no other ever had. Every moment he'd spent with her—every kiss—had been worth it. His only real concern was for Maddie. He didn't want to cost her anything, neither the esteem of others nor a business that consumed most of her waking hours.

He glanced across the train car at her. She immediately turned her head and met his gaze directly.

No coquettishness. No pretense. Just an open expression of curiosity and warmth.

Then she lowered her eyes for a moment and studied his mouth. He fought the urge to cross to her bench and kiss her, but they weren't truly alone. A porter or other passenger might pass by the compartment window at any moment.

He'd promised Cora he'd take more care, and he intended to. His worries now were for Maddie's sake. She might think her independence was unquestioned, but he knew society was unfair to women. Men like his father could treat life as a series of drunken revels and be thought of as *good fun* or *a jolly fellow.* He'd lied and boasted, and his circle of friends had only grown more devoted. After taking mistress after mistress with only the merest attempt at discretion, other men didn't disdain him. In fact, they envied his prowess.

Whereas if Will's mother had eked out some little bit of pleasure for herself and taken a lover, she would have been reviled, condemned, and ostracized from all good society forever.

He suspected Haven Cove did allow a certain leeway for Maddie, a capable young woman and business owner who contributed in a dozen ways to the town. But she was also unwed and independent, and a hint of scandal might be enough to bankrupt Ravenwood's and ruin her in the eyes of her noble patrons.

Will would never allow her to pay a price for his desires.

He wanted her as he'd never wanted a woman in his life. There was no denying it. The longing only intensified each moment he was near her. If he thought of it—and he tried not to—he couldn't quite imagine returning to a life that didn't include her.

Could his life include her? He recalled his conversation with Cora. Maddie would make a remarkable duchess. And while he knew marrying was his duty and he could easily imagine spending the rest of his days with her, he knew her priorities were in Cornwall.

He could see how Maddie would fit into his life, but where would he fit into the life she'd made? It was a selfish desire of a man who would soon leave her to her very full life here.

"What are you learning in that book?"

When he hadn't spoken after they settled into their train carriage, she'd pulled out a book that, according to the title, recounted the history of the county.

She centered her bright blue gaze on him, set the book aside, and leaned forward eagerly. "Bodmin is one of the oldest towns in Cornwall and is the only large Cornish settlement listed in the Domesday Book. If we have time, perhaps we could visit the church. Part of the original Norman tower still remains as part of the current structure, which was built in the fifteenth century, and it was the largest church in Cornwall until the cathedral built in Truro a few years back."

He let out a chuckle that felt good rumbling in

his chest. Historical relics generally didn't interest him, but her enthusiasm was utterly convincing. "If you like."

"Did you bring any drawing materials?"

Will patted the pocket of his coat. "A small notebook and pencil."

"Perhaps you could sketch the tower. I owe the Historical Society an article for their quarterly newsletter, and I could write about the church."

"I'll draw whatever you like." Most of all, he wanted to draw *her*.

"Thank you." She offered him a smile that once again made him want to touch his lips to hers. He would never forget the taste of her.

But he'd promised himself this outing would simply be about enjoying their time together. He had no right to want or expect anything more. At least this far from Haven Cove, there would be no one to observe them together and gossip.

One perfect, private day together, and he'd keep his promise to attend the hotel event and then return to London.

"There's a little map here." She'd picked up her book again. "The festival site is a bit far from the station. We may need to rent a carriage."

"I know you'll insist on driving," he told her in a teasing tone, "but I promise I'm better at it than rowing."

"Are you still trying to impress me?"

"Very much so." His voice had roughened because the ways he wished to impress her had little to do with driving a carriage and much more to do with thoughts he had no right to be thinking.

"Fine. I shall let you drive," she announced with mock seriousness.

"So very gracious." He simulated doffing a hat, though he hadn't worn one.

For a moment she simply watched him. Her gaze was brazen, curious. She studied his face, swept her perusal down his body all the way to the spot where his outstretched legs tangled in the hem of her frilly yellow skirt. Whether she knew it or not, she'd bitten her lip as she studied him, and his own desire to sink his teeth into her plush pink lip in the same spot made him hard and heated.

"There's room over here." She didn't wear gloves, and her bare palm stroked the empty spot on the velvet carriage bench next to her. "We could share the book."

Will wasn't sure she knew what a temptress she was, but he told himself he could sit next to her and remember he was a gentleman.

He leaned forward, got to his feet, and took the spot next to her.

On the boat, they'd both been soaked, and yet he'd caught a floral scent on her skin. Now it was sweeter, a fresh yet subtle perfume that made his mouth water.

"We won't be near enough to Bodmin Moor to roam its wild terrain, but it's a unique kind of beautiful."

She was a unique kind of beautiful.

After studying her profile for a moment while she read, Will withdrew his notebook and pencil.

"What are you doing?" she asked worriedly.

"We have hours on the train, and now I have the perfect view of you for sketching."

Nearly tipping her book from her lap, she gestured jerkily at the view rolling past the train windows. "Draw the countryside."

"You're not moving past me at thirty miles per hour. You're a much better subject."

"I very much doubt that." With a contemplative frown, she glanced down at the notebook in his hand.

"You are."

"I have trouble sitting still for photographs."

"This isn't a photograph, so you needn't hold completely still." Will tipped his head to study the curve of her lips as he roughed out their shape in his sketchbook. "I've drawn you from memory, but it's much better to have you in the flesh."

His pulse rushed in his ears at the wantonness of his words and the images they sparked in his head. Then his body thrummed lower when her lips parted, and she flicked her gaze his way.

"Is there any particular way you'd like me to pose?"

Will swallowed hard as he contemplated the question—long and hard contemplation. Oh, the ways he would love to sketch her.

When she turned her head and sat up straighter to offer him her profile, he couldn't resist reaching for her. He touched his fingertips to the edge of her jaw.

"Relax. It's just me."

She let out a breath, and the tension seemed to leave her body on the exhale. Settling back against the carriage seat, she opened her book again and began scanning the pages. But she nervously swept back a strand of hair, then toyed with a button on her bodice.

With a peek at him from under her lashes, she asked, "Will you let me see after you're finished?"

"Of course." Will stilled and waited until her gaze seemed to be scanning the words and images in the book. But as soon as he began moving his pencil across the paper, she peeked at him again out of the corner of her eye.

"You're a very great distraction," she whispered.

"I can move back to the opposite bench."

"No." She swallowed after saying the single word.

He began to draw in quick, light lines to capture the shape of her face and the lovely tumble of red curls she'd arranged in a knot above her nape. As he added shading, he found himself returning to her lips.

For a man who didn't believe in fanciful nonsense, he would swear he could still feel the soft, sweet memory of them on his lips. As if she'd branded him as her own.

She kept sneaking glances at him, and he liked it. They were playing a game of glances. He looked up; she looked away. He turned his attention to his sketch and immediately sensed her gaze on him.

"Tell me more about Ravenwood Nursery," he told her, as much to distract himself from the need to touch her again as to make her forget she was being sketched.

The way her body stiffened at the question surprised him.

"When my father died nearly two years ago, it fell to me. I try to maintain it as he and my mother would wish. They worked very hard to build Ravenwood Nursery into an enterprise that supported our family."

"Mmm." Will had surmised that much, but he wanted to know what she wasn't saying. "But it's been difficult?"

"No." She blinked quickly, and color rushed into her cheeks. More quietly, she admitted, "Yes. I thought I would be better at it, honestly."

"Are you not good at it?"

Her fingers ran along the spine of the history book in her lap, and Will suspected she was censoring herself, weighing what to say. More than anything, he wanted her to trust him enough to tell him the truth.

Just when he was on the verge of saying something to reassure her, she let out a long sigh.

"Sales have fallen off. Customers have gone elsewhere. The hotel has been our saving grace. They've given us the biggest orders Ravenwood's has had in years, but I fear . . ." She looked at him, wary and uncertain. "I fear I don't have the passion for it that my parents did."

Was that why she did so many other things? Because running her family's enterprise did not bring her any joy?

"I think I understand."

"You do?" Her gaze was dubious.

"In my experience, taking on the responsibility of what someone else has created is a challenge. If I could have picked a fate other than taking on the chaos my father wrought, I might have."

"Taking on the mantle of someone else's chaos had to have been daunting. Especially since it included taking on his title. The name that represented all his infamy now represents you."

"Exactly. Redeeming that title seemed important to me. I would like people to hear the Ashmore name and think of something other than scandal, especially for the sake of my sisters."

"I'm sure they will eventually. And while a dukedom may be a burden, by mere advantage of your position and wealth you can do so much good."

Ah, Miss Ravenwood and her tendency to put him straight.

"You're right. And considering that the title would have fallen to a rather dreadful cousin who would have left my sisters penniless, I'm better off where I am." As he said the words, he glanced down at the mere inches that separated their bodies.

"I'm sure you work hard to do your duty."

Will couldn't resist smiling at that. "That's an odd thing to say to a man you've only seen while away a week sketching and soaking up sunlight and sea breezes."

She laughed. "That's what one does on holiday."

"So I am doing something right at least."

"I'm sure you do a great deal right."

His mouth went dry. She seemed to catch the double meaning too and darted her gaze back to her book. Good grief, he would not make it through this day without touching her again. Kissing her, if he was lucky.

After allowing her to read for a bit, he couldn't resist learning more.

"What are you passionate about, Miss Ravenwood?" There was no double entendre intended. She'd said the nursery wasn't her passion, and he wanted to know. What made her happy besides volunteering on every committee she could?

Her eyes flashed a look he could only call dubious, as if she doubted that he truly cared to hear her answer.

"Designing flower gardens," she finally said with an emphatic certainty that made him smile. "If I could just consult and design flower gardens for clients, I'd be content. And creating new roses, of course. Though it's not just roses." She leaned toward him ever so slightly, as if preparing to divulge a secret. "I've been experimenting with hybridizing rhododendrons too."

"That's a flower?"

She laughed indulgently. "A flowering shrub, but very hardy. Some grow to enormous heights."

"What if you narrowed your endeavors to design and hybridizing?" In sorting through all that needed to be done to restore the dukedom, he'd had to employ a kind of tactical precision to get anything accomplished.

She fell silent, and he wondered what ideas were spinning in that clever mind of hers. When she put the book aside and stared at the passing landscape, he wondered if he'd sparked some idea or, worse, brought something unpleasant to mind.

"It struck me as something that would appeal to you, but it was the suggestion of a man with no real knowledge of the challenges you face. Of course, I trust that you know best."

"Oh, it does appeal to me. I never thought I would inherit the nursery, you know. I suppose I thought he'd sell it, and I'd always imagined I might study landscape design or art or botany. But then I lost my mother, and my father was content with me helping him run the business. If his heart hadn't failed him, I still believe he would have been persuaded to sell eventually."

"Were there ever interested buyers?"

"Mostly a man named Longford." Her forehead puckered in a frown the minute she spoke the man's name.

Remembering his brief encounter with the man, Will didn't have trouble imagining why. "I've met him. In the pub."

Her eyes widened in surprise. "It must have been the day he came to persuade me to sell to him."

Will understood now why Maddie felt such a sense of responsibility to run her family's business, yet it was also clear that it wasn't her passion. Perhaps Longford sensed the truth, and it made him believe she'd capitulate and sell. From the stubborn set of her chin, Will suspected that she never would.

"Ravenwood's was left to me, and abandoning what my parents made feels wrong. A betrayal. As if I'd be letting them down."

"But it's yours now. You must choose what's best for you. Would that not be their wish?"

Maddie glanced at him, her gaze weighted and worried, but she said nothing. He wished he could soothe away whatever troubled her. Was it guilt because she could imagine a different life for herself than the one that she'd inherited? That he understood.

Her book slid from her lap, and Will reached out to catch it. Unintentionally, he caught a swath of her skirt and yanked it up so that her boots and white stockings were momentarily revealed.

Their gazes clashed, and for one wild moment he considered continuing. Dropping the book and lowering his hand to her lap, hitching the fabric of her skirt up higher, and sliding his hand underneath.

At the sound of a man clearing his throat, they both snapped their gazes toward the sliding door of their compartment.

"Hello, mister and missus. When we arrive in Bodmin, will you need any assistance with luggage?"

"No." Will realized he'd growled at the man, but the racks above them were empty. Their lack of luggage was obvious, and the man's timing was bloody maddening. Or perfect, if he intended to keep his promise to himself to behave like a gentleman today.

Maddie settled her skirt and offered a little sympathetic smile toward the porter as he departed.

"I shouldn't have been so short with him." The man she'd met those many months ago growled at others as a matter of course. Hell, he'd shouted at her that night. She had every right to fear that deep down he was still that gruff, curmudgeonly man.

But he wasn't sure he truly was that version of himself anymore. Certainly not with her.

"Thank you for coming with me today," he told her softly. "I know your time is precious."

"I would never have thought to take a day and visit a festival, but I wanted to come with you."

He wouldn't have sought an outing like this on his own either. If these days had been any sort of holiday, it was the time spent with Maddie that made it so.

Tomorrow, he had no doubt, she would go back to busy days of work and preparations for the royal visit.

He knew what his duties were to the dukedom, and he'd return to them soon.

But not today.

Awhile later, the train slowed as it drew into the station, saving him from having to say more. Instead, he stood, shrugged into his suit coat, and offered her his hand. "Shall we?"

MADDIE SLID HER fingers against Will's, and a rush of desire for him made her shiver.

From the moment they'd settled into the train carriage, there had been a strange energy between them. She'd struggled to concentrate on anything but his scent, the warmth in his gaze, and the way her pulse sped every time he looked her way.

Attraction was undeniable from the moment she'd first seen him, but now she knew how it felt to kiss him, to have his hard, heated body against hers.

When he'd hitched up her skirt, it had taken every ounce of restraint not to reach for him. She knew it had been an accident. Will wasn't the sort of man who needed to rely on ham-fisted fumbling to get a woman to lift her skirts for him.

He was tempting. More so than any man she'd ever known, and Maddie hadn't wanted him to stop.

A silly wistful notion had been with her all morning. A wish that they could spend more than a few hours on their journey. What would it be like to spend days together exploring the moors and all the historic sites nearby?

More and more, she was imaging him as part of her future days. But that wouldn't be. Their lives were too different, their commitment to the responsibilities they'd inherited too great. Besides, how could she be a duchess? She hadn't been born into his world, the one her own mother had left behind.

She knew she should simply be content with today and the possibility of seeing him again before he departed.

Of course, she didn't have days to spare. Part of her still felt guilty for allowing herself the pleasure of this one.

"I think this must be the way." Will hooked his arm through hers and tugged her out of the path of a couple barreling past them.

A little procession was heading up the lane toward a sign with an arrow pointing toward the Bodmin May Festival.

They joined the line of people walking past the sign, mostly couples and a few families.

"I hope we're not late for their flower event." He scanned ahead, and there was real concern in his voice.

Maddie smiled. "I had no idea you'd taken such an interest in flowers."

"I haven't. But I'd hate for you to miss it."

He was being too sweet. How was she expected to concentrate on anything but him?

The lane ascended and wound past stone houses and then smaller cottages, and just when her legs began to ache, Maddie spotted the festival grounds. A long grassy field contained stalls with items to purchase. The first few they passed featured food: local honey, eggs, savory pies, and fruit tarts that looked too perfect to be real.

Next came fabrics and woven items. Maddie stopped to look at a basket, and Will stood by her side, perusing a pamphlet he'd somehow acquired since they'd entered the festival grounds.

"What do you think of this one?" Maddie held the basket on her arm.

Will reached out to run his hands around the handle, but somehow ended up trailing a line of warmth down her arm and across her wrist with his fingertips. His gaze was appreciative, but he wasn't looking at the basket.

"Very fetching." He lifted a coin and handed it to the basket weaver.

"No." Maddie reached for his hand. "I didn't mean for you to buy it for me." The nursery wasn't doing so poorly that she couldn't purchase a little basket.

Will took her hand gently in his—the one that wasn't passing the coin to the appreciative craftswoman. Then he led her down the row of vendors, still holding her hand.

"Thank you," she finally said, "but—"

"You're welcome, and I meant to buy you a souvenir anyway, so don't chastise me."

She was too distracted by the way their fingers had entwined so naturally, as if they'd held hands in just this way a hundred times.

"Free bouquets," a young man called as he made his way through the crowd. "Flower show at the top of the hour. Free bouquets for all who attend."

"Where is it, lad?"

"Behind the carousel, sir. Can't miss it if you keep on the way you're going."

Will nodded at the boy, then glanced at Maddie. "Carousel, my lady?"

"Yes, please." She felt the same thrill of excitement she'd felt as a child the first time she'd seen a carousel.

"Listen." Will pulled her closer. "Do you hear that?"

Maddie heard the music, a deep resonant throng of sound from a pipe organ. Will looked as eager as she was. He led the way, and he was such a sizable man that others parted as he approached.

"There."

Maddie tracked her gaze in the direction his finger was pointing and let out a little gasp. It was a lovely, gleaming mechanism of the brightest colors. Reds and purples and royal blue, all topped by a spinning gilded crownlike top. Passengers were just stepping onto the polished wood floor. Ladies fussed with their gowns as they settled on wooden horses. A girl ran toward a black horse and squealed when she finally reached the wild-looking wooden creature. It was the fiercest of those Maddie could see, with a tousled mane and bared teeth, but the girl patted its neck lovingly.

"We have to have a ride," Will said decisively.

"Is there enough time?"

"Should be."

They started forward as one, and he squeezed her hand when they got in line. As the carousel started spinning, children began to laugh. One lady in a lavender gown let out a little scream and then joined in the laughter. Steam poured out of the top of the spinning crown, and the pipe organ played a livelier tune.

Maddie bounced on her toes. The only other time she'd seen a carousel at a fair she'd been quite young, and her parents hadn't let her ride. "Have you seen one before?"

"Yes, at Brighton. My sisters rode, but I didn't."

"Why not?"

He looked uncomfortable and loosened his grip on her hand. "I was a bit of a miserable snob. I thought it was silly."

"And now?"

"Nothing could stop me from riding it with you." There was something different in his gaze today. On the train there had been a heated intensity that mirrored everything she was feeling. But now he was watching her as if he feared she might dart off and disappear.

"It's our turn."

Passengers stepped off the carousel, and those waiting climbed on.

"The white one?" Will pointed to a white horse with a unicorn horn.

"The black one." Maddie scooted onto its back and sat sidesaddle.

Will took the roan next to her. She tried not to giggle at the sight of him, with his long legs and broad shoulders, seated on a horse that was smaller than any pony she'd ever seen.

"Don't laugh," he told her playfully. "I'm planning to enjoy this."

"You might like it more than you think." Her words wobbled at the end when the carousel began to spin. The horses moved up and down on golden poles at a speed that made some of the younger riders cry out in fear or delight, but Maddie found herself wishing it would go faster. She hadn't had the time to ride a horse across a field on her own in so many years she could barely remember. As a girl, it had been one of her favorite things. Giving a horse its head, letting it take the length of a field as fast as it liked while the wind pulled her hair out of its braid.

"You look serene." Will's voice was clear above the din of music and squeals.

Maddie turned to find him watching her with a kind of awestruck grin, as if seeing her enjoy herself truly brought him pleasure.

"I was remembering how much I like to ride and how I haven't done so for pleasure in such a very long time."

He arched one brow. "We have beautiful fields for that in Sussex. Hills that rise gently, field grass that gives off the sweetest scent in the summer."

"Your home is there?"

"The family estate. Eastwick. It's not Norman or medieval, I'm afraid. Just a Jacobean pile, but I think you might appreciate its history."

There was more. Something weighed on him, bothered him when he discussed the estate. Perhaps, like Carnwyth, it reminded him of his father.

Maddie realized he was waiting. Watching her as if he'd asked a question and she'd not yet replied. But then the carousel slowed. They climbed off their horses, and Will started off first, descending to wait for her on the grass nearby.

When she reached his side, she considered how to ask what had happened. His whole manner had altered when he'd mentioned his estate.

But he turned to her with a smile and offered his arm. "To the flower show, Miss Ravenwood?"

After a moment's hesitation, Maddie laid her hand on his forearm. It was very formal. The way her mother had taught her to take a man's arm if he asked her to partner him at a dance.

Perhaps this was how they should have behaved from the beginning.

Had discussing Eastwick reminded him of the life he was on holiday from, the one he'd soon return to? A life of duty and propriety.

Maybe it was for the best. It was too easy for her to forget herself when she was with him, and if he felt the same, then they should remind themselves that one day soon they would return to a life that didn't include each other.

But Will didn't seem to agree. He reached up to clasp the hand she'd placed on his arm, and then he twined their fingers together. They held hands as they had when they'd entered the festival grounds and made their way toward the flower show.

Chapter Sixteen

*F*lowers loved her as much as she loved them. Will watched Maddie move from entry to entry in the Bodmin May Festival Flower Show and consider each plant with the same curious interest. She liked to touch them, even if it was simply to run her finger along the edge of a leaf. They all looked a little brighter after she had showered them with attention.

He recognized roses and tulips and lilies, though he couldn't have named most of the other blooms. But Maddie seemed to know them all.

"My youngest sister has a book of flower meanings, but I can never recall which is which," he admitted.

"The language of flowers. My mother loved the notion that flowers carried meaning. Oh, look at this one. The scent is heavenly." She bent, closed her eyes, and breathed in deeply.

The sight was so lovely that Will tried to sear it in his mind's eye so he could draw the moment later.

"Smell." She pointed to the delicate white bells surrounded by enormous green leaves.

He was quite content watching her enjoy herself,

but he obeyed. Heady sweetness, soft and yet powerful, wafted in the air.

"Spring flowers are so delicious," she told him. "Hyacinths have such a perfect scent, but *Convallaria majalis*, lily of the valley, will always be my favorite."

As with most things that caught his eye lately, Will considered how he'd sketch it. The leaves were almost as appealing as the flowers, and he mimicked Maddie's tendency to reach out and touch.

"Don't." Her hand came down over his when he reached for another flower. "It's quite poisonous."

Will stood and stepped away from the delicate little blooms. "Apparently I'll need you to accompany me on all my visits to flower shows so I don't touch something that will do me in."

"I have a terrible habit of touching everything."

He was acutely aware that she was still touching him, and he didn't mind at all.

After they attended the flower judging, they shared a bag of roasted chestnuts.

"What did you think of the roses?" he asked her, knowing she must have been acutely aware of each specimen and the way each was judged in the show.

"I saw nothing to compare to my Victoria rose." She reached into the bag in his hand and looked at him with an almost giddy grin. "I'm even more confident now."

"You named it after the queen?"

"Princess Beatrice's daughter is named Victoria too. Does it seem silly?"

"I think it's a lovely gesture."

A girl came along soon after, handing out cups of honey mead, and another followed with flower crowns strung on her arm.

When Maddie took the drink but not the floral crown, Will reached for one.

The girl shook her head. "Oh, they're only for those of us who are unwed, sir. So we don't become miserable, childless spinsters."

Maddie shot him an inscrutable look over the edge of her cup.

The girl's assumption that they were married pleased him for some reason. Maddie merely looked contemplatively and slightly bemused.

When the girl had gone, she explained, "I suspect they're preparing for a maypole dance. Usually, May festivals are at the start of the month, but apparently Bodmin is catching up now."

The explanation was well and good, but he was more concerned with the effect the girl's words had on Maddie. She seemed unbothered, but she did pull her watch from her skirt pocket for the first time.

"The train comes at four. We still have time to walk to the church."

The closer they got to the edge of the festival grounds, away from the chatter of voices and laughter, the more it felt like the beginning of the end. And he didn't want their time together to end.

"Looks as if this leads through the forest." She turned back, and he noticed she'd taken a few blooms from the bouquet they'd been given at the flower show and put them in her hair.

She should have had one of those bloody crowns if she wanted one. There was nothing she should be denied.

As they walked on, they both fell silent. Perhaps she too was sensing that this might be the last private moment they'd share. Or maybe she was simply worrying about the upcoming royal visit. He'd pulled her away from last-minute preparations, but knowing how deeply committed she was to everything she did, it couldn't be far from her mind.

"Maddie."

"Yes?" Her expression tightened in concern, as if she could read in his face all the jumbled emotions he'd been feeling since Cora's visit.

She let him lead her off the path toward a stand of trees surrounded by some forest flower she would surely know the name of.

"I need you to know . . ." What? Inside him, there was a gnawing need, but the words wouldn't come. Instead, he touched her, reaching out to stroke his fingers against her cheek. She was warm and soft, and denying himself suddenly seemed like madness.

When he slid his hand down along her neck, she let out a little gasp and dropped her basket and bouquet.

Will held her gaze and hunched down to retrieve the flowers, pulling out a few. "You should have had a flower crown if you wanted one." He stood and placed a purple flower in her hair. Then a pink one with a frilly dark rose middle.

"I didn't want one. I'm not a child who fears spinsterhood or thinks a dance around a maypole will change my fate."

He stilled, and she took the last flower from his hand.

"Bluebells," she said as she reached up and slid it into the buttonhole on his lapel. "They mean . . ." She paused, curling her fingers around the fabric of his coat and pulling him closer. "Gratitude."

Then she stunned him by rising onto her toes and pressing her lips to his. All the worry and uncertainty within him seemed to quiet, and he wrapped his arms around her. He wanted her, and she wanted him. Nothing else mattered more than that.

Will cupped her cheek and kissed her again, losing himself in her sweetness.

"I didn't want you to stop," she whispered against his lips. "On the train, I didn't want you to stop. Please touch me."

He nuzzled her cheek, and his breath came in fast, sharp gasps. All of his intentions of propriety evaporated.

Dipping his head, he stroked his lips against her neck and reached down to tug at her skirt. He turned with her, keeping her back against the trunk of a tree, shielding her body with his. His fingers edged under the fabric, but her white stockings still separated him from her flesh.

Then he reached higher, fingers brushing her bare

skin and the ribbons of her drawers. She was so soft.

She gripped his shoulder, twined her other hand in his hair. He kissed her the moment he found the slit in her drawers. He told himself to go slowly, but his hand was trembling and her breath hitched as he slid his finger against her. Every instinct told him to take her, pleasure her, make her cry out in the bliss of release.

"Don't stop," she told him, squeezing his shoulder when he stilled.

He chuckled softly and took her mouth, parting her lips with his tongue as his finger slipped inside her slick heat. Slowly, gently, he waited for her reaction and was answered when she let out an impatient little moan.

"I want you," she whispered.

"And I want you." More than he'd ever wanted any woman. At this moment, more than he'd ever wanted anything in his life.

Whatever he was, whatever his duties, what mattered most was being the man she made him want to be. Kinder, better, more patient and curious.

He kissed his way down her neck, licking at the heady scent of her skin at the base of her throat. She'd begun to gasp. Little catches in her breath that told him she was close.

Will nipped at her earlobe, then placed a kiss just behind her ear. That seemed to undo her. She tugged at his hair, clutched at his shoulder. She began to quiver, her body tensed, and then she let go. Her mouth opened, but he could tell she was trying not to cry out.

He pulled back to watch her, needing to see her in that sated moment of release. Gently, he began to pull her skirt down between them.

"Don't go," she said breathlessly.

"I'm not going anywhere, sweetheart."

He held her for a moment and tried not to think about how the words would soon be untrue. She laid her head against his chest, and he felt the racing thud of her heartbeat.

"There's a hotel in town." She lifted her head, and the heat in her eyes made his mouth water.

God, yes. One night with her. What he wouldn't give for one night with her. His body was screaming for release, and even now, chest to chest, he didn't feel close enough to her.

But in his head, he was already battling himself. *Let her go back to her life.*

If he took her to bed, it would change everything. He couldn't leave her, and he might put a babe in her belly that would change both of their lives forever. And if he asked her to stay with him forever, would he be asking her to forfeit too much? Would he be trapping her in a life of duty that he sometimes wished to escape himself?

The sound of voices startled both of them. A couple was approaching down the same path they'd taken.

Will drew Maddie deeper into the tree cover and hoped the couple would pass without noting their presence.

"Shall we go?"

"We should," he told her regretfully. "Only a quarter of an hour before our train departs."

"So we're going back."

"If I take you to that hotel—and I assure you, every bit of me wants to—there will be no going back for either of us."

Will held his breath. If he hurt her, there would be no peace for him. Causing her pain was precisely what he was determined to avoid.

"You're right. I know you are." There was no anger he could detect in her tone. In fact, she smiled at him, but it wasn't the bright, open expression he was used to from her. "I was thinking impulsively."

Will took her in his arms, and she came willingly and easily. He kissed her forehead, the tip of her nose, and then let his lips rest against her cheek. Breathing in her scent. Savoring the moment, sealing it in his memory.

Chapter Seventeen

After returning to Carnwyth, Will had filled pages with sketches of moments he remembered from the day he and Maddie had visited Bodmin. Then he'd walked the path to the beach and stared at the sea until the sun sank toward the horizon and the sky bloomed with shades of lavender and rose.

The next day, he'd done much the same. And the next day as well.

In essence, he'd sulked like a lovelorn fool and argued with himself about why he should leave Maddie to the life that mattered to her and go back to his life in London. Though, he knew that life would never be quite the same, because he'd changed.

Workmen were beginning to replace the broken windows, and while he checked on their progress and the new items they'd discovered that required repairs, Bly had their supervision well in hand. Will agreed to everything Bly suggested, and the manor house now hosted carpenters, masons, and a man to examine the ballroom's damage.

Maddie hadn't come to call or sent a note or contacted him in any way.

She was busy, of course. A princess of the realm

and her entourage would descend on Haven Cove in days. And *he* had been the one to stop what would have been a point of no return for both of them.

For two long days, he'd alternated between regret about that decision and relief that he hadn't been reckless. Both of them wanted that moment, of that he had no doubt. The consequences—that was what he could not bear.

He missed her. So much so that he'd ventured to Ravenwood Nursery, hoping to see her and, if he was lucky, get a tour of the nursery's fields and flower beds from the proprietress herself. But she'd been gone, busy with one of her myriad commitments in town.

When a note had arrived an hour ago, he'd hoped it was from Maddie. Instead, it was a letter from the proprietor of the Haven Cove Hotel, Mrs. Reeve, requesting that he join her for a meeting to discuss the event he'd agreed to attend at the hotel.

He didn't give a damn about a meeting with Mrs. Reeve, but he'd told Maddie he would attend the hotel's previsit celebration, so he would go.

Now, standing in the busy hotel lobby, he scanned faces like a starving man, hungry for the sight of Maddie. The mere thought was fanciful. She'd be at her nursery hard at work. He had no logical reason to think she might—

"Mercy." She stood across the hotel lobby from him, and he found he wasn't truly prepared for the sight of her.

She looked lovely, as she always did. But now, seeing her brought a rush of longing. A desire to be near her, a realization that the days since they'd last spoken had lacked something. Even standing so far away from her felt wrong. It took extraordinary self-control not to stride across the lobby and pull her into his arms.

There was no indication she'd noticed him. In fact, she looked distracted. Her arms were full of documents, and she glanced again and again at an elaborate clock on the hotel wall.

"Miss Ravenwood." An older woman with dark blond hair nearly the same shade as her gold-rimmed spectacles approached Maddie. They spoke to each other quietly for a moment, and then they turned their gazes on the guests in the lobby.

Will waited impatiently for Maddie's gaze to find him. When it did, he saw the flicker of a smile, then she shocked him by raising a finger and pointing him out in the crowd. The woman with her turned and immediately began sailing his way, her chin up and her elaborate gown swishing around her ankles.

"Your Grace," she announced loudly, "how good of you to come."

Will felt the effect of her words on the others gathered in the hotel lobby. It was a little too much like the effect his presence had on a London ballroom. People stared. Whispers rose around him. Apparently, any anonymity he'd enjoyed in Haven Cove was at an end now.

"Jane Reeve. Welcome to my hotel." She held out her hand boldly, just as Maddie had that day in the cottage.

Will tried to focus on the hotelier and not the woman who'd been on his mind for days.

"Mrs. Reeve, thank you for the invitation."

"I believe you and Miss Ravenwood are acquainted." The hotelier gestured to Maddie.

"We are."

The look Maddie shot him was unreadable, but she didn't look quite as pleased to see him as he was to see her.

"If you'll both follow me."

Will waited for Mrs. Reeve to pass, and he and Maddie followed her, walking side by side.

"I didn't realize you'd be here," he whispered. "I'm glad you are."

At that admission, she snapped her gaze his way. "I knew she'd invited you. I didn't know if you'd come."

He held in the words gnawing at him but finally whispered, "Have you been avoiding me?"

"No. I've been busy." She gripped the papers she had in her arms tighter.

Will sensed her glancing at him out of the corner of her eye.

"I thought perhaps *you* were avoiding me," she said quietly.

He slowed and reached for Maddie's arm to slow her too. "Not at all. I even went to the nursery hoping to see you, but you weren't there."

Mrs. Reeve stopped before ornate double doors, took hold of each latch, and pushed the doors open dramatically. "This is the ballroom where we'll host the celebratory event," she said as she stepped into the enormous room, the clip of her heels echoing to the high, gilded ceilings. It was twice the size of the cluttered ballroom at Carnwyth, at least.

Tall arched windows along the far wall contained dozens of panes that looked out onto the sea. It was a stunning view, even if the water would be difficult to see at an evening event.

"We'll also host a dance here during the princess's visit, but that guest list will be far more manageable. For the previsit event, all hotel visitors are welcome."

Will sensed Maddie watching him, as if waiting for his reaction.

"It's an impressive space, Mrs. Reeve."

"Thank you, Your Grace." A moment later, she stepped from the room and snapped the doors shut. "Just this way to my office."

To his shock, Maddie moved close enough for her body to brush his, but they didn't slow their pace as they followed behind Mrs. Reeve.

"What you've agreed to is sufficient," she told him in a rushed whisper. "She's going to ask you for a great deal, but you needn't agree to any of it."

"That doesn't sound reassuring."

"It's not meant to be."

Will shot her a frown at the same moment Mrs. Reeve glanced back to see if they were still following.

"Here we are." With an outstretched arm, she ushered them into a lushly appointed office. The pastel damask wallpaper was dotted with cheerful watercolor paintings. A curving walnut desk didn't dominate the space so much as enhance the office's welcoming air.

The chairs in front of the desk that Will and Maddie sat in were as overstuffed as the chaise lounges at Ashmore House. Once Mrs. Reeve settled into the chair behind her desk, she squared her gaze on him so assertively, Will had the urge to bolt.

"First, Your Grace, let me welcome you to Haven Cove."

"Thank you."

"Though, I suspect Miss Ravenwood has already offered that welcome. You two met soon after you arrived, is that right?"

"Yes," Maddie put in before Will could answer. "We met by chance on the day he arrived."

Will shifted in his chair as Mrs. Reeve glanced between them, gazing first at Maddie and then at him, and finally nodding as if she accepted Maddie's explanation.

"Now, as I understand it, Miss Ravenwood has spoken to you about doing what we can to mitigate the rather ramshackle view of your manor from the hotel."

Ramshackle? Will didn't even particularly like Carnwyth and he was a little offended on the house's behalf.

On the verge of considering how to respond, he noticed Maddie lean forward.

"As we discussed, Mrs. Reeve, the duke and I agreed that Ravenwood Nursery will provide some mature potted sycamores to present a pleasing vista to anyone looking toward Carnwyth from this side of the cove."

"I've also decided to make more substantive repairs to the manor," Will added, "though they won't be finished in time."

Maddie turned her gaze on him, and when Mrs. Reeve took up her pen to scratch out notes, Will offered her a quick smile. She looked surprised but, more importantly, pleased.

"I'm glad to hear you'll revive the manor, Your Grace, but obviously my main concern is what can be done before the royal visit. However, I've invited you here to discuss what happens after the princess arrives too."

"I've agreed to attend the event at the hotel."

"Yes, so Miss Ravenwood informed me." She consulted the sheet of paper she'd been writing on. "Would you be willing to participate in an auction? Or even a contest?"

Maddie inhaled sharply. Will didn't understand the odd sort of contentiousness between the two women, but he was on Maddie's side whatever the conflict.

"I have not broached those subjects with the duke," Maddie said in a clipped tone that told him she was trying to hold her emotions in check.

"Yes." Mrs. Reeve smiled tightly. "That's why I'm broaching them now." She lifted a slip of paper and slid it to the front of her desk. "What do you think of these ideas, Your Grace? Both for a very good cause, of course."

Listed under the word *Auction* were such details as *The highest bidder shall win (1) a dance with the duke, (2) a private luncheon with the duke, or (3) a promenade with the duke on the hotel balcony at dusk.*

Will blinked.

Maddie whispered, "No," in a quiet tone he wasn't even certain he was meant to hear.

He forced himself to read on. The word *Contest* was next to *Auction*, and below that were details of how one would win. *To dance with the Duke of Ashmore, one lady must win at archery? Darts? Croquet? Tennis? Runner-up will sit with him during the previsit dinner. Monies will be collected via tickets to enter the tournament, whatever the chosen method of competition.*

"Mrs. Reeve—" Maddie was sitting so close to the edge of her chair, it was a wonder she was still in it.

"I know it may seem unusual."

"It seems inconsiderate." Maddie glanced at him before continuing. "As a woman, I would not wish to be a prize at an auction or a trophy after a contest."

"But His Grace is not a woman." Mrs. Reeve swept him with an appreciative gaze that held on his shoulders and face as if to confirm her claim. "And this is for charity. Nothing is promised to the winner but a few moments with the duke at a very public event. Surely, no harm would be done to his reputation or theirs."

The obvious solution in Will's mind was that he would agree and somehow ensure that Maddie won whatever contest or auction they decided upon. He'd happily dance or dine or promenade with her.

"I know your father wasn't very charitable," Mrs. Reeve said matter-of-factly. "But you seem quite different, so I must admit to hoping you will be more so."

Will curled his fingers into fists against the arms of his chair. There was nothing subtle about Mrs. Reeve or her desire to leverage him and his presence at the hotel's events to her advantage, but he was willing to be agreeable for Maddie's sake. "I'm happy to be charitable. I agree to whichever you choose." He slid the paper back onto the edge of Mrs. Reeve's desk.

He'd shocked both women. Maddie tapped her fingers nervously against her thigh, and Mrs. Reeve went silent a moment before collecting herself.

"That's excellent news, Your Grace. Thank you." She beamed at Maddie who returned only the slightest of smiles. "Now, that brings us to another matter. Miss Ravenwood tells me that you have decided to return to London before the princess arrives."

"I had." Or at least that had been his plan before attending the festival with Maddie. Considering that they hadn't seen each other in days, he couldn't bear the notion of departing early and costing himself even a moment with her.

The hotel events were to unfold the day before the arrival of the princess, and he'd hoped to be out of Haven Cove just as the royal entourage arrived.

"I take it Miss Ravenwood did not convince you on this point."

"I understand that you have matters to attend to in London," Maddie said to him directly, and Will turned toward her in his chair. Truth was he wanted to lock Mrs. Reeve out of her own office and have a moment with Maddie alone.

"I should return soon." He heard the regret in his voice. It was a truth he had been avoiding.

"But that won't do." Mrs. Reeve's voice had risen. Rather than a persuasive tone, her voice tipped toward irritation. "You're the nobleman of rank in Haven Cove, and meeting with you would likely put the princess at ease."

Will doubted that was true, particularly since he was now the subject of whispers in London, according to the scandal-rag clipping Cora had shown him.

"Even if you can't host a party at the manor, we could offer you space here to arrange a luncheon or a soiree—"

Will found he couldn't remain in his chair. He stood and Mrs. Reeve gasped, no doubt assuming he planned to walk out. But all he really needed was air. A window stood open, and he approached to look out on a view of the hotel's long veranda crowded with guests taking tea in the sun.

"Lady Trenmere is also willing to host Princess Beatrice, and she's invited you to join them."

"Has she?" That was unexpected news, considering that he'd had no contact with the countess since that night when he'd stalked out of her party without even taking proper leave.

"Yes, of course. And I understand Viscount Prestwick is returning from a hunting expedition to visit with the princess too. You're the odd man out, Your Grace."

Will laughed because the woman seemed to have no notion of how right she was.

"We could arrange it so that it only required you to stay a couple of extra days. None of us wish to inconvenience you."

That was precisely what she wished to do, but it was hardly polite to say so.

How did he make them understand that by remaining and meeting the princess, he'd likely make things worse?

Maddie shifted in her chair. He was aware of her every movement, and she was the reason he was biting his tongue and not being as blunt as he might have been with Mrs. Reeve. What he truly wanted to know were Maddie's thoughts, not just about how he might make the royal visit a success but whether *she* wanted him to extend his stay.

"What do you think I should do?"

Mrs. Reeve spoke up immediately. "Well, of course I—"

"Miss Ravenwood? What's your opinion? Should I remain a few days beyond my planned departure and entertain the princess?"

MRS. REEVE GASPED.

Maddie dropped her pen and froze the moment she realized the question was for her.

"I'd like to hear your thoughts on the matter." His voice had gone quieter, deeper.

She'd been thinking of *that* voice, remembering the things he'd said, and most of all the things he'd done, to turn her bones into melted syrup. And she had worked for three days to push thoughts of him aside.

When Will finally turned away from the window, he focused on her as if Mrs. Reeve wasn't in the room.

Maddie swallowed against the tremor that ran through her.

She'd been trying to control her reactions from the moment she'd spotted him across the hotel lobby. But how could she be unaffected when she'd thought of him for days? Hadn't stopped thinking about him since the day he'd arrived in Cornwall? Even as she told herself that she'd been impulsive in Bodmin, that he'd soon leave, that their connection would soon come to an end, the thought of him and the moment they'd shared played over and over in her mind.

What could she say? As a member of the Royal Visit Committee, her role was to support Mrs. Reeve and the success of the visit. But asking him to stay meant he would need to commit to do more. She had no right to demand that of him, even if she wished to. Perhaps there *were* matters in London that required his immediate return. Mrs. Reeve wouldn't care about that, but Maddie cared about him, so what he wanted mattered most.

Maddie took a breath to speak, glanced at Mrs. Reeve, whose eyes were bulging expectantly, and then at Will.

"Would you excuse us briefly, Mrs. Reeve?" Shockingly, he strode toward her and offered his hand.

Maddie was stunned by the moment, but he looked at her with such need and determination that she reached up and took his hand.

Without waiting for Jane's answer, he tucked Maddie's arm in his and walked out of Mrs. Reeve's office down the corridor opposite of the way they'd come, around a corner, and pushed open a door that led to the hotel's broad terrace.

Still holding her arm, he led them to a spot at the edge of the balustrade, away from the guests at tables and on the promenading path.

She was breathless when they stopped, not because of the journey but because of how good it felt to be near him again.

"I don't give a damn what Mrs. Reeve wants," he told her earnestly, "and there are good reasons that I shouldn't meet with the princess." He hesitated before continuing. "One of the princess's entourage, Lord Esquith, is a nobleman who dislikes me immensely. I have a kind of reputation in London and at court for being rather . . ." Emotions shifted in his gaze, and Maddie had the sense his mind was sifting unpleasant memories. ". . . heartless and glum."

"We both know you're neither." Maddie felt from the first night they met that the claims of the noblewoman who'd jilted him cut deep, but she'd doubted them even then. Now she was certain of the sort of man he was.

"It matters to me that *you* believe I'm neither. And I'll stay if you wish me to."

Maddie knew he didn't mean forever. Only a few more days. But, at the moment, that seemed like enough.

"Yes." The word came out on a whisper, but she meant it with her whole heart, so she said it louder. "Yes."

He smiled a disarmingly knowing smile.

"I do like that word on your lips." He brushed the backs of his fingers against her cheek, then a finger along the edge of her mouth.

Maddie couldn't resist reaching for him. The moment she placed her hand against his waistcoat, the strange unease of the last few days melted away. All that time telling herself she shouldn't want to be with him and yet the moment she was, it all felt right.

"What if I kissed you? Right here and now." He watched her eyes, waiting.

Maddie wrapped her fingers around the lapel of his waistcoat and glanced around to see if anyone was watching them. To see if Mrs. Reeve had come to find them. She hadn't as far as Maddie could see, but someone was looking their way. More like scowling their way.

Maddie had seen him at the hotel previously. He was a nobleman who'd been sent on behalf of the princess to ensure that her accommodations, the menu, and the schedule were acceptable.

"Someone is coming this way," Maddie said, wishing they'd chosen another spot to talk.

"Who?" Will turned to look in the direction of her gaze and tensed.

"I suspect it's the same nobleman you just spoke of."

"Esquith." Turning his body, he stood in front of her, blocking her from the other man's view. He reached back for her hand. "Maddie, go back inside. Tell Mrs. Reeve I've agreed to stay."

"Will?" Maddie entwined her fingers with his.

After a moment, he released her and said again with an anxious edge in his tone, "Go, Maddie."

"DAMN YOUR BLOOD, Ashmore." The man had seemed haughty in the Countess of Trenmere's drawing room, but today he looked like a hound who'd scented blood.

"Keep your voice down, Esquith." Will worked to temper his own tone. "I know you like contributing to the gossip mill, but I do not."

The older man gave him the same sneer he'd offered each time they'd been in each other's presence. "Is that so? Seems you've left off destroying your father's reputation for the sole purpose of coming here to create a scandal."

"You have no notion of what you're talking about."

"I've seen you with the girl. Pretty thing. Can't blame you for the impulse. But for as long as I've known you, since you were a pompous little whelp living in your father's shadow, you've needed to be taken down a notch."

Will knew the man had been his father's crony, but the loathing for him personally was more of a mystery.

"Why have you spread rumors, Esquith? Surely, my interest in one woman is nothing to what you witnessed as a friend of my father's. You were quite content to keep his secrets."

The mention of secrets caused Esquith's eyes to widen.

So that was it. Will hadn't wasted time searching out the misdeeds of his father's friends or business associates, but occasionally such information was uncovered during his investigations. Perhaps men like Esquith and Davina's uncle were simply terrified he'd expose them.

Will leaned a bit closer, lowering his voice. "Whatever you did that's causing you so much fear of discovery, you can stop worrying." He straightened again. "I don't know many details of your connection with my father." Though, what he did know was bad enough. "And I have no plan to expose any deeds but his."

Esquith worked his jaw as if he was grinding his teeth, but his gaze suddenly looked more exhausted than hateful. "Have you no sense of honor toward the man?"

"Only as much as he had toward my mother and his title and all the others who trusted him and were betrayed."

Esquith squinted at him but seemed deflated, as if he had lost the fire to fight this battle.

"Stop the rumormongering, Esquith. You want to loathe me or speak poorly of me at your clubs, suit your bloody self. But leave Miss Ravenwood's name off your tongue, or—"

"Or what? You'll spread rumors of your own?"

Will had never spread gossip in his life, but apparently, for men like Esquith, telling the truth when it was something they wished to hide equaled rumormongering. There was a sort of code among the aristocracy that called for protecting their own. In the eyes of men like Esquith and Davina's uncle, Will had breached the code merely by seeking the truth.

He had no desire to be in the business of retribution, but he would go to any lengths to protect those he cared about.

"If you force my hand, yes," he told Esquith, hoping the man was smart enough to heed his warning so he wouldn't have to be the monstrous ogre everyone seemed to think he was.

Chapter Eighteen

*W*ill crouched on the edge of the cliff on the east side of Carnwyth, considering whether the work done matched the drawing he'd made. The masons he'd hired had removed most of the fallen stones and were making swift progress in rebuilding the structure that supported the seaside portion of the house. But Will had made some changes. The elaborate buttress wasn't necessary. He possessed enough knowledge of architecture to know that much. Like everything at Carnwyth, the exterior of the house was overdone.

With the slimmer, less obtrusive supports, there would be room for the tree cover Ravenwood's would provide. According to Bly, the trees to cover the view were due to arrive today, and Will expected—hoped—that Maddie would come to oversee their placement.

Though their attempt to have a moment alone the previous day at the hotel had been interrupted by Esquith, Will felt there was a great deal more to say. He suspected Maddie did too.

And if she didn't come to Carnwyth, he'd visit Ravenwood's. Since coming to Haven Cove, patience no longer seemed a virtue. Though he'd agreed to extend his stay, there were still only a handful of days remaining, and those days would be busy with the hotel events, the flower show, and the presence of a member of the royal family in the town.

"They're here, Your Grace."

Will looked up to see Mrs. Haskell poking her head out of a window on the second floor. It was the room where he often sat to draw.

"Send them around."

"They'll have to trample around the back terrace." If she was worried about the manor house's grounds, there wasn't a great deal to damage. A few low boxwoods and the enormous hedges, but they could skirt around them easily enough.

"I'll meet them and oversee the work." It had been his intention all along, but if Maddie had come, he would undoubtedly be distracted.

"Let's start with four, James."

Will heard Maddie's commanding tone from the other side of the house. He swiped at his dusty trousers, pulled down his sleeves and buttoned the cuffs, then made sure his waistcoat wasn't a crumpled mess.

When he rounded the house, he was surprised to see three young men already removing potted trees from the long-bed cart they'd driven over. The trees were bigger than he expected, and with the progress the workers had made, he wasn't even certain they were still necessary, but he hadn't been sure they'd make such quick headway.

"That way." Maddie pointed, and the men proceeded with their wheelbarrows, but she stopped the moment she spotted him.

"Good afternoon, Miss Ravenwood."

"I hope this is a good time," she said in an affable but professional tone. "Mr. Bly said we should come at one, but judging by the weather, I thought it best to come early."

As had many mornings since he'd arrived, the day dawned with clear blue skies, but dark clouds had begun to appear midmorning.

"It's a fine time." When he drew close to her, one of the young men from the nursery turned his head to watch them, and Will resisted the urge to reach for her as everything in him wanted to.

"I should go assist them and make sure they place the trees correctly." Without another word, she tore off at a smart pace toward her employees.

Her reaction confused him, but he still wanted to see what she thought of the work that had been done to repair the facade. Stretching his long legs to catch up with her, he touched her elbow lightly as he fell into place beside her.

"Something's upset you."

"It's nothing."

Will let her walk ahead, waiting until she could get around the corner and see the work that had been done. When he caught up to her, she was directing James and the others to place the trees as close as possible to the cliff's edge, since it was the most even patch of ground.

"With a storm coming, we should weight the pots." She looked back at Will. "You've started repairs on the wall," she said matter-of-factly. "And it looks like they've removed most of the fallen stones."

"There are a few that remain." Will pointed to a spot farther along the house where they'd stacked some building stones that were unbroken and could be used in the repairs.

In truth, he'd done little to effect the changes but suggest how the wall could be repaired and provide the funds. With her standing near, he felt the need to do more.

Maddie approached one of the young men in her employ and spoke to him, no doubt asking him to retrieve some of the stones. But Will was already striding toward the pile, rolling up the sleeves he'd buttoned just moments before.

"You needn't bring them yourself," she called to him.

"I prefer to not be merely decorative, Miss Ravenwood." He tipped a grin at her over his shoulder and felt, for a moment, the usual reaction when their gazes met.

She gave him a half smile and turned back to direct the placement of the potted trees.

Will had collected and transported two piles before he sensed her following him back to the stones.

"Can I help at all?" The wind was picking up, and the straw hat tied with a ribbon under her chin had broken free. Strands of her red-gold hair fluttered in the wind.

"I think this is the last pile we'll need." Will bent at the knees to collect the carved stones. "I've got them."

"At least let me take one." She reached for the one on top and took it into her arms before he could protest. He knew it was bloody heavy, but she seemed to manage well enough.

"You'll ruin your dress."

"I came here to work, and I want to be more than decorative." At that, she gave him a saucy grin.

Will was glad that the easiness between them had returned, though she resumed her professional mien when she sat the stone in place and directed James to adjust the farthest tree so that it wasn't too close to the cliff's edge.

"That all, then, Miss Ravenwood?" Another of the young men had collected the straps they'd used to secure the trees to the wheelbarrow and gave the darkening sky a glance.

"Thank you, Thomas. The arrangement looks good, and the stones should hold them in place despite the weather. Take all the wheelbarrows but one, and leave me the pony cart. And be sure to secure the greenhouse and cover the new plantings when you get back."

"Yes, miss."

The three young men piled into the long-bed carriage, and James gave one last glance and a nod of his head toward Maddie and Will before they departed.

Will was so pleased that she'd stayed, he was almost afraid to ask her why she had.

As if she'd read his thoughts, she turned back to him and said, "It's time for me to take the roses."

"Will you allow me to help you?"

"I hoped you would."

She was different now that the others had gone, and he understood that she played many roles within the town. How people perceived her mattered to her, despite her claim that she was viewed as a spinster and could do as she wished.

He should have taken more care to protect her reputation.

Maddie retrieved several wooden crates from the back of the small cart. "Would you carry the shovels? I didn't know what tools you might have here."

Will followed her to the rose garden next to the cottage. Most of the area was stony grass or overgrown shrubs, but the area around the rose bushes had been tended.

"You take care of them."

"I thought my mother would wish it." She lifted her hand and pointed to the spades, and he handed one of the shovels to her.

"Tell me about them." Will positioned his shovel near a rose, but Maddie stopped him with her hand on his arm.

"A little farther out. We don't want to damage the roots."

Will began digging gently. Maddie worked more quickly. Her experience and skill were obvious. She had two roses out of the ground and was settling them in burlap inside the crates before he'd gotten his loose.

"You want to know about my parents?" She watched him with her hands folded over the top of her shovel handle.

"Yes. Distract me while I make a mess of this." He could feel the edges of the rose's roots and worked the soil around them as carefully as he could.

"My mother was very attentive. Very interested in what I thought and read and had to say." She paused so long that Will glanced back at her. She gave him a tight smile. "My father was very busy. He worked long hours building up the business. When I think back to my childhood, my mother sweetens every memory, and my father is absent or disapproving."

"What did he disapprove of? You seem a most dutiful daughter."

She surprised him by laughing.

"I wasn't always. Father said I was too fanciful, and I wasn't interested in the things either of them wished me to be interested in."

Will finally got the root ball of the rose loose, reached for a crate, and crouched down to pull the plant out. "Well, that begs the question." He glanced up at her for confirmation he was proceeding correctly.

Maddie nodded but let him unearth the rose on his own.

"What were you interested in?"

She nudged her chin toward the rose in his hands. "I dreamed of traveling to see gardens around the world. Even back then, it was as I said on the train: flowers and designing gardens. Father didn't mind that part, but he wanted me to appreciate trees and ground cover and all the practical plants Ravenwood's tended to sell. And Mama would have preferred that I showed more interest in ladylike accomplishments. Dresses and dancing. At one point, I think Lady Trenmere convinced her I could be a debutante."

Will stood and felt quite accomplished once he'd secured the final rosebush in its crate. "You didn't want to be a debutante?"

"I didn't think I'd be very good at it."

After dusting off his hands, Will took the shovel from Maddie's hands. "You would have taken London by storm."

She laughed again, a deep, throaty sound that he didn't hear from her nearly often enough. "I love to dance but don't do it well, I have no sense of fashion, and I prefer digging in a garden or designing one more than almost anything else."

"So you decided to run the nursery."

"It wasn't so much a decision as a necessity. Something that I felt I must do."

"I know." Will swallowed hard. "I understand that feeling."

The sky let out a distant rumble above them, and a moment later the air crackled and lightning lit the cloud-strewn sky.

"We should get inside." Maddie rushed toward the cart and rather than worry over the roses, as he expected, she began removing the harness on the single horse. "Mabel doesn't like storms. Can we put her in the stable?"

"Of course." She began leading the horse up the drive of Carnwyth, but Will found himself worried about the roses they'd carefully pulled from the ground.

"Will they be all right?"

"Lift the tarp over the top, and they should be fine. They're much hardier than they look."

Will did as she asked, pulling the tarp tight, edge to edge across the bed of the cart. Then he ran to catch up to Maddie. Raindrops began to fall in a gentle shower at first but soon turned into a downpour.

Maddie had already tied the mare to a post in the stable when he reached her.

"Shall we run for it?" Will grinned at her and shrugged out of his linen suit coat, lifting it over his head and stretching the fabric out to urge her closer.

Maddie looked up at the coat, returned his smile, and then stepped out into the stable yard. "I'm not afraid of a little rain, Your Grace."

Will lowered his coat and stepped into the rain next to her. "Nor I, Miss Ravenwood." He was so happy to have her close to him that for a moment he stood still, watching her.

Maddie tipped her face up to the sky, closed her eyes, and her mouth curved in a soft smile as if she was enjoying the warm cascade of a soothing shower rather than the chilled pellets of a fierce Cornwall storm.

Her hat had fallen back and several of her hairpins had come loose. Long strands of wet auburn waves clung to her shoulders and neck.

Will couldn't resist sweeping a strand aside and letting his hand linger on the lovely slope of her neck. She tipped her head and looked at him, her eyes impossibly bright.

Mercy, how he adored this woman. There was no denying the power of his feelings for her. When she was near, his heart was fuller. His life was fuller.

Their breaths joined in cloudy puffs between them. Will's teeth began to chatter.

"Let's go inside and get warm." He reached for her hand, and Maddie twined her fingers with his. "Quickly?"

She chuckled and nodded, and Will squeezed her hand. They both broke into a dash across the swatch of grass between the stables and the front door of Carnwyth. Before they could reach for the latch, the door swung open.

"My goodness, you're both drenched as bilge rats." Mrs. Haskell headed down the hall quickly and returned with two towels. "I'll have some tea brought to your room right away. I've already asked Kate to lay a fire."

"Send more towels up too." Will laid a hand on the small of Maddie's back, and she looked at him with an emotion he couldn't name. But he knew for certain what he was feeling. He needed her—time with her—more than anything.

MADDIE FOLLOWED WILL up the stairs and decided this was where she needed to be. Over the past few days, she'd almost convinced herself that his presence in Haven Cove and her life was a distraction she didn't need. Despite how much she enjoyed his company. Despite how she'd come to care about him. Despite how much the thought of his departure disturbed her.

That's what she couldn't abide. No matter how she thought about him or felt about him, there would come a day when he would leave Haven Cove, and she didn't know if she could get back to the life she'd had before meeting him and not feel that something essential was missing.

Would he miss her after he left? She had no real notion of what his life in London was like. Lots of parties like those at Lady Trenmere's, perhaps. An estate to manage. Eastwick, he'd called it. He'd mentioned his sisters, but what else filled his days? What did he wish filled his days?

"What would you have been if you hadn't been destined for a dukedom?" Maddie asked as soon as they entered a large room with a four-post bed against one wall and red and gold wallpaper dotted with chips of mirror.

A fresh fire crackled in the grate, and Maddie drew close and held out her hands while she waited for his answer.

He'd stopped in his tracks and spun to face her the minute the question was out. But then he said nothing while he freed the knot of his tie before dragging the soaked fabric from his neck. "I always knew I would inherit the title one day. I didn't let myself think of other possibilities."

"Never?" Maddie had worked the towel Mrs. Haskell had provided downstairs over her hair, and the fabric was quickly becoming as wet as her dress. "What would you have wished to do if you hadn't inherited the dukedom?"

Will stared a moment at her rain-soaked gown and strode to a huge carved wardrobe hugging one wall of the room. He pulled a blue velvet robe out and handed it to her. Then he yanked the coverlet from the bed.

"If you move to the corner, I'll hold this up and you can get out of those wet clothes."

It seemed an elaborate effort of propriety when he'd already touched her in the most intimate of ways.

"Couldn't you just turn around?"

The muscles in his neck shifted and his jaw tensed as he contemplated the question while watching her with a look full of need and uncertainty. "Of course."

He turned and Maddie made quick work of unbuttoning her bodice and slipping the hooks of her skirt. The wet fabric was heavy and slid to her ankles immediately, followed by her petticoat. She peeled off her bodice, then unfastened the hooks on her corset.

The room was quiet but for the sparking fire, and she was intensely aware of her breathing. And his.

"Architecture," he said, though his voice had suddenly gone raspy and low.

When she slipped the last hook on her corset and let it fall to the floor, his breath hitched. Could he identify the pieces of clothing by their sounds as they struck the carpet?

"So your skill at drawing is more than a pastime. Did you study the subject?"

"I did for a while."

Even her stockings were wet, so she bent and removed her boots, slid out of her drawers, and stripped off each stocking. When she stood, Will inhaled sharply. That's when she noticed the chip of mirror on the opposite wall, and the reflection of his gaze as he watched her.

"How much did you see?"

Tipping his head to the side, he didn't turn around but said, "I tried not to look."

"I'm not sure I would have done the same." In the forest in Bodmin, she'd wanted to touch his bare skin the way he'd stroked hers. "Help me into this robe."

He turned, lifted the robe, and crossed the inches between them. Maddie noticed he was still trying to avert his eyes. She wore only her chemise now. Though her mostly bare legs were beginning to warm from her nearness to the fire, the wet fabric of the chemise still clung to her breasts.

"You're being terribly proper," Maddie whispered as he stretched the robe out for her to step into.

"I promised myself I would be."

"After the forest?" Maddie slowly slipped the knot holding her chemise in place, waiting for him to glance her way.

"Yes." He glanced at her but then immediately turned his head again. "I struggled with that decision. I'm struggling now."

"I decided something too."

"Did you?" He met her gaze, seeming to forget his determination to avert his eyes.

"I decided to focus on work and preparations for the visit. I was determined to not be distracted."

Maddie reached out and touched her fingers to the edge of his jaw to keep him from turning his head again, to keep him looking into her eyes. "But now I've made another decision."

"Tell me."

"Right now, this is where I want to be." With a tug on the ruched neck of her chemise, Maddie loosened the garment enough for it to slip from her shoulders. The soft fabric skimmed over her breasts, her belly, her hips, and then joined the rest of her clothing at their feet.

Resisting the urge to cover herself, she stood still, waiting for him to see her, wanting him to. Because this might be the one night they'd ever have together like this, and she didn't want to withhold anything. No worries about propriety or what came next. Just this moment between them.

Will stepped closer and reached for her. One hand came up to caress her cheek, and he pressed another to the curve of her waist. He stroked his fingers across the edge of her jaw, down her neck, then swept a fall of hair over her shoulder. "How utterly gorgeous you are," he murmured as he pulled her closer.

Maddie began working the buttons of his shirt, but she gasped when his fingers traced the curve of her breast before she filled his palm. His hands were deliciously warm, and Maddie arched into his touch.

When he bent to brush his lips against hers, eagerness made her body tremble.

But instead of kissing her, he whispered against her lips. "I'm glad you've decided this is where you want to be because I don't want to let you go."

Chapter Nineteen

*W*ill couldn't let her go. It was the problem that had been before him since the day he'd met her. Even at that moment in Lady Trenmere's conservatory when she'd been nothing more than a pretty stranger, her claim that she might never return to London had unsettled him.

He'd never considered himself a man who luck favored, but perhaps he was.

With Maddie in his arms, he was.

She rose on her tiptoes to kiss him, and he pulled her into his arms and got lost in the way her kisses set his blood aflame. When she shivered, he released her, remembering his clothes were still damp and she was gloriously bare.

He wrapped the velvet robe around her shoulders, but it almost slid to the floor when she reached up to work the buttons on his shirt.

"Now you're the one who should get out of your wet clothes." Her gaze had turned hungry and bold, and he loved letting her take control.

"There's only one robe," he said before taking her lips for another taste.

"Hmm. We'll have to devise some means of keeping warm. Any suggestions?"

"A few, actually."

She laughed, and Will held her close because the sound of her amusement lightened something in him. He couldn't imagine a future without Maddie and her laughter as part of his days.

"What is it?"

The sentimental turn of his thoughts must have shown on his face. She reached up and laid her palm against his cheek.

Before he could answer, someone knocked on the door.

"Tea, Your Grace."

Will buttoned his shirt halfway and waited until Maddie had cinched the belt of the robe and strode to the opposite side of the room near the fire.

Kate bustled in with an enormous tray with a teapot, a tureen of what he guessed was soup, and a loaf of bread that was still warm enough to scent the air. "Mrs. Haskell thought you might be hungry."

Behind her another maid entered, carrying towels and what looked like a dress. "For the young lady," she said quietly before offering a curtsy and leaving the room.

"Anything else you'll be needing, Your Grace?" Kate didn't blink an eye at Will's partial undress or Maddie standing in a robe that hung too long at her arms and pooled at her feet.

"That will be all, Kate."

She smiled, nodded, and turned for the door.

"Oh, I almost forgot. I drew a hot bath for you, miss." With that, she left the room and pulled the door shut behind her.

"A hot bath," Maddie said in an almost longing tone.

Will smiled and took up the ties of the robe and reeled her in closer. "For all its oddities, Carnwyth was outfitted with a few of the latest amenities." Wrapping an arm around her shoulders, he led her to the door in the guest bedchamber that connected to an enormous dressing room. The entire space was tiled in peacock blue, and it had been equipped with both an elaborate shower that shot water out of a metal structure down the length of one's body and a ceramic tub large enough for several bathers to get into the water at once.

Thanks to Kate's forethought, the heat of the tub water had turned the room into a steamy, soothing haven.

"Goodness," Maddie breathed. "This is quite a room. And that tub is extraordinary."

Will went to test the water with his fingers. Very warm but not scalding. He lifted a hand, urging Maddie closer.

"I'll help you in." He stood and tugged at the ties of her robe, and the sight of her beautiful curves and freckled skin sent a shot of lust through him.

She braced a hand on his arm and stepped into the tub. As she settled in, her long hair spread out around her, undulating in the water, and Will felt as if he'd interrupted a bathing goddess.

"Heaven," she whispered, closing her eyes as she swept her hands through the water.

It was. Watching her blissfully ensconced in the steaming water, the lush swell of her breasts peeking above the waterline, and her long legs moving beneath, Will once again felt that rush of some twist of fate favoring him with this unexpected bliss. He wasn't certain he deserved it, but he was damn well determined to savor it.

Maddie opened her eyes, and the blue of them seemed darker. "Come join me."

His very own siren.

She pointed at him. "But you'll have to take all of that off."

Unlike earlier when he'd tried—and failed—to avert his gaze while she undressed, Maddie seemed determined to enjoy every moment. She scooted back in the tub, sunk a bit lower, and rested her back against the ceramic.

Will worked the buttons and removed his shirt and waistcoat quickly while toeing off his boots. When he reached for the fastening of his trousers, she sunk her teeth into her lower lip. He stilled, not because he had any hesitation, but because he wanted to indulge her.

Slowly, purposefully, he loosened the fastenings of his trousers and then slid them down his body along with his drawers. He was hard and aching, and when he straightened, Maddie swept her gaze down his legs and then fixed her focus on his sex.

The longer she looked with a deliciously pleased expression on her face, the more his patience waned.

"Is all to your liking, Miss Ravenwood?"

"Very much so, Your Grace."

Somehow, from her sweet lips, in the husky voice of desire, the honorific shot a shiver of anticipation down his spine.

Will approached the edge of the bathtub in two long strides, and he stepped in, facing Maddie, his legs between hers. The tub was so long and wide, he could seat himself opposite or next to her and not touch her at all. But he needed to touch her, and she seemed eager for him to. She slid her legs along his, and then sat up to rest on her knees between his legs.

He reached for her, but she was busy looking around the edge of the tub. She found a bar of soap and began building a lather on her arms and neck. Then she shocked him by lifting his hand, placing a bar in his palm, and pulling his hand toward her.

Will ran his hand over her breast, feeling the peak of her nipple against his palm. He cupped water to rinse away the soap and drew Maddie closer. She came to him, allowing him to lift her, until her thighs were on either side of his. Their bodies slid together, his length stroking at her center. She gasped and adjusted her body so that she could reach between them, her fingers seeking him.

He groaned at the feel of her hand around his cock, but he let her explore. She stroked him tentatively, all the while watching his eyes as if gauging his reaction.

"Do you like this?"

Will laughed and stroked his hands up the supple lines of her back. "More than I can express. But if you don't stop . . ."

"I just needed to touch you." She released him and braced her hands on his shoulders. "But now I want to feel you," she whispered. Rising on her knees, she positioned herself above him. Water sluiced down her breasts and belly, and Will couldn't resist taking one sweet, taut nipple into his mouth.

Maddie gasped, and he dipped his hand under the water to trace his fingers up to the apex of her thighs, even as he teased against her with his cock. He yearned to arch up into her, to claim her and pleasure her as he had longed to for so long. But he waited, determined to let her choose the pace of this moment.

"I want you," she whispered against his lips as she lowered her body and took his length.

"And I need you," Will told her before taking her mouth.

She moved against him tentatively, letting out little gasps and mewls of pleasure. Will fought the urge to lose control and focused instead on watching her. She closed her eyes as she built a rhythm and twined her hands around his neck, stroked at his hair, and clutched his shoulders as her pleasure built.

"Will," she said on a breathy whisper. She gazed

at him steadily, and the look of trust and desire unraveled his last bit of self-control.

Under the water, he curved a hand around her backside and arched up so that he could get closer to her. Being with her, their bodies joined, their breathing racing in sync, was as right as he'd ever felt.

"Yes," she whispered as he lifted his hips to arch into her again and again. She tipped her head back, and he kissed her neck, nipping at her skin. A moment later, she cried out, and her body tensed and shuddered with her release.

Will nestled his face against her shoulder, licking at her skin, kissing another trail along her neck. The water had grown colder, but he didn't want the moment to end.

But neither did he want her shivering.

"We should get out."

"Mmm." The little murmur of agreement came with the stroke of her fingers down his back. "And go to bed?"

"If you like."

"Not to sleep," she said, her gaze bold.

"Not to sleep, sweetheart. At least not for a while."

At her words and the hunger in her eyes, he was hard and aching for her again. He loved her boldness, loved her determination. He loved *her*, and the realization didn't come as a revelation but settled inside him like a truth that had been there all along.

Will stood and Maddie came with him. After

they were out of the tub, she offered him the robe, but he wrapped it around her again and led her to the bedroom. There was a step up to the four-post bed and she slid the robe off as she stepped up.

Her comfort with his gaze on her excited him as much as the sight of her. She crawled onto the bed and then turned, resting into the coverlet, and then lifting a hand to draw him closer.

Will needed no encouragement. He was on the bed, arching over her body, nestling his hips between hers, and she was wet and ready for him.

"Maddie." He breathed her name, then took her mouth.

She was sweet, soft, and everything he could ever want. Just her. Just this closeness, tasting her body, watching her find her pleasure day after day, night after night. What more could he ever need?

Chapter Twenty

Will woke as morning edged toward noon and found Maddie gone. The memories of their lovemaking played in his mind, but her absence left an aching hollowness inside him. Memories weren't enough. He wanted her next to him when he woke, and not just today.

There had to be a way. Could he return to visit Cornwall soon? Or could Maddie find the time to visit London? Even as his mind sifted possibilities, none of them truly brought any satisfaction. Stolen moments with her wouldn't be enough. He hated the prospect of parting from her at all.

He wanted her for his own, but asking her to sacrifice the life she'd built felt wrong. Selfish. And he'd vowed never to be a man who allowed his selfish desires to cause others pain, as his father had.

A note he found on his bedside table confirmed that she had a busy day ahead. The words had been written hastily in his sketchbook and told him that she needed to go home, dress, and then head to the hotel. The celebratory event would be this evening, and tomorrow the princess would finally arrive.

Will glanced at the clock, counting the hours until he could see her again.

After he dressed and went downstairs, Mrs. Haskell caught him heading to the dining room.

"Your Grace, a messenger came this morning. A telegram for you was received at the train station." She anxiously waved the slip of paper in the air in front of him. "From your sister, I believe."

Will suspected what its contents would be but waited patiently for the housekeeper to calm herself enough to hand him the telegram.

He skimmed the brief message, and not a single word came as a surprise.

Even if Esquith had taken his threat seriously and stopped spreading rumors all the way back to London, the city's gossip mill had done its worst, and what started in a scandal rag had no doubt made its way through salons and dinner parties and ballrooms.

UNPLEASANT RUMORS ABOUT YOU AND MR CONTINUE TO SPREAD PLEASE RETURN TO LONDON FORTHWITH —CORA

"Shall we prepare your traveling trunk, Your Grace?" The housekeeper twisted her hands nervously. She'd clearly read the contents of the message too.

"Prepare the trunk, but you needn't make arrangements for a carriage to the station immediately. I've agreed to attend the hotel event tonight, and I intend to keep that promise."

"Very good." She nodded, but her wrinkled brow

remained furrowed with concern. "What about the flower show?"

Will stared at her as his chest tightened with a messy wave of emotions. Guilt for worry he'd caused his sisters. Concern for Maddie and how she'd fare at the event that meant so much to her. And, most of all, yearning to turn back the clock and have her in his arms.

"I'll stay for the flower show." He hadn't thought the decision through, and he knew Cora would likely resent him for delaying his return by another day, but he wanted to be there for Maddie. Even if she hadn't asked him to be.

"So departing in two days?"

Dread seeped into his bones. Two days wouldn't be enough, and he couldn't even fathom how he'd say goodbye to Maddie, but he offered Mrs. Haskell one firm nod. If Cora was in distress and had taken the time to send a telegram, the underlying implication was that Esquith's rumormongering might harm Daisy or cast a shadow over her coming wedding. Her nuptials and happiness had been his and Cora's singular focus for months.

But he worried for Maddie too. Esquith would leave Haven Cove soon, but would his whispers cause her lasting damage?

"We've made progress on the ballroom, Your Grace. Would you like to see?"

Will's attention snapped back to the here and now as he followed the housekeeper down the hall to the ballroom.

"You and the staff have been busy." The room had been transformed, at least in terms of cleanliness, but clutter too.

"The carpenter you hired too."

"Where did everything go?" The towering pile of broken furniture had dwindled down to a red damask settee and an overstuffed chair.

"Some of it has been repaired and placed back where it started. Other pieces are with the carpenter so he can fix them in his workshop."

"It looks like a ballroom again." Will didn't have any urge to attend a ball or host one, but he could imagine dancing with Maddie here. Just the two of them. Hadn't she said she liked dancing?

"Aye, it does." Mrs. Haskell sounded almost wistful, as if she was recalling the space with the sconces lit and full of dancing couples. "But there's more to show you."

She proceeded toward the far-left corner, the spot where they'd discovered the kittens and the hole in the floor. Will knelt to examine the wood. He'd be hard-pressed to find the spot where the hole had been. The repair to the flooring and wall were that seamless.

"I can't believe the repair happened so quickly."

"Sometimes, once change has begun, the transformation comes quickly."

There was no indication the housekeeper meant the words to have some deeper double meaning, but Will couldn't help but apply them to himself. Good grief, the man who'd arrived in Cornwall a dozen days ago wouldn't recognize the man who'd paid to repair his father's Cornish hideaway and spent all his days thinking of one overly busy, flame-haired businesswoman.

Will stood and dusted off his trousers. "Thank you, and convey my thanks to Mr. Bly too for overseeing these repairs. I should begin preparing for the festivities at the hotel this evening."

"Going early, are you?"

"I'd hoped to, yes."

The housekeeper smiled knowingly and reached into the pocket of her apron. "Mitchum found these in the stable yard. I'm guessing they might be Miss Ravenwood's."

She raised her hand, Will did the same, and she deposited a handful of silver hairpins in his palm. The wry smile on her face he expected, but not the flash of pink on her cheeks.

"Are you blushing, Mrs. Haskell? After years of living here while my father held raucous parties?"

Will felt no self-reproach for what he and Maddie had shared. Every moment with her had become precious, and he would never regret them. And he did trust the staff of Carnwyth to be reasonably discreet, but inside him there was still a flare of doubt and concern for Maddie's reputation. Though the townspeople of Haven Cove accepted her independence as a businesswoman, he was less sure they'd allow her other sorts of freedoms without casting judgment or aspersions.

"I blushed quite a bit then too," Mrs. Haskell

finally admitted. "If I may speak freely, Your Grace, your father was not an easy master. I was quite pleased when you came. We'd heard you were quite different." She smiled, but her words unsettled him.

"I am different, Mrs. Haskell. I'm not my father."

"Of course you're not, sir. I meant no offense." The look she gave him was truly contrite. "None of us think you're like him."

Will wasn't certain if that referred to Carnwyth's staff or the entire town. But all of them were watchful, and nothing happened in Haven Cove, it seemed, without everyone knowing it.

"I suppose it's pointless to ask that the staff not spread gossip about Miss Ravenwood's visit." He didn't expect to speak so bluntly about the topic with his housekeeper, but he saw no reason to prevaricate with a woman who'd seen so much during her time at Carnwyth.

"I give you my word that I understand discretion, Your Grace. But the young staff . . ."

"Of course." Perhaps privacy in such a small town was a futile hope. Maddie had reminded him of how quickly news spread on that first night he'd arrived.

"I assure you, Your Grace, Miss Ravenwood is well-loved in Haven Cove."

She would be. Was there any cause she wouldn't join or any effort she wouldn't take upon herself to accomplish?

Before heading upstairs to wash and dress, Will

asked Mrs. Haskell to find something he might take as a contribution for the auction at the hotel.

"The late duke hoarded quite famous brandy, Your Grace. Will that do?"

"That will do nicely."

He'd almost reached the top step, when he heard her footsteps quickly receding down the hall and then, oddly, returning to the bottom of the stairs.

"Speaking of offerings, Your Grace, I thought you might wish to see this and consider it for Miss Ravenwood." She tipped her head to indicate a painting on the wall near the staircase. "The same artist who left the drawing supplies you've found quite useful sketched and painted it during a visit to Carnwyth."

She hefted the painting up for his perusal. Its colorful palette was accented by a pretty gilded frame. And the subject was the small cottage where Maddie had grown up and Carnwyth's grounds from a high vantage point, as if the artist had simply glanced out his guest chamber window and re-created what he saw in lighter, looser brushstrokes. Among those strokes was a woman with auburn hair occupied with pruning a rose bush.

"It's Mrs. Ravenwood, Your Grace."

Will couldn't resist a smile. "Thank you, Mrs. Haskell."

"Miss Ravenwood, have you seen the bunting?"

"The bunting?" Maddie held a crate full of small

handmade candles that were to be distributed at each table. The local candlemaker had created them especially for the event, and Mrs. Reeve didn't trust them to the few dining-room staff members who were helping arrange the room for the evening's meal.

"It's white and gold. We were supposed to have nearly forty feet of it delivered for the evening's auction."

"I can help look for it as soon as I place these candles, Mrs. Pendenning."

"Will you have time? Mrs. Reeve told me you're to assist her with the seating plan. Apparently, the hotel staff has made a muddle of it."

Maddie walked a few steps, rested the edge of the crate she'd been carrying on a table, and let out a little sigh of relief.

"I'll let you finish this. Come find me in the gold room, won't you?"

"I will. I promise." Maddie blew a wayward curl off her face and picked up the crate again. And then stilled again for a moment. Through the long windows looking out toward the balcony, she watched the sea.

Her body ached in new ways, and all day the world around her had looked a little different. She was always so busy rushing from one thing to the next, she rarely savored moments. But she'd let herself savor the hours with Will last night. Making love in that ostentatious bathtub, then the more ostentatious bed, and again in the early-morning hours when the bed had become familiar and warm with the heat of their entwined bodies.

Leaving him a few hours later had been one of the hardest things she'd ever done.

But there'd been no other option. She'd promised to come to the hotel early and help with all the preparations. She'd been doing so for hours, but the thought of him was constantly there in her mind. She found herself smiling, lost in memories of their lovemaking. More than once, Mrs. Reeve or one of the other committees had asked her what was so amusing.

"Miss Ravenwood!" The shout came from across the long hotel dining room and nearly made Maddie tip all the glassware off the table.

"I'm so glad I found you." Miss Dixon worked a fan aggressively against her face but still looked overheated. "I have something rather delicate to ask." She looked either way as if to see if they could be overheard, though they were quite clearly alone in the room but for a staff member shining silverware on a cart near the door.

"Well, as you said, you found me. How can I help?"

"It's not help I need. It's your permission."

Maddie carried a candle to the next table and cast a bemused grin over her shoulder at the older woman who touted herself as Haven Cove's most content spinster. "What ever do you need my permission for?"

Miss Dixon stepped closer, gulped, and whispered

from behind her fan, "I plan to win the auction for the duke."

A flare of irritation made Maddie clench her hands into fists. Jealousy, potent and unbidden, made her instantly irked with Miss Dixon. "Do you, indeed? Others will be bidding too. You might be outbid."

Miss Dixon's chin wobbled, and she whispered, "Do you plan to win him?"

Maddie ignored the implication behind the question. "Mrs. Reeve encouraged us to let others donate, and I can't spare the funds anyway. I've already made my donations in time devoted to the committee."

"But you don't wish anyone to win him, do you?"

Maddie felt little beads of perspiration at her nape, and she knew her cheeks were flaming despite her attempt to stem the silly moment of jealousy. "I don't know why I would have any say in the matter."

"Don't you, my dear?" Miss Dixon laid a hand on Maddie's shoulder and then instantly let her go as if uncertain whether Maddie would allow the intimacy. "It's been quite obvious since he arrived in town that there is a . . ." Her gaze softened. "A tenderness between you. Affection."

Maddie found she couldn't meet the woman's gaze. The jealous anger of a moment ago was replaced with a rush of something else. Tears threatened to well in her eyes, and she drew in a sharp breath to collect herself. Goodness, what an emotional storm she was today.

"There is affection," she finally admitted. "But our friendship"—it was far more but she didn't know what to name it—"will soon come to an end when he returns to London in a few days."

"London isn't so terribly far."

"Perhaps not in miles. But it's a world away. When I visited Lady Trenmere in London, I realized how different all of it is." Maddie smiled because she'd had this argument with herself many times. Yes, she could visit the city again. The thought of seeing more of London and of Will thrilled her. But what of when they parted again? What would they be? Lovers? He needed to choose a duchess and marry, and all her responsibilities were here. People relied on her.

"I haven't been in many years, but I could see you fitting in quite well."

"That's kind to say, Miss Dixon." Maddie chided herself for overreacting a moment before. "Win the auction for the duke with my blessing."

Miss Dixon let out a surprisingly girlish giggle. "Thank you, my dear."

After she'd gone, Maddie continued placing the decorated candles on each table. As she was placing the last few, one of the hotel staff members approached.

"Mrs. Pendenning sent me, miss. She says you're needed in the gold room."

Mrs. Pendenning had possibly less patience than Maddie, and that was saying a great deal.

Five minutes later, she started on her way after

taking a last look at the dining room. Maddie glanced at the clock in the lobby as she passed through. Soon, she'd have to take time to go to Mrs. Reeve's office and change her dress before the events got underway. The day dress she'd thrown on after rushing home to wash and dress quickly this morning was far too frumpy to wear to the dinner and dance.

Halfway across the lobby, her breath tangled in her throat, and her heart leaped in her chest.

Will had arrived early. He looked as he had that first night they'd met. Dressed in formal black and white, with a crisp snowy tie tucked under his throat and a bright white waistcoat hugging his broad chest. Now he wasn't merely a perfect statue of a man with broad, view-blocking shoulders, he was a man she cared for. Yes, with tenderness and affection as Miss Dixon had said. But it was more. Somewhere between stumbling out from behind a potted palm and boating with him in the cove, she had fallen in love.

The sight of him made her smile, and it also made her mouth water. *Mine*, her heart seemed to shout, whether it was true or made any sense at all.

He turned his head to scan the lobby, and she knew he was searching for her.

How lovely it would be to steal away with him for a few moments, but until this night was over, there would be no free moments.

Finally, he spotted her, and such pleasure filled his gaze that Maddie found herself striding toward him. He started toward her too, and they met near the center of the lobby. They joined hands wordlessly, and Maddie watched his gaze flicker to her lips.

I want to kiss you too.

"Miss Ravenwood."

Maddie closed her eyes and let go of Will's hand.

"Did the hotel girl not come to fetch you?"

Maddie turned to face Mrs. Pendenning. "I was just on my way."

"But you got . . . distracted, as I see." Mrs. Pendenning offered Will a tight smile. "Welcome, Your Grace. You're quite early."

"Yes," he said with a half smile. "I thought I might be able to help."

Mrs. Pendenning took him in from his polished boots to the wild waves of his overlong hair. "Perhaps you could assist us with the bunting."

He looked at Maddie, searching her gaze, and she gave him the minutest of nods and tried to signal *please* with her eyes. She didn't mind helping with preparations in any way she might be needed, but spending time alone being barked at by Mrs. Pendenning held no appeal.

"Well, come along," Mrs. Pendenning told them. "We don't have much time before guests begin arriving."

Chapter Twenty-One

*W*ill hoped to never see a length of bunting again in his life.

An hour after arriving at the hotel, he was still tangled in the stuff, or rather he and Maddie were doing their best to untangle and repair the twisted mess that someone had left the bunting in days before. The flags along the strip of bunting were fragile, so untangling them had to be undertaken with care.

When Maddie tried to cover a yawn and gripped the back of her neck, he was ready to abandon the whole thing. He wanted to soothe away those knots in her neck. They could do without the bloody bunting for the night.

Mrs. Pendenning had her back turned, so he reached over to massage Maddie's nape.

She let out a little moan of pleasure, then covered her mouth. But like some unexpected blessing, the Pendenning woman had left the room.

"Do you think we'll ever get to the end?" she asked him playfully.

"God, I hope so, because I'm on the verge of tossing the whole of it into the sea."

"You did agree to help." She laughed and her eyes danced with amusement. The sound of her laughter would always undo him a little.

"I only agreed in order to spend time with you."

"And you have."

"Alone."

"We're alone now." She glanced at the door where Mrs. Pendenning had exited and scooted her chair closer to his.

Will dropped the strand of bunting in his hands and reached for Maddie. With one hand wrapped around her waist and another at the curve of her neck, he kissed her. Then again. When she opened her lips to deepen the kiss, Will felt himself tipping over the edge. He wanted her. Would he ever stop wanting her?

At the sound of footsteps, they stilled.

A few moments later, Mrs. Pendenning entered through the far doorway.

He immediately released Maddie, and they leaned away from each other.

"I need to change my dress," Maddie told the older woman when she came to check on their progress. "There's only a little bit more bunting to untangle."

Mrs. Pendenning seemed on the verge of protesting, but Maddie stood with a regal kind of poise and laid down the line of flags she'd been working to untangle.

"Don't stay here much longer," she whispered to him. "If she's determined to use this bunting, she can finish it herself."

Will smiled. "Quite right, Miss Ravenwood."

"I'll see you at the auction before dinner." Without waiting for his reply, she swept across the room and past Mrs. Pendenning.

"Might you take over, Mrs. Pendenning?" He stood and gestured toward the small length that hadn't yet been straightened and was strung out on the floor.

"Yes, Your Grace." She tried for a disappointed look, but he didn't give a damn what the older woman thought of him. Only that she didn't think poorly of Maddie.

But he was still happy to escape the woman and the maddening task. He inquired of a busboy where he might find Mrs. Reeve and was led to the same grand room he'd been shown a few days before. The space was different now. Half had been dotted with tables set elegantly for dining, and parquet flooring was revealed in the other half, obviously for dancing later in the evening.

He'd never felt more like a man transformed than at that moment, when he actually had a flash of yearning to take a turn on the dance floor with Maddie. He'd managed to avoid dancing despite attending numerous balls since inheriting his father's title. Maddie had said she wasn't good at dancing, and Will knew he was almost certainly worse. But he didn't care. He just wanted to have Maddie in his arms again.

"Your Grace, you're here. Excellent." Mrs. Reeve swept toward him in a stunning silver gown. "There is the dais where you'll stand while we perform the auction announcement. We've had so many donations. You're quite the draw." Unlike the rather staid, sharp-edged businesswoman he'd met a few days before, Mrs. Reeve was practically giddy.

She led him toward a little platform that had been laid at the front of the tables. Though the event wasn't set to begin for another half an hour, curious ladies and gentlemen were peeking in or milling about the room as if scouting for the best seats.

"Is it dinner or dancing with whoever wins me?" Will asked with as much equanimity as he could manage. All he wanted was to find Maddie, but he'd agreed to this, and he'd keep his word.

"We decided on both, if you don't mind, Your Grace."

Will nodded and cast his gaze around the room, but he didn't see Maddie.

After what seemed an age of Mrs. Reeve advising him on what to say, where to sit, who to speak with, and which dance he would be dancing with the evening's winner, the attendees began streaming into the room and taking seats at the tables.

Will scanned the room for the one person he most wished to see. His heart knocked against his ribs when he spotted her. Pride rushed through him. As if she was his, and in his heart, she was.

Maddie wore a yellow gown and peach-hued roses in her hair. She looked exquisite, not just because of the gown but in the way she held herself, that poise and grace that made her stand out despite the crowded room. She smiled at him, and he loved that she didn't try to hide her happiness at seeing him.

Long moments passed while they watched each other. Mrs. Reeve was still speaking to him, finishing her instructions about how the night would proceed, and Will tried to focus. Maddie was swarmed by other ladies, and when he glanced at Mrs. Reeve to nod at something she said, he lost sight of Maddie.

"Once again, Your Grace, you'll sit just there with whoever wins you in the auction." The hotelier pointed to a table near the dais, close enough to the windows for a striking view of the sea rolling under a sky just turning a dusky gold. Another woman rushed and passed a note to her, and Will took the opportunity to step away.

He was still trying for a glimpse of Maddie when Mrs. Reeve stepped up onto the dais and called for the guests to quiet and give her their attention.

"If you'll join me, Your Grace," she said to him quietly.

When he joined her, she gestured toward him as if he was a prize pony and said in an overloud voice, "The Duke of Ashmore joins us this evening, and he will be joining one of you for dinner and a dance soon."

That drew a small round of applause and a few titters of laughter from ladies among the guests. As he looked toward one giggling woman, a flash of yellow drew his attention to Maddie. Just finding her in the crowd sent warm relief washing over him.

"Thank you to all who donated," Mrs. Reeve

said to the crowd. "Your donations will be given to a charity of the princess's choosing in honor of her visit and will hopefully remind her of Haven Cove in years to come."

After a dramatic pause and a glance Will's way, she unfolded the note in her hands.

"The Duke of Ashmore raised the most of all our auctioned items for a total of one hundred and forty-five pounds."

A whoop and cheer went up. Will never imagined the prospect of spending time in his company would result in such charitable fervor after all of London's aristocrats had decided he was odious and avoided him assiduously. His acceptance in this little seaside town, by those who knew of his family and those who didn't, was something he'd carry with him after this sojourn.

He sought Maddie's face in the crowd, and her gaze locked with his. *She* was the real boon of coming to this little town. Every moment with her had been a revelation.

"The winner of dinner and a dance—only one dance, mind you—with the duke is . . ." Mrs. Reeve flipped the note in her hand. "Our own dear Miss Dixon."

Mrs. Reeve waved at the giggling lady seated next to Maddie. "Come up to the front table, Miss Dixon."

Miss Dixon was beyond the bloom of youth, but she had a cherubic, happy face, and the pink gown she wore only heightened the sense that she must be a jolly lady. She stood, but rather than respond to the hotelier's command, she spoke up and gestured to Will.

"I've saved a seat at our table. Won't you join us, Your Grace?"

Mrs. Reeve frowned when Will shrugged in her direction before striding immediately to Miss Dixon and Maddie's table. To his shock, the older woman vacated the chair she'd been sitting in and invited him to take the spot next to Maddie.

She was either an angel or this was a blatant attempt at the most unnecessary matchmaking he'd ever experienced.

He slid into the chair next to Maddie, and something inside him slid into place as well. It always felt right to be near her. He could admit to himself now that it had that first night in London. As the others at the table introduced themselves, the sight of her in his periphery made his mouth twitch into a smile.

Miss Dixon peppered him with questions, and Will told himself to do better at conversation than he usually did in London ballrooms. The difference here was that no one seemed to resent him or look at him and see only his father. And, of course, Maddie sat at his elbow. He could sense her gaze on him, and every time he turned to catch her eye, she shot him a look as hungry as his own. At one point, his desire to touch her was so great, he made a fuss about dropping his napkin, just to have an excuse to reach for her under the table.

He slid a hand along her thigh, and she let out a stifled gasp.

When he sat up again, he spent most of the rest of the meal considering some other surreptitious way to touch her. But mostly he took comfort in her nearness, her scent, and the sound of her voice as she joined the conversation at table.

It was, without a doubt, the most pleasant evening he'd spent at a soiree for as long as he could remember.

"How much longer will we enjoy your presence in Haven Cove, Your Grace?" a gentleman asked from across the table.

Will felt Maddie tense beside him. Miss Dixon seemed to notice the change in both of them.

"Yes, Your Grace, having you here has proven so beneficial. Might we convince you to stay longer?" she asked with genuine warmth.

His heart, which he rarely consulted, was telling him quite loudly that remaining longer was exactly what he wanted. More time with Maddie in a place where people didn't think him a bore seemed like perfection.

But inside his waistcoat pocket, the folded telegram from Cora lay snugged against his chest. He'd vowed when he'd become head of the family after his father's death that he would not abandon them as their father had. Most especially, he would not let them suffer because of his actions.

"I plan to depart in two days." Will forced the words out and was acutely aware of Maddie's stillness beside him. "If we could find a time to talk—"

"Excuse me." Mrs. Reeve had positioned herself on the dais again. "While dinner service ends, the dancing will begin."

Will had been too distracted to partake in much of the meal. Still, the prospect of dancing unsettled him at any time. However, Miss Dixon had proven herself to be kind, and he didn't wish to disappoint her, despite how much he needed a moment to speak to Maddie. She hadn't looked his way since his declaration about leaving Haven Cove.

Perhaps it was the notion of them finally saying goodbye, and perhaps she suspected that he wished for more, and she knew she couldn't leave her home and business behind.

He stood from the table. Maddie was engaged in conversation with the woman next to her and seemed to not even notice.

"Miss Dixon, if you're ready to dance, I'm ready to partner you." He spoke the words as jovially as possible, but Miss Dixon looked at him with concern. Her gaze settled on Maddie, then up at him, and she gave a quick nod as if she'd come to some decision.

"Your Grace, I fear the caramel pudding has done me in. I have no idea what Mrs. Reeve's rules are about the matter, but I designate Miss Ravenwood as my proxy for our dance."

MADDIE HEARD THE words but it took her a moment to register their meaning. When she looked at

Elmira Dixon, the older lady beamed a mischievous smile her way. Then she stood and moved to the other side of Maddie's chair.

"I hope it's all right, my dear," she whispered in Maddie's ear. "But you looked so forlorn, and so does he. Have a spin around the dance floor together."

"Until today, I had no idea you were such a schemer, Miss Dixon."

Elmira chuckled. "We spinsters must stick together, Miss Ravenwood." She patted Maddie gently on the shoulder by way of encouragement. "Now, go and enjoy yourself. That would be the finest reward for my donation."

Will moved to stand a short distance away and wait for her. When she stood, he beckoned her with a lifted hand.

Maddie took one long look around the room. As she suspected, many faces were turned their way. It wasn't that she minded that anyone knew what was between them. She'd chosen to spend every moment she had with him knowing that rumors might spread like fire in dry tinder. But the risk had been worth it because every chance to be with him had seemed like a gift she couldn't deny herself.

What she feared now was making a maudlin fool of herself. She'd wanted to be in his arms all night, and once she was, she suspected letting him go again would end in tears.

But she went to him, took his hand, and walked with him to the dance floor.

He held her closer than propriety would demand. "Remember," she said quietly, "I'm bad at this."

"There's something I haven't told you." He rested a hand against her waist, and Maddie placed her hand on his shoulder. "I'm terrible at this."

The utterly sincere declaration made her laugh. "Then, we shall be awful and enjoy it."

When the music started, it was a waltz. "This is one I know, but again, I can't vouch for my skill."

Maddie loved dancing the waltz, or at least she had when her mother had taught her as a child. As an adult, she'd had few opportunities to dance. "I know this one too. We'll be fine."

They started the box step pattern, and Will only went to lead her astray once.

"Well, I know you're skilled at other things, so I won't judge you too harshly for this."

His eyes turned a molten dark chocolate brown, and a wolfish smile tipped his lips. "How very gracious of you, Miss Ravenwood."

Maddie felt her cheeks warm, not just because of the naked desire in his gaze but because the memories of his body against hers doing a different sort of dance were suddenly playing in her mind. But it was what his nearness did to her heart that affected her most. It felt fuller when she was with him, and it beat wildly now that she was in his arms.

There was no denying it. She had fallen for him completely.

Chapter Twenty-Two

"Thank you so much for coming this morning." Lady Trenmere stood beside Maddie as she checked one last time on the camellias the countess planned to enter in the flower show. One particularly healthy and promising specimen had been potted and made ready for presentation. But Maddie had potted two more just in case something went amiss with the favored plant.

"Of course I came." They'd both been looking forward to this day for months.

"I know you have a great deal to do and must be filled with worries about your roses, just as I've worried about these silly beauties."

"I'm not worried." It was true, but Maddie had no desire to explain why. It wasn't that the flower show didn't matter to her anymore, but her perspective about it had shifted. She'd put all her hopes into winning and finding favor with the princess, but would it be the answer to all of her problems? It no longer seemed the cure-all she'd once imagined it to be.

"You do always manage to work things out in your mind and think more logically than I do."

When Maddie slid off her work gloves and turned to the noblewoman, she found the countess assessing her with a pinched brow.

"Do you have time for tea?" she asked brightly, the worried frown slipping from her features.

Maddie wasn't certain she did have the time to spare. She needed to be at the flower show early to help with any last-minute preparations for the welcoming of the princess. But she rarely told Lady Trenmere no. The countess had done so much for her.

"If I don't linger too long, I do."

A maid brought a tea tray quickly, and Lady Trenmere poured as she usually did. Her hands moved purposefully over the porcelain, and it was a bit like watching an elegant ballet.

Maddie felt the anticipatory air that usually came when Lady Trenmere was working up to some topic she wished to broach but didn't wish to speak bluntly.

When they were settled and Maddie had taken her first sip of the lovely floral jasmine tea, Lady Trenmere laid down the spoon she'd been swirling around her cup and smiled.

"Is that what you're doing in regard to the duke?"

At the mention of Will, Maddie took a long sip and felt the stinging burn on her tongue. "Pardon?"

Surely she'd missed something.

"Oh, I was saying you manage to think more logically than I do. I wondered if you're doing the same with Ashmore."

There were so many thoughts and feelings she

had about Will, and now memories too, but none of it was particularly logical. None except the one unwavering inevitability between them. He must return to London and do his duty, and she must stay in Haven Cove and do hers. They'd never spoken of it to each other that plainly, but she sensed they both knew it. And she suspected their final conversation would be about that inevitably.

"My goodness. It has gone far, hasn't it?"

Maddie took another sip of tea and realized she'd drained her cup. Lady Trenmere lifted the pot to pour her more. When she settled back in her chair again, she didn't wait for Maddie to answer her previous question before lobbing another.

"You haven't fallen in love with him, have you?"

That was one thing she couldn't deny. The realization hadn't come in a single moment she could identify. It had been inching toward her for days. But now the clarity of it was blindingly bright.

"I have, my lady."

Lady Trenmere breathed in a long, slow breath and let it out just as slowly, as if calming herself. "And does he return your feelings, Madeline?"

"I haven't told him." She regretted that, and finding a way to speak to him had been on her mind from the moment she'd awoken. But she'd had this commitment to meet with the countess, and the flower show would come soon after.

The countess arched one delicate brow. "But he probably knows, don't you think? He can't be an easy man to fall in love with."

"But he is. He was. I was falling from the minute I met him all those months ago, I think."

"Months ago?"

"I met him in your conservatory. Purely by happenstance. I witnessed . . ." Maddie took a sip of tea. In for a penny, in for a pound. "I observed his conversation with Lady Davina."

"Mercy. That must have been a bit of a spectacle."

"She was very angry."

"Who could blame her?"

"She was concerned for her family, I understand."

Lady Trenmere sat her teacup on the lacquered table at her side. "Oh my dear. You really don't know him at all, do you?"

"I do." Maddie clamped her teeth together to hold back her anger and keep from saying more. She did know Will. She knew he was tender, wry-humored, kind to animals, committed to his family, and talented at art. And talented at other things that made her toes curl just to think about.

"Tell me what it is that you think I don't know." That day at the nursery, Will had been resistant to speak of his father and all that he'd done to restore the family name. Was Lady Trenmere one of the aristocrats who blamed him for seeking out the man's secrets?

"I rather think William should tell you, but I care for you too much to leave you wondering."

Maddie couldn't stay mad at the countess long. She could see in her soft gaze and in the evidence of all she'd done for her over the years that she truly did care. "Please do tell me."

"After the death of his father, who was a quite terrible man, as I think you know by reputation—"

"Yes." Though, it was almost impossible for Maddie to reconcile what she'd heard about Stanwick Hart with his son.

"Will resented him. Perhaps he hated him. No one would begrudge him that. You see, the late duke's antics broke his wife. She grew inconsolable as his infidelities were revealed. So miserable she didn't wish to eat or speak to anyone or accept the advice of her doctors. She grew ill and lost the will to get better."

"He blames his father for the death of his mother." Maddie realized that in all her discussions with Will, he'd never mentioned his mother at all. Now she understood why. She couldn't imagine the pain of knowing one parent had so thoroughly harmed the other.

"Entirely." Lady Trenmere sipped at her tea and stared off into the distance thoughtfully. "I can't say he's wrong. Josephine was a strong, beautiful woman, but Stanwick's betrayals were the death of her."

Maddie's heart ached for Will, and for his sisters.

"Will became vengeful when he inherited. He set out to expose his father's misdeeds, which were tangled with the misdeeds of many others of the nobility. In pulling back the curtain on his father's sins, others feared exposure."

"Surely Will can't be blamed for merely telling the truth and trying to put right what his father had done wrong."

"It does seem that simple, doesn't it? But reputations are currency among the aristocracy. Often it's not our actions that destroy us but what others do with the knowledge of them."

Maddie felt her cheeks warm, and then the heat rushed down her neck. "Are there rumors about Will and me now?"

The countess's gaze grew sad, her expression bleak. "Yes. I'm sorry, dear, but there are. Most don't name you. Just initials or a more oblique reference to a young businesswoman in Cornwall. But Will and his sisters have been careful not to allow any whiff of scandal since their father's death."

"This isn't a scandal."

That caused the countess to stare into her dainty porcelain cup as if she was reading tea leaves.

Finally she said, "Perhaps that's true in Haven Cove. In London, it would be. And if you'd allowed me to give you a coming out as I suspect your mother would have wished, it would have been more than a scandal. Ashmore would have done his duty and married you."

"Marriage shouldn't be a duty." Maddie understood duty, knew it was important. But it could become a burden, like the nursery. And if her mother had imparted anything, it was the insistence that Maddie should marry for love.

"Marriage *is* a duty, Madeline. Even if we marry

for love, wedlock comes with its duties. And for a man like Ashmore, the very act of marriage is a duty. He cannot merely choose to be a carefree bachelor." Lady Trenmere paused and looked at Maddie sympathetically yet pointedly. "If he does not marry, the title will pass to—who knows?— some male relative or child on a distant branch of the familial tree."

That didn't sound like the absolute worst fate that could befall a dukedom, but she understood that it could be for those who relied on Will. His sisters, any extended family he was benevolent to, and to those who worked the ducal lands on the estate of Eastwick.

While Maddie contemplated Will and the duties of his role and imagined how many people relied on him making the right choices, Lady Trenmere contemplated her.

"Are you happy with the life you've chosen here?"

The question caused Maddie's jaw to slacken and her mind to spin. She rarely pondered that question, or at least she tried not to. She kept busy so that she didn't have to consider it. Because what was the point of the answer? This was the life she had. Ravenwood's. Being of service where she could. Roses and responsibilities.

And she would have called herself happy. Until fourteen days ago.

"Mmm, I thought as much."

"I didn't give an answer." Maddie found herself gripping her cup too tightly and speaking with too indignant a tone. There was no reason to be angry with the countess. She'd asked a reasonable question.

"But it's all written on your face, my dear. You're an open and honest person. And I could see hints of it before now. It's why I offered you another way."

"That offer was impossible once Father died."

Lady Trenmere averted her gaze and nodded. "I know. I understand."

Maddie wasn't certain she did, but she always appreciated the tenderness in her tone.

"I suppose there is only one other key question," the countess said as she tapped a long, slender finger against the edge of her cup.

"What's that, my lady?" Maddie found that the conversation had washed away some of her anticipation for the day and the flower show she'd been working toward for so long. A sort of sad weariness swept in to take its place.

"If Ashmore offered for you, would you marry him?"

WILL SAT ON the enormous gold settee in what he'd come to think of as the front sitting room. Heaven knew what it had been designated as in Carnwyth's heyday. The staff had done their best to revive the space. They'd taken out some of the more overdone furnishings and even replaced the heavy plum velvet draperies with a lighter fabric in a cool peach shade. The color of the roses Maddie had worn in her hair at the hotel last night.

Without trying, Will had managed to connect everything he saw since waking with her. His bed, of course. Though he would likely never sleep in it again after tonight, some part of him now thought of it as theirs. They'd claimed the grand ceramic tub as theirs without a doubt. Of the drawing materials he'd decided to pack for his train ride, all the pages were covered with images of Carnwyth or sketches of her, and, in truth, all of it had been drawn while she was on his mind.

"I should have found her and said goodbye last night," he told the kitten sleeping in the corner of the settee, its paws resting against his thigh. It was the only one of the litter that hadn't found a home, not because they couldn't find a willing family but because Kate and Mrs. Haskell had taken such a liking to the little runt of the litter that they'd decided to keep her. They'd asked his permission, and Will had given his blessing. He no longer felt loathing for Carnwyth, and the wee thing thought of it as home in the same way that Bly and Haskell and the rest of them did.

He'd never found the land agent as he'd intended, and now he wasn't certain he would anytime soon. His feelings for the manor house had changed dramatically because of Maddie, and he suspected he wouldn't be eager to dredge up memories of the house or make any final decisions about it for a while. When he got to a day when he didn't think of her from waking until night, he'd consider Carnwyth again.

But, in truth, from where he sat now, with his heart as torn in two as it was, he wasn't certain that day would ever come.

"Visitor to see you, Your Grace." Mrs. Haskell, quiet treader that she was, had approached the threshold without catching his notice.

"Who is it?" He wasn't in any state to receive guests, but there was one visitor he desperately needed to speak to. He held his breath as he waited for the housekeeper's answer.

"It's Lady Trenmere."

Will closed his eyes and let out a frustrated sigh. Then he stood, careful not to disturb the kitten, and rolled his shoulders. Might as well make amends with the lady if he could. He'd seen her at the hotel the previous night, but she'd been ensconced in conversation with another nobleman.

"See her in."

The countess swept into the room in the commanding way she sailed into any space.

Without any preamble or niceties, she gave him a tight smile, stripped off her gloves, and took a seat in the overstuffed gold chair that matched the settee.

"Welcome, Lady Trenmere. It's been a long time."

"Don't look at me that way, Ashmore. We both know Davina's brother is close friends with my nephew. I could hardly take your side."

Since she had seated herself, Will resumed his spot on the settee, stretching his arms along the back and crossing one leg. This conversation would likely be irksome, and he wanted to start it as comfortably as possible.

"I never meant for there to *be* sides."

She waved the gloves clutched in her hand at him. "William, intentions are well and good, but our actions matter most."

He couldn't and wouldn't even attempt to argue with her on that point.

"Well, I'm glad you're here now. That night was actually fortuitous, despite how others characterized it later. Davina and I were never well suited."

She squared her vivid blue gaze on him. "But you and Miss Ravenwood are?"

"Yes." The word slipped from his lips before he could weigh or temper it. They did suit each other. However their outer circumstances might differ, their hearts—and what was essential about each of them—were connected.

"Then, what do you plan to do, Ashmore?" She edged forward a few inches in her chair. "Because that young woman means a great deal to me. Her mother meant a great deal to me. I do not wish to see Madeline hurt or discarded by you."

"She means a great deal to me too. The last thing I wish is to cause her harm."

Discarding her had never been a consideration. His head ached with the conundrum of how she could maintain her life in Cornwall while he did his duty back in London and Sussex. They couldn't make a life out of visits across England. At one time, he might have believed in the sort of marriage so many aristocrats had, with one's wife in the countryside so that a nobleman might do as he pleased in town. He couldn't bear that kind of life with Maddie. The prospect of spending even a handful of nights without her was almost as unbearable as walking away from her altogether.

"Then, you do plan to marry her?"

He couldn't simply make that plan because it required him to ignore what was important to her. Her business and connection to Haven Cove. He'd considered it. Hell, the idea had practically possessed him when he woke in his bed late in the night. Last night—dancing with her, watching how she spoke tirelessly with person after person, even after helping with preparations all day—he realized what a fabulous duchess she would be. To hell with what anyone else might say.

But there was a sticking point, a barrier that seemed immovable.

"She wouldn't accept such a plan."

Lady Trenmere started to speak but then turned quiet and contemplative. Even she couldn't deny what Will suspected.

"She wouldn't, would she, Lady Trenmere? She would refuse my offer even if I asked her to marry me."

"I honestly don't know." Settling back into her chair, she looked as defeated as Will felt. "I can see that you care for each other a great deal."

"It's more than that."

"Love?"

He'd already revealed more to the countess than he'd intended, but he refused to confess the depth of his feelings for Maddie to any woman other than Maddie.

When he didn't answer, she gathered her gloves and scooted to the edge of her chair as if she was prepared to depart just a few moments after arriving.

She stood and Will did the same.

"I'm sorry to be hurried, but I must make my way to the hotel for the reception of the princess and the flower show."

Of course. It was all finally happening today.

A thought came to Will, a suspicion about what had prompted Lady Trenmere to come to him today of all days. "Have you spoken to her?"

She busied herself with buttoning her gloves. "I saw her this morning."

"And? How is she?"

Head tilted as if considering her reply, she finally said, "I see the same thing in her eyes that I do in yours. It's a pity there isn't a way for the two of you. But your duties lead you in opposite directions." She cast a gaze around the room and finally glanced at the kitten, as if noticing it for the first time. "You're leaving tomorrow, I understand."

"Yes." He'd sorted most of his things this morning, and a maid was working to fill his traveling trunk as they spoke.

Hat tipped back on her head, she gazed up at him, and her eyes were sad but somehow resolute. "I think that's for the best. The sooner you go, the sooner the both of you can get back to living your lives."

Chapter Twenty-Three

This was the moment they'd been hoping for, planning for, and dreaming about for nearly a year, but Maddie was still tempted to pinch herself as Princess Beatrice stepped into the hotel lobby surrounded by her entourage and looked around with a glint of admiration in her eyes at the clean lines of marble, the sparkle of gilt, and the decorations that had been specially placed for her arrival.

She looked like her mother, or at least every photograph and etching Maddie had ever seen of the aged queen. But Princess Beatrice was prettier. All of the features the princess had inherited from her mother were softer than the queen's, a contribution from her father's masculine beauty, no doubt.

Though she was now a woman of middle age, there was still a youthful, rounded quality to her face, and Maddie could easily believe she had been the most favored child of the queen and prince consort.

Mrs. Reeve stepped forward, and Maddie and Mrs. Pendenning, as the two other founding members of the Royal Visit Committee, followed her as she presented a bouquet of flowers, some of which would appear at the flower show later in the day.

A single bloom of Maddie's Victoria rose was among the bunch.

The princess nodded and regarded the bouquet for a long moment. "These are exquisite," she declared in her polished accent.

Craning her neck, Maddie noted that she was pointing to one of Lady Trenmere's camellias. She felt a swell of pride. Yes, of course she still hoped the princess might smile as favorably on her tea roses, but she'd helped cultivate the camellia that drew the visitor's notice, and she couldn't help but be happy for Lady Trenmere and the work they'd done together.

Mrs. Reeve introduced all of them and gestured to the other members of the Royal Visit Committee who stood nearby watching—more like gaping—as the princess entered the hotel.

"Your Royal Highness, we are honored by your visit," Mrs. Reeve said in an awestruck tone. Then she turned to a regal-looking attendant among the princess's party. "The bellboy will show you to rooms we prepared for Your Highness." The lady nodded, but the princess had taken a few steps away and continued perusing the hotel's interior.

"Might we have a tour of your dining-room balcony, Mrs. Reeve?" she asked. "I've heard so much about it."

It was the first time Maddie had ever seen Jane Reeve rendered speechless. "Y-Yes, of course, Your Highness."

Jane shot Maddie a questioning glance as if to say, "I suppose I'm doing this," and Maddie nodded at her eagerly. Showing off the hotel was one of the things Mrs. Reeve loved best, and to have a request from the princess she'd transformed her hotel to accommodate must have made her downright giddy.

The tour of the hotel was actually a godsend for Maddie, since she needed to slip away from the welcoming party and get down to the portion of hotel grounds that they'd designated for the flower show. Some committee members wondered at her involvement with the preparations for the event, since she would also be a contender, but no one else had volunteered to oversee the setup for the show.

All she needed to do for her own preparations was to ensure that her flower was properly tagged and set in place, ready for judging. But making sure everyone else's was tagged and ready would take a while.

She rushed through the lobby as quickly as she could, then down the stairs and around the corner to the long swath of glossy green grass where they'd decided to host the event.

Other contestants were gathered, some looking anxious, others hopeful.

"There she is," Miss Dean from the Horticultural Society called out as Maddie strode across the grass. "Have you seen her yet? The princess?"

"I did. She's lovely."

"Not an intimidating judge, then?" Miss Dean let out a low, ornery chuckle. "Not as intimidating as her mother, in other words."

"Not by a mile. She seems happy to be here."

"Perfect." Miss Dean smiled and clasped her gloved hands together. Then she looked up, past Maddie's shoulder, and her eyes widened.

Maddie turned to see what had so shocked Miss Dean, and her blood warmed in her veins.

"Every time I see him, my breath just whooshes from my lungs," Miss Dean murmured. "My cousins in London say he's a bad-tempered, penny-pinching killjoy who his own sisters ran out of town so they could have a proper party for Lady Daisy. But look at him," Miss Dean continued in a gusty whisper. "How can a man who looks like that be someone you'd wish to avoid?"

Since the last thing Maddie wished to do was avoid him, she couldn't think of a single answer to offer Miss Dean.

"He doesn't seem like an ogre, does he, Miss Ravenwood?" Miss Dean seemed to read her mind.

"Not at all." He was the warmest, kindest man she'd ever known.

"Was he pleasant to dance with? I heard you stood up together last evening?"

"He was." It had been extraordinary to whirl around the dance floor in his arms, even if she stumbled through some of the steps. He always caught her, and it would forever be the best dance of her life.

"I do believe he's spotted you," Miss Dean whispered.

His movements had been leisurely, the same relaxed movement of the other guests who were not
contestants in the flower show or business leaders
hoping to get a glimpse of the princess. But the minute he spotted Maddie, his stance and movements
changed. He lengthened his stride and approached
with singular determination blazing in his dark
eyes.

THE SUNLIGHT ALWAYS made her skin glow and
her hair sparkle with flecks of bronze and gold.
She wasn't wearing a hat, which meant her freckles
were on full display, and Will loved each and every
one of them.

He fought the urge to sweep her into his arms, but
the lady staring wide-eyed at him from over Maddie's shoulder told Will that such brazen displays
would only fuel more gossip.

"You came," she said when he drew up next to her.

"Of course I did. I know this day means a great
deal to you."

"It does, but I don't feel anxious anymore." She
lifted a hand to look up at him, shading her eyes
from the sun. "I tell myself I've done my best. And
if that's not enough, then so be it. At least *I* know
I've done what I can and didn't give up."

He tried to read her gaze, to see if she genuinely
felt so sanguine or was simply putting on a good
face for the lady standing behind her, listening to
every word they said to each other. But when he

looked up, the woman was gone, and Maddie still looked calmer than he would be on a day that was so momentous and meant so much to his future.

Noting that no one was close to them or seemed to be paying them much mind, Will reached for Maddie's hand. She didn't hesitate to take his, and then she placed her other on top of their laced fingers.

"I know you've done well because I know you and your determination are a force to be reckoned with, but may I still wish you luck?"

"Yes, always."

He leaned closer and couldn't resist brushing his lips against her cheek. "Good luck, sweetheart." The scent of her skin made his mouth water, and being near her soothed something inside him. For a moment he pushed away how much the prospect of saying goodbye to her filled him with misery.

Maddie seemed to need this closeness too. She reached for him, gripping the edge of his coat, and Will wondered if he should dare a true kiss. Though he worried that if he started, he wouldn't wish to stop.

Then, unsurprisingly, someone among those gathered on the green called to her. The same lady who'd stood behind her just moments before.

"Maddie, come quick! Some of the entrants say they've lost their tags, and Mrs. Hobbs has filed a complaint to pull your plant from the competition since you are a co-leader of the Royal Visit Committee."

"That's outrageous." Will was ready to find Mrs.

Hobbs, whoever she was, and give her a piece of his mind. Maddie stilled him with a quick brush of her hand against his.

"Don't worry. I can handle this. Mrs. Hobbs knows her complaint has already been heard and rejected. She's just trying to rattle me."

"Are flower shows always this cutthroat?"

Maddie smiled. "You have no idea." With that she joined the young lady and strode away.

Will noticed she rarely took her leave of him properly. Perhaps she was as loath to say their parting words to each other as he was. "Good luck!" he called as she retreated.

After circling the green for half an hour, Will had consumed enough lemonade to make him sick. Finally, the guests were allowed into the flower-show area.

Will didn't know one flower from the next, though some looked like varieties he'd seen in London parks or at the gardens at Eastwick.

He finally found Maddie's rose. It was the same flower she'd worn in her hair last night at the dance.

Crouching to get a better look, he read her description—the same one she'd told him—of how she'd blended two varieties of rose to get this lovely frilled peach and coral beauty. He still thought calling it the Victoria rose was a clever choice.

Someone approached to stand next to him, and the sun cast their shadow across the flowers. For a moment, Will was too engrossed in studying all the little details of Maddie's rose to look up. Finally, he stood and turned to find Lady Trenmere at his side.

"If you'd like to give my entry your ducal blessing, it's over there." She pointed with an amused grin that softened her face.

"What are they?"

"Camellias, of course. The previous owner of Allswell imported a few varieties from China, and they're the only specimens of that particular strain living in England."

"They are beautiful."

"Thank you," she beamed proudly, as if he'd just complimented her child. "It's such a momentous day that it's hard to believe it will all be over in a matter of minutes."

"Do you really believe a nod from her can change someone's stars?"

"It could change everything for Maddie. I suspect it will no matter how the princess judges."

"How so?" Will took a few steps toward the countess's camellias. With their dark glossy leaves and bright pink coloring, they were striking.

"If she does win, she'll feel compelled to stay at Ravenwood's and make it the success her parents always dreamed it could be." Lady Trenmere tipped her head and studied him. "And if she loses, would she really wish to stay? Don't we both agree that running the nursery is not the fate Maddie had envisioned for herself?"

Garden design. Flowers. He knew those were her passions. And helping wherever she could.

"You think she'd consider leaving Cornwall?" He tried to temper the hopefulness in his tone.

Lady Trenmere reached out to slide one finger along a camellia petal as if offering it a nudge of encouragement. Then she stood and faced him with a bold, expectant look on her face. "You mean you haven't asked her?"

Will stared at the noblewoman a moment and couldn't find the words to answer because it suddenly felt as if the weight of the sea itself was pressing down on his chest.

A ruckus of noise forced his attention to the far edge of the grass. A woman with the younger, softer face of Queen Victoria was entering the area where plants were set out for her to judge.

This was Maddie's moment. He watched her enter the judging area and take up a spot with a group of other ladies and gentlemen who he assumed were also entrants in the show.

It was a long, harrowing process as they all watched and waited as the princess walked from entry to entry, sometimes bending down to get a closer look, even using a magnifying glass to study the tinier blooms, and all the while whispering to Lord Esquith, who scribbled down notes as she spoke.

When she finally came to Maddie's rose and read the tag, she wore a genuine smile. The bloom was too lovely to spark any other reaction, but he suspected the naming of the new strain might have tickled her too.

But as with all the blooms, she looked, pondered, spoke to Lord Esquith quietly, and then moved on to the next. Will rapped his finger rhythmically against his thigh and watched Maddie lift a hand to nibble at her nails and then force her fisted hands to her sides.

After viewing every flower, the princess moved to a seating area under the shade of a white canopy to take refreshment and rest. The waiting was agony. Meanwhile, Mrs. Reeve consulted with Lord Esquith, even looking with him at the notes he'd made in his notebook.

She mouthed what looked like *Are you certain?* and then nodded before stepping into the center of the judging area. A young woman approached and presented her with three ribbons.

"May I have everyone's attention, please." Her usually confident smile wobbled a bit, and she took a deep breath before continuing. "Mrs. Hobbs's peony, Pink Sensation, takes third place in the competition." A round of lukewarm applause was the only response as Mrs. Hobbs approached to retrieve her ribbon.

"In second place, we have Mr. Peregrine's poppy." A short, gruff-looking man immediately stalked toward Mrs. Reeve and practically snatched the ribbon from her fingers.

Will watched Maddie. She had given in and was chewing her nails now.

"For the first time in Haven Cove Flower Show history, we have a tie for first place. We don't have enough ribbons, of course, but we'll amend that as soon as we're able." She swallowed hard and continued. "The first prize goes to Lady Trenmere for her Extraordinary camellia and to Miss Ravenwood for her Victoria rose."

Yes! Will's heart burst with joy as if he'd been the one to win the award. He started toward her, but others were swarming close by, offering congratulations and praise. A moment later, the winners were trotted past the princess and either bowed or curtsied to show their gratitude for her efforts.

Just when he spotted an opening that might allow him to get close to Maddie, she turned in the crowd and sought out Lady Trenmere. They held on to each other a moment as if they were long-lost family.

"Your mother would be proud of you."

Will was close enough to hear Lady Trenmere's voice, and he noticed Maddie let out a sigh as she heard the countess's words.

"I think so too. And now Ravenwood's will thrive, and my father will be proud too." Maddie smiled so wide that her eyes crinkled.

Lady Trenmere laid a hand on her cheek. "Yes, my dear. The nursery will be the success that your parents wished it to be."

He'd known that if she won, she would be even more committed to staying. It made perfect sense, just as Lady Trenmere had said.

How could he quash her joy by asking her to leave Cornwall now?

Backing away, Will headed for the spot where he could exit the grass and reach the road back to Carnwyth. He had been preparing himself for the moment when he would have to say goodbye to Maddie. But not here. Not now.

He'd almost reached the far edge of the hotel property, and the longing for Maddie deepened with every step.

"Will!"

Maddie's voice stopped him in his tracks, and when he turned, he found her rushing toward him, her color high and that same beaming smile she'd offered Lady Trenmere on her face.

She didn't stop until he caught her in his arms.

"You did it," he whispered against her hair.

She held him tightly, and he wrapped her closer in his arms. Neither of them wished to let go. But finally, she was the first to loosen her hold. Her gaze was serious when she looked up at him, and he was simply glad to have her in his arms again.

"When do you depart?"

"Not long from now. First thing tomorrow."

She pulled farther away, bit her lip, and cast her gaze out toward the sea.

"Maddie . . ."

"Yes?" Her voice emerged on a raspy whisper.

"You're the most extraordinary woman I've ever known. My feelings for you—"

"I know." She reached for his hand and came into the circle of his arms again. "I feel the same."

He knew that. He'd never doubted that what was between them was powerful and entirely mutual.

"I'm proud of you," he told her. For the first time, he noticed the first-place ribbon someone had pinned to her bodice. "And as much as I'd like to never part from you, I cannot ask you to forfeit your own life. Your business. Your goals. This little community that relies on you so much."

He was shocked he'd gotten the words out. Even as he spoke, part of him wanted to ask her, plead with her, to be with him. To stay with him, whatever it cost. But he loved her too much to let his selfish needs cost her anything.

She'd seamed her lips together, and her eyes had gone glassy with unshed tears.

Drawing her close, he waited, hoping she'd tell him what was in her heart.

"You're right." Finally, she looked up at him as a tear slid down her cheek. "I have so many commitments here, not just my duty to carry on my parents' business but to people in the town. I know who I am here, and it's the only place that's ever felt like home."

Duty. Commitment. He'd come to Cornwall as the stuffiest man in Britain and had somehow fallen in love with a woman more sensible than he was.

"You'll do wonderful things here, sweetheart. You already have." He stroked his fingers against her cheek, and she drew closer and wrapped her arms around his neck.

"Don't say goodbye. Let's not say those words," she said with her lips near his ear. Then she pulled back and kissed him.

Will poured everything he felt for her into the kiss and hoped she knew and could feel how much she meant to him.

When they finally caught their breath, her tears had dried, and she offered him a sad but resolute smile. "Safe travels. Send me a note, perhaps, to let me know you arrived safely."

"I will." He kissed her lips once more, a too-quick brush of his mouth against hers. Then he pressed his lips to her forehead and lingered there before forcing himself to take the first step away.

As he retreated, he glanced back once. She waved, and he nodded, swallowing down the pain welling up inside him. Farther on, he looked back a second time, and she had gone. He could just glimpse her in the distance, entering the hotel grounds and the throngs still gathered after the flower show.

It was, Will told himself, the belonging she needed in her life.

Chapter Twenty-Four

*M*addie woke, squinted at the clock, and groaned. It couldn't be that late. The clock face read nine thirty, but she always woke up before the day had dawned. It had been her way since she was a child, mimicking her parents' habit of rising early to begin work at the nursery.

Today, her eyes were sore from the tears she'd shed when she'd returned home exhausted after the events at the hotel.

After winning the flower show, she and Lady Trenmere had joined a celebratory luncheon, had their photograph taken, and been interviewed for a London newspaper. Then they'd been asked to join Princess Beatrice for dinner in her private dining room.

Giddiness had kept her going all day, but it dipped into sadness whenever she cast a gaze toward the grassy area outside the hotel and remembered Will walking away.

Today he would leave Cornwall, perhaps for good, and she decided that as painful as it would be, for his sake she would wish him well and find some measure of contentment in knowing he was going back to duties and a life that mattered to him. Maybe he would go back as a changed man. Their relationship had changed her, reminding her of the joys life could bring. She hoped it had done the same for him.

She washed, dressed, and put her hair up into a simple knot before heading to the office to see Alice. The young woman was in the office, just as Maddie expected. She seemed full of energy and was busy tidying the space and watering the plants she kept inside to make the building cheerful.

As soon as Maddie stepped through the door, Alice dropped her broom, turned, and dashed into her arms.

"Congratulations! I am so proud of you."

Maddie held her tight and smiled. "Thank you. But I couldn't have done it without you. This nursery wouldn't run smoothly without you here, and I could slip away to work on my roses knowing everything would be in capable hands."

"Nonsense," Alice told her bashfully.

Maddie held the girl's pretty face between her hands. "I mean it. Listen to me."

Alice lowered her eyes and grinned. "Thank you, Maddie."

Maddie turned to check the pile of mail Alice had left for her at the front edge of the desk. There was nothing of particular interest until she reached the bottom and found a letter with a return address from Longford Farms.

"He just won't give up."

"The man is irritatingly tenacious." Alice picked up her broom again and began sweeping.

"Even if I was to consider selling Ravenwood's, it wouldn't be to him. Goodness, my father loathed him. It would have to be to someone who loved the place." *More than I do*, Maddie stopped herself from saying. Perhaps it was that her head and heart were still full of Will or that she'd accomplished what she'd worked so long for with her roses, but something in her could no longer escape the truth that running the nursery was not her passion.

"You'd consider selling?"

It was terrifying to answer in the affirmative, and she couldn't quite get the words out, but she offered Alice a quick nod.

Resting her hands on the top of the broom, Alice watched Maddie as if waiting for her to say more. After a long, tense silence between them, Alice asked softly, almost timidly, "Would you ever consider selling to my father?"

"He's the only person I can honestly imagine selling the nursery to." The fleeting thought had come to her many times, especially when the duties of running the nursery felt like drudgery to her and still seemed to give Eames enormous satisfaction every day.

"Is this because of the duke?"

Before Maddie could answer, Alice's eyes went wide.

"Heavens, I almost forgot." She rushed to the side of the room, hefted a large oblong, paper-wrapped package, and set its edge on her desk. "This came for you."

"What is it?"

Alice giggled. "I thought you might open it and see." She looked at Maddie and in an almost conspiratorial whisper said, "I think it's from *him*."

Maddie began to shiver. It was odd and unbidden and made no sense since it was a warm, blue-sky day. But something about the package felt ominous. Final.

She moved to the desk and began tearing at the paper. A gilded frame emerged in one of the corners.

"A painting." Why would he send a painting? Maddie continued tearing at the paper and realized it was a depiction of the rose garden near the cottage where she'd grown up. At first, she thought it was a painting Will had created himself, but then she noticed a figure in the garden. A woman crouched before a rosebush, one hand lifted to tend to the plant.

"It's my mother." Maddie could hardly get the words out. Her throat was tight, and tears burned in her eyes.

The woman had her mother's burnished auburn hair. Someone must have painted her when Maddie was a child. Some artist who'd been among Carnwyth's visitors, no doubt.

Maddie collected and wadded the wrapping paper as she stared at the image of the person who'd loved her most in the world. It made her heart full to see her represented so lovingly and doing what she adored.

"You dropped something." Alice bent next to her and scooped up a folded piece of paper from the floor.

The shivers returned. This was what she'd been dreading. A gift. A note. They hadn't said the words because she'd insisted, but this felt very much like a goodbye.

Darling Maddie,

I find I cannot tell you goodbye, so I'll tell you instead that you have changed me for the better. Softened my heart, fired my blood, turned my mind to things I'd forgotten. Such as the truth that love matters most. So while I wish to stay or wish for you to come with me, loving you means letting you have the life you choose, even if it's not with me.

Mrs. Haskell tells me that the painting I'm enclosing portrays your mother and the roses she tended. The painting, like the roses themselves, should have always been yours.

Like my heart.

Ever yours,
Will

Maddie held the note, staring at the words until they blurred. Then she folded it, placed it inside her bodice next to her heart, and looked up at Alice, who stood watching her anxiously.

"Are you all right?" she whispered.

Maddie nodded and pressed a hand to her chest where her racing heart was making her a bit light-headed.

"When does the train leave?"

Alice rushed to the desk, pushed papers aside, then folders, then a seed catalog, and finally seized a train timetable.

Maddie bit her lip and clenched her hands, willing herself to manage any measure of patience.

"In half an hour." Alice shooed at her. "You need to go. Now."

Maddie turned and ran from the office toward the barn where they stabled their workhorses. James was returning from a delivery with the pony cart, and she nearly got herself run over by jumping in front of him and forcing him to stop.

"I need the cart."

"'Course, miss." He jumped down with a dumb-founded expression on his face.

If she looked as wild as she felt, she must have been a sight to behold.

Once in the cart, she led the horse back onto the main road, and Mabel seemed to sense Maddie's urgency. The trip to the train station from Raven-wood's took half an hour in good weather, assuming the train was running right on time.

But she had to make it. She had to tell him what was in her heart.

WILL PICKED UP a newspaper another passenger had discarded in his train car and tried to read the words to no avail. Staring at the newsprint, he saw only Maddie. The note had been a coward's way out. He should have confessed his love for her, and he feared he'd avoided it not to spare her pain but to keep himself from falling to pieces.

The fact was that he couldn't say goodbye to her. Even if she hadn't insisted that they avoid the word. Speaking those words to her would break something inside of him. It felt wrong. It was wrong. Parting from her was wrong.

He hadn't even asked her if she'd leave Cornwall. He couldn't bring himself to make her choose. Or, worse, force her to refuse him.

"May I see that newspaper, guv?" The Londoner across from him took the paper when Will didn't answer. "You all right, sir?"

"No." He wasn't. Not in any way. It was like he'd left a piece of himself behind, and every other part of him was protesting.

"A lady, is it? Did she leave you high and dry? Run off with your best mate?"

Will frowned at the boisterous young man who suddenly sounded as bitter as Will did when speaking of his father.

"No, nothing like that."

The young man crinkled his brow. "Well, what then?"

Why was he even contemplating sharing personal matters with a boorish stranger?

"She refused you? Is that it?" He asked the question with a kind of glee.

"I never asked her."

"But you wanted to?"

"Yes."

"In that case, you're daft as my aunt Minnie."

Will groaned and considered escaping to another train car.

"Never give up an opportunity, my ma always says."

"Oh bloody hell." Will stood, retrieved his bag from the rung above him, and stalked from the compartment. The hallway was fairly empty of passengers. Most people were settled into their seats, waiting for the train to depart.

Will spotted a porter and opened his mouth to shout and tell the boy he needed a new seat.

But that's not what he needed. Not truly. He needed Maddie.

His annoying compartment companion had a point. He was daft for not even trying. Good god, how could he give up what he wanted most, the person his heart had been meant for, without truly trying? Even if it meant her refusal destroyed him?

He should have given her a chance to choose.

Rushing down the narrow hallway, he called to a young train worker. "I need my trunk removed from the train."

"Sir?"

"I've changed my mind."

Steam started to roll across the platform, and the train's wheels began to squeal. In a panic, Will shoved open the nearest door and jumped onto the platform. Soon after, he saw a porter staring at him from the far end of the train. The London boy stood beside him pointing at Will.

He ran a hand through his hair and searched the line of cabs and carriages that waited near the station to deliver people to wherever they needed to go in Cornwall. Striding to a small carriage, he told the man beside it he wished to hire him and be taken to Haven Cove.

"It's quite a distance, sir, and I was just off for a spot of tea."

"I'll pay you double. Whatever amount you name." Will was overheated and frustrated as hell. *Maddie.* He needed to get back to her. Even if she said no, even if her feelings weren't as deep as his, she deserved to know how much he loved her.

Will glowered at the carriage driver, who slid a brow skyward as if contemplating how much to ask for.

Will's nerves were fraying by the minute. Drawing in a sharp breath, he caught a floral scent on the breeze.

Then he heard her voice.

"But I must board the next train."

"The train is leaving, miss. If you've no ticket, you cannot board."

Will couldn't quite believe she wasn't simply a

beautiful mirage. She stood on the platform at the ticket window shouting at the man behind the panel.

"Maddie." He breathed the word too low, and she didn't hear him. But when he strode toward her, she turned and reeled back in shock.

"I thought you'd gone." She rushed toward him and looked as dazed as he was.

"I tried. I truly did. But I just couldn't do it."

"You couldn't?"

A train on the opposite track steamed into the station, white smoke billowing around them.

"Come," Will urged her as he grasped her hand. Her skin was deliciously warm, and touching her instantly eased his racing heartbeat. He led her to a bench and they sat, their bodies turned so they could face each other.

She waited for him, and he understood. He was the one with the explaining to do.

"I was a fool to send you that painting and note."

A little sound of protest came from her throat. "I love that painting."

"I knew you would, but I should have come to speak to you again. To tell you—"

"To tell me?"

"I'm not sure why it's been so difficult. Perhaps because I've never felt this way about anyone before. Never spoken the words and meant them in this way."

With the backs of his knuckles, he skimmed the

silken curve of her cheek. "You are unique in my experience."

"As are you," she whispered and reached for his free hand.

"In the time I've known you, I've become a different man. A better man. A truer version of myself."

"Will?" She'd slid her fingers under the cuff of his shirtsleeve and stroked his skin in a mesmerizing rhythm. "Tell me."

Her eyes were so full of impatience that he couldn't help but smile.

"What an insistent woman you are." He nuzzled his nose against hers and pressed a soft kiss to her lips.

"Do you mind?"

"Not at all."

Wrapping a hand around his neck, she pulled him in for another kiss, then arched back. "Good. Now tell me. Please."

"Madeline Ravenwood?"

"William Hart?"

"I love you." Will lifted her hand and kissed the backs of her fingers. "I adore you." He raised his head and kissed the tip of her nose. "And I've realized"— Will kissed the corner of her lush mouth—"that I simply cannot imagine my life without you. Not a single day."

Maddie closed her eyes and smiled, and when her lashes lifted, her gaze was bright and full of everything he craved. Love. Trust. Desire. "So, if I understand correctly, you love me."

"Mmm. I do."

"And you don't think we should be apart."

"Correct."

"But how do we manage that?"

"I was hoping you'd be amenable to becoming my wife."

She let out a long shaky breath. "A duchess."

"My wife." Will leaned in to tuck a stray strand of her gorgeous hair behind her ear. "You will be a glorious duchess, but most importantly, I want you to be my wife." Will realized she hadn't said yes or agreed in any way. "If you wish it."

She laughed, that low resonant laugh that wound through him all the way to his groin. "I suppose it's my turn to make myself clear to you."

He waited, yearning, hoping.

"I love you." Her brows tipped together in a mock serious look. "Now, don't take this as license to be grumpy, but I think I may have loved you from the moment we met."

"The first time."

"Yes."

Will grinned, and Maddie covered his mouth playfully with her hand, then replaced her hand with her lips.

"I couldn't stop thinking about you after that night," he confessed. "Probably terrible to admit because my fiancée had just jilted me. But that night was the beginning."

"And now here we are."

"Did I miss it, or did you agree to be my wife?"

Maddie bit her lip and looked skyward as if considering the question. "Yes. There, I have now."

"I'm the luckiest man in England." Will kissed her then, caressing her jaw, stroking her hair, and fighting to maintain control when she opened to him and deepened the kiss.

When they pulled away from each other, Will realized the London train had departed and the arriving train had left too. They were virtually alone on the train platform, so he kissed her again. And once more for good measure.

Maddie noticed his bag. "You're coming back to Haven Cove with me?"

Will squeezed her hand and looked off into the distance where the train had headed.

"Or do you need to go to London?"

Will nodded. "I should."

"Shall I come with you?"

"Would you?"

Maddie drew a finger along his jaw that sent a shiver down his spine. "Of course, you silly man. I realize we've much to decide, but the one thing I know is that I don't want us to be apart. Not if we can help it."

"We should be together."

"Today."

"And tomorrow."

Maddie leaned closer. "And tonight."

"Always." They came together in a kiss. Then another.

All the decisions would come later. They'd made

the most important one of all. She wanted to be with him as much as he wanted her, and he would make sure she didn't give up her passions, just as he would never stop being the man she inspired him to be.

Epilogue

Six months later
Eastwick Estate, Sussex

Will checked his tie in the hallway mirror and smiled at the sound of voices emerging from the drawing room.

What sort of man had he turned into that he was looking forward to a dinner party? In his own home? No, no, that wasn't right. In their home. For the first time in . . . forever, Eastwick did feel like a home. They hadn't made any drastic changes to the decor, and Maddie hadn't even fully revamped the gardens and landscape around the estate yet, but it was home because they were together. They'd found a home in each other.

Maddie's throaty laughter caught his ear, and he wished he could entice her out of the gathering and have a few moments with her to himself.

As if she'd read his mind, he saw her in the mirror's reflection slipping out of the drawing room.

"There you are," she said as she came up behind him and wrapped her arms around his middle.

"You're needed in the drawing room. Your sisters are crushing me at whist. Well, Cora is."

"Cora beats everyone at whist." Will turned so that he could gather her in his arms. Her sweet flowery scent filled the air, and he couldn't resist lowering his head and kissing the delicious curve of her neck.

Maddie let out a little gasp and reached for his hand. After a glance at the drawing-room doors, she tugged him into the morning room across the hall. The rich scent of blooms and greenery assailed them as they stepped inside. She had made this room her office and studio. Each day, she spent time answering correspondence, writing articles about rose hybridization, and designing gardens for several noble ladies Lady Trenmere had introduced her to.

Will chuckled as they slipped inside, and he kicked the door shut with his boot.

"I thought I was needed in the drawing room."

"Change of plans," she said breathlessly before kissing him. "I need you for a moment first."

"And I need you." He cupped her face and bent to kiss her properly. When she opened to him and stroked her tongue against his, a shot of heat through his body made him moan. "My wife," he breathed against her lips. He still marveled at the fact that she was his.

Maddie laughed and pulled away long enough to slide her hand between them. She stroked her fingers against his length, and her eyes took on the molten look that he'd come to love. "My husband." Her voice had gone deep, raspy, possessive. And he suddenly didn't give a damn that half a dozen nobles and his sisters waited for them in a room across the hall.

He began pulling at the skirt of her gown, even as he tightened an arm around her waist and moved her toward her desk. She let him lift her and helped him gather the fabric of her dress. When his fingers slid against the warm, silky flesh of her thigh, she clutched at his shoulder and gasped. He peppered kisses along her neck and swept his tongue against the spot where her pulse thrummed at the base of her throat as he slid a finger into her gloriously wet heat.

"Will," she whispered, "I love you."

"And I love you, sweetheart. Always."

Maddie tipped back, bracing a hand on the desk. But a moment later, she squealed when her hand slipped against a stack of papers, tumbling them to the floor.

Will ignored them and kissed her. He stroked his fingers against her warmth as he deepened the kiss. When she moaned against his lips, he knew she was close. He wrapped his arm around her more tightly.

"I've got you, love."

She quivered against him, her body tensing and then letting go. He wished the room wasn't dark. He loved watching her when she let herself fly over the edge. Being this close to her, hearing her sounds of pleasure, knowing she was his and he was hers and nothing could part them brought him a contentment he'd never expected to know. A happiness he still wasn't certain he deserved.

When he'd righted her skirt and given her one last thorough kiss, she tipped her head as if concerned about the papers that had fallen.

"I'm sorry, Maddie." He stepped away and bent to retrieve them. "Are they important? I don't think any are torn or bent too badl—"

Before he could gather them, she jumped down from the desk and darted in front of him, gathering the papers to her chest.

"Just some correspondence."

Will swallowed hard, and a foreboding sense of unease settled in his stomach. They were open with each other. Honest. They kept nothing from the other.

"Correspondence that you don't wish to show me."

"It's not that." She bit her lip, sighed, and shoved the papers toward him.

Will squinted at what seemed to be a letter in the dusky light of early evening that illuminated the room. The letter was in Maddie's neat, sloping hand and was addressed to Miss Dixon.

"The woman who giggles a great deal?" Will recalled how she'd taken on a matchmaker role—though unnecessarily—the night of the celebratory event at the hotel.

Maddie nodded. "That's the one."

As he skimmed the contents of the note, he found what didn't surprise him at all.

"I know what you'll say," Maddie told him in a rushed voice. "I've committed to too many things. But you did say we might go back if the weather isn't awful in early winter."

"I did." They'd agreed early on in their marriage that they would return to Cornwall as often as they were able. Mr. Eames had taken on the running of Ravenwood Nursery, but he had insisted on maintaining Maddie as co-owner, and she oversaw the not-unexpected success of her Victoria rose, which had proved a boon in income for the nursery after the princess's visit.

"It really isn't a terrible inconvenience. A couple of days at most." Her tone brightened, and she smiled. "You could help too, if you like."

"I think I will." He stood and offered a hand to help his wife up. Then he looked at the letter again. "After all, I've always wanted to be a member of"—he read directly from the letter to get the name right—"the Haven Cove Midwinter Decorating Committee."

Maddie hooked her arm through his and grinned up at him. "Don't worry, husband. I'll teach you as much about red bunting and holly-and-ivy bundles as you could ever wish to know."

"I'm counting on that." Will covered her hand with his where it rested in the crook of his arm as they started toward the door. "As long as you're there, it's where I wish to be."

**The next breathtaking romance in *USA Today*
bestselling author Christy Carlyle's**

Love on Holiday series

Arrives Fall 2022

*Next month, don't miss these exciting
new love stories only from
Avon Books*

Highland Wolf by Lynsay Sands

In all her daydreams about her wedding day, Lady Claray MacFarlane never once imagined being dragged to the altar by her greedy uncle and forced to marry a man she didn't know. But that's what would have happened had a handsome Highland warrior with black-as-sin hair called Wolf not snatched her up at the last minute and ridden off with her in his arms . . .

His Lessons on Love by Cathy Maxwell

The Earl of Marsden—better known as Mars—has lived his life by his own rules . . . until he is presented with a very big problem in a very tiny package: his baby daughter cast off by his ex-mistress. Mars doesn't know the first thing about babies. Panicking, he turns to Clarissa Taylor, village spinster, matron-in-training, and Mars's greatest critic. Still, who better to tend a motherless child than a woman who was abandoned as a babe herself?

Discover great authors, exclusive offers,
and more at hc.com.

RELB 12 21

Author photo ©2001 Paul F. Blouin

Fueled by Pacific Northwest coffee and inspired by multiple viewings of every British costume drama she can get her hands on, *USA Today* bestselling author **CHRISTY CARLYLE** writes sensual historical romance set in the Victorian era. She loves heroes who struggle against all odds and heroines who are ahead of their time. A former teacher with a degree in history, she finds there's nothing better than being able to combine her love of the past with a die-hard belief in happy endings.

christycarlyle.com

 authorchristycarlyle   writerchristy   writerchristy

ISBN 978-0-06-305449-3

USA Today **Bestselling Author**
CHRISTY CARLYLE
dazzles with the first romance in her enchanting
Love on Holiday series

William Hart, the Duke of Ashmore, is everything his father wasn't: scrupulously honest, forbidding, and apparently joyless. As a duke, he's a catc but as a grumpy stick-in-the-mud, no lady knows quite how to catch his e When his sisters concoct a plan for him to holiday in a run-down family prope in Cornwall, he reluctantly agrees, hoping it will be a chance for him to rediscov the carefree man he once was.

Madeline Ravenwood believes she can do anything she puts her mind including running the gardening business she inherited from her father a being a founding member of the Royal Visit Committee. Hard at work prepari for the princess's visit to judge their annual flower show, Maddie finds the appe ance of a stern, handsome duke, a man she almost kissed months ago in Lond to be a distraction she doesn't need.

Determined to convince the duke to repair his ramshackle manor house time for the royal visit, Maddie agrees when Will enlists her to join him he explores Cornwall. Spending their days, and nights, together, Will's love Maddie becomes too strong to ignore. But when the burdens of his title reapp and the differences in their worlds become all too real, can Will persuade Mad that she's the woman he's been waiting for?

An Avon Romance

AVON BOOKS

 AvonRomance

 AvonBooks

 AvonBooks

avonromance.com

Available from HarperAudio and HarperCollins e-books

DISCOVER GREAT AUTHORS, EXCLUSIVE OFFERS, AND MORE AT HC.CO

ISBN 978-0-06-305449-3

50899

9 780063 054493

Historical Romance | USA $8.99 CAN $11.99